Curlew Dreaming is the eagerly-awaited fourth instalment in the Curlew Series by Don Douglas. The action begins in 1928 after the Tomahawk Plains races. Nettie Chambers and Northern Territory cattleman Eric McDonald begin a love affair that has evolved from a teenage crush over a period of years.

The death of an Aboriginal elder leaves Eric with a solemn duty and also a legacy of profound connotations in the form of the Crocodile Blood Diamond. Initially sceptical, Eric's subsequent experiences lead him to acknowledge that the talisman has supernatural powers.

World War II intervenes in Nettie and Eric's lives and their separate experiences test their mettle, their resolve and their fidelity. Nettie undergoes another uncanny experience and is no longer the straightforward young woman she once was.

Cover design: James Barron

Cover Artwork by: John Morrison

Typeset in 12/16 Bembo

CURLEW DREAMING

DON DOUGLAS

Also by Don Douglas

Boolarong Press

Curlew Enigma

Curlew Calls

Curlew Fugitive

Amazon Publishing Services

Gone Cop

Stories of Oz Publishing

The Copper Crossing Mystery

This story is dedicated to the memory of all those brave men and women, many of them unsung, who defended our country from foreign invasion during World War II.

McDONALD FAMILY TREE

EDGAR (b) 1801 (d) 1847
(m) ALICE

ELIZA (aka ELIJAH HENRY) (b) 1-8-1840 (d) 29-10-1939   CLAYTON
= ELMORE HENRY   (b) 1842
    (m) PATRICK O'REILLY (no issue)

RANALD (BUSTER) (b) 10-1-1856 (d) 1-3-1942   JANE   dau #2   EDGAR
(m) TOBY

BEN   ELIZA JANE   HENRY   JAMES   ROSE
(b) 10-1-1885   (b) 2-2-1888 (d) 1945   (b) 30-6-1889   (b) 1-6-1892   (b) 6-3-1900
(m) SARAH TAGGERT   (m) JAMES GORDON   (aka JIMMY HENRY)
                                               (aka EL JIMMA bin HENRY)
                       CLARE   (m) daughter of AHMED MUHOMMAD BEY
                       (m) HAMISH LOGAN
                                               BEN ABDUL HENRY
                       MARK

ERIC   GORDON (GORDY)   JANETTE   RACHEL & THOMAS
(b) 1-10-1905   (b) 6-1-1908   (b) 15-2-1909   (Twins) (b) 2-2-1920
(m) ANNETTE CHAMBERS
(NETTIE)

LENNY & LILY   NAT   ELIZABETH SARAH
(Twins) (b) 15-9-1930   (b) 20-10-1932   (ELIZA) (b) 20-7-1946

CHAPTER 1

April 1928

Eric McDonald and Annette Chambers watched as Eric's parents Ben and Sarah taxied onto the Tomahawk Plains strip in their light plane. The sun had just risen on a fine morning at Eric's north-west Northern Territory home adjacent to the East Kimberley, across the border.

Sarah waved out the window as Ben gunned the motor and the plane gained speed as it ran down the strip and took off, leaving a trail of fine clay-pan dust in its wake. They watched it go low over the Aboriginal camp down on the bank of Sandy Creek before climbing and turning south-west, setting course for their distant home at Kalgoorlie. Ben and Sarah were now mining magnates who had eventually prospered despite often encountering almost insurmountable odds along their troubled way.

'I'm glad I met your mum and dad Eric,' Nettie said.

'Yeah, it was good they come up for it, been twenty-one years since Mother won the cup an' that long since the last Tomahawk Plains races. That was just before everythin' went haywire for 'em an' they lost Sarah Springs because of that bastard Southerland who owned this joint back then.'

'I like 'em both.'

'Yeah an' they like you too so that's all good. Glad I decided to get the races goin' again for more reasons than one.'

'Yeah, me too Eric.'

Ben and Sarah had flown up a week before the bush race-meeting which had been held two days previously after a long gap in what had once run annually until it had been ended by a tragic sequence of events involving Ben and Sarah and Southerland.

As they turned to walk back to the homestead they spotted a young girl running from the direction of the Aboriginal camp.

'That's young Daisy comin' an' she looks like she's in a hurry. Wonder what's goin' on down at the camp?' Eric said. 'She definitely ain't doin' it for the exercise.'

They waited for the girl who arrived breathless. 'Better come quick-feller boss,' she gasped.

'What's up Daisy? Just take your time so I can work out what you're sayin' ay.'

'Me proper old-man father bin all finish up 'e reckon boss an' 'e reckon gettim bossman come.'

Her father Captain was the senior elder of the tribe, an old man who once had reputedly been one of the best stockmen on the place before Eric's time. Captain had befriended Eric when he had first arrived to take over the running of Tomahawk Plains when Eric was only thirteen. That had been during the war when Ben had been away fighting the Turks at Gallipoli and in Palestine. The previous manager Jack Miller had come off second best in a clash with a scrub bull and was out of action as a result.

For quite a while, in more recent times, Captain had supplied Eric with diamonds that he found over the border on the Ord River and with the depressed state of the economy these had provided Eric with his main source of income in recent years.

'Did Captain reckon come quick or is that just what you're sayin' Daisy?'

His experience was that often a casual message was given more urgent connotation in the translation, usually to give the messenger higher status.

'That what 'im sayim, boss. Reckon not long now ay? 'Im proper feller old-man this one time.'

'Alright I'll come with you.'

'You want me to come too or stop here Eric?' Nettie asked.

'No, sounds like old Captain's gonna snap the hobbles an' he must wanna talk to me about somethin' important before he goes.'

'Man talk?'

'Yeah man talk I reckon. You know what they're like.'

'Righto.'

He went with the girl to the camp, where the old man sat on the ground with the embers of a small fire smouldering between his big bony feet. His spindly legs protruded from an old army greatcoat. It was a still and humid morning almost at the end of the wet season, but the old man was shivering. Eric had seen men dying before and thought Captain had that air of death about him.

His wives and children and the others of his clan hung back, watching from a distance. He was alone at the fire when Eric joined him.

'Minjurra you wanted to see me?' Eric spoke in the tribal dialect.

Captain's bony old head lifted, displaying his opal eyes which were now totally blind.

'My ears saw you coming Boss-Eric.' He ran the name together like he always did.

'Daisy reckoned you was all bin finish up.'

'She's only a girl but sometimes even women have some sense, and she has been my eyes for a long time now. She is all right as women go.'

'Are you leaving us Old Father?'

'It is cold here and I am going to a place where it is warm but there are things you must know. And there is also a favour I ask of you.'

'What is the favour Minjurra?'

'When my spirit is no longer in my body, will you take me to my burial place?'

'Why me? Why not one of your own people? One of your sons?'

'You know that we are the Crow people and that is our dreaming. My mother was of the Crocodile people from the direction of the sunset where I get the stones you call diamonds.

'Long ago ... before your time ... when the first Kitja★ came to our country they took my mother and my sister and they shamed them. I killed those men and other whites.

'Then more whites came and I came to know that not all white men were bad. The one I call King made his home here and he named me Captain. He was King and I was Captain. That was what he said. We were friends. We had respect for each other as equals. He taught me things about white man ways … I taught him things about the knowledge of my people here, my country … and there was harmony in this place.

'Then he went away … not much later his son came … but he was a white devil. You have seen the scars on my back from his whip.

'He used my daughters and the other young women for his pleasure … I no longer trusted the skin name of their children.'

'I know about your dreaming but when it comes to skin name it's too complicated for me,' Eric replied.

'By that time my eldest son was dead … killed by that Kitja devil-man. All the men of the tribe were afraid of him.

'Then because of his disregard for the women my own sons and the other young men followed his example … mated with many women of all skin families. Our tribal lore was breaking down … I knew the spirits were angry.'

Eric knew from the records in the homestead office that Lord Southerland had taken up the first lease on Tomahawk Plains. Before that it had been Crown Land, peopled only by Aborigines and mustered for cleanskins by Durack's Argyle Downs stockmen from over the border. It also had occasionally been mustered by Legune Station or Victoria River Downs stock camps and traversed from time to time by drovers heading west with breeders or east with bullocks; as well as explorers, duffers, fugitives and prospectors coming and going periodically.

'The man you call the white devil was Basil Southerland?'

'Yes that was his Kitja name … I blame him for the breakdown of my people's ways. My own sons are no longer here where they were born … they quarreled with me over the skin of their wives. That is why I ask you to bury my body in my mother's country … where skin is still important to the people.'

'I will do what you ask Minjurra because we are friends of long standing. You have been a good friend to me in all the years I have been here, and you have taught me things that my father was not here to teach me.'

'You are as a son to me … I will give you something that will protect you and your sons and daughters. It will link you to our dreaming … our country and yours.'

'I don't have any sons or daughters Minjurra.'

'When you take the girl Nettie as your wife you will have.'

How could the old man know about that? He and Nettie had only begun their tentative relationship two nights earlier at the race-night festivities and that had only amounted to kissing and professing their feelings for each other. They had known one another for the past nine years or so since he had come to manage Tomahawk Plains but had both been too shy to make that first amorous move. They had become good mates in that time but before the races, mateship was all it ever had been.

Minjurra took a pouch made from crocodile belly skin on a plaited horsehair thong from around his neck and handed it to Eric.

'This will protect you from the crocodile spirit of my mother's people … it will also allow you to go into their country to find the diamonds when I have gone. Her brother's son is the wise man of the crocodile people now … he will know you have my blessing.'

'How will he know? Will I have to show him this pouch?'

'He will know without seeing it … open it and see its power for yourself.'

Eric opened the pouch and took out the most exotic diamond he had ever seen, a perfect clear cubic crystal with faces an inch across. In its heart it contained a perfect blood-red garnet crystal. He had read of such inclusions but had never expected to see one. Deep in the bowels of the earth a garnet had formed in a volcanic pipe and then had been swallowed by an evolving diamond crystal, as heat and pressure reached extremes capable of converting pure carbon atoms into crystalline form. Such stones were rare and keenly sought after by collectors because of their scarcity and exotic beauty.

'The red of its heart is the blood of the crocodile spirit Boss-Eric …

whoever carries it is safe from the crocodile people and the crocodiles in the river … it has no power for anyone who steals it. You will need that protection when you bury my body there … you will also need it when you go there to get more diamonds.'

'One of your sons should have this Minjurra. I am only a white man, a Kitja.'

'You are my only son now. I have disowned my blood sons … you also have the blood of our race anyway.'

How could Minjurra know that he too had Aboriginal blood? His grandmother was half-caste from a distant area and while Eric had never been ashamed of that blood very few people in this part of the country even knew his bloodline.

'You are a wise man Minjurra and I am proud to be your son.'

'Bury my body in a cave … high up on the cliff … on the sunrise side of the crocodile hole in the river.'

'How will I know the place? I've never been there.'

'You will know it when you see it … you will know Yamburra, my mother's brother's son in the same way.'

'I'll do as you ask Old Father.'

'Go now Boss-Eric. I cannot leave this world while you are here with me.'

They clasped hands and the surprisingly powerful grip of Minjurra's huge scrawny claw of a hand drew blood on the back of Eric's rough hand, as his long talon-like nails bit into the skin.

'Go to where it's warm Minjurra. I will remember you and respect your memory.'

Eric pondered what he had learnt and the responsibility he had undertaken as he walked slowly up the rise to the house, where Nettie waited on the verandah.

'Everythin' alright Eric? You got it sorted out?' she asked.

'Yeah, except that it's maybe changed our plans Nettie.'

They had planned to spend the next week or so in each other's company exploring their new-found love.

'How do you mean change our plans?'

'Old Captain's dyin' an' I gotta take his body an' bury it over on the Ord River.'

'Why you Eric? How come they ain't gonna do it? It sounds a bit funny to me gettin' a whitefeller to do it.'

'He asked me to do it an' he reckons I'm his only son now. He's blued with his own sons over their women. Their wives ain't all the right skin.'

'How can you be his son? You ain't even a blackfeller.'

'He somehow knew that I do have black blood an' he also reckons his own sons have shamed him by marryin' out of their skin code.'

'You know I got black blood but I never knew you did too. I don't know nothin' at all about this skin business just the same. It's outside of anythin' I understand even though I sorta know what it's about.'

'Yeah, me too. It's pretty complicated an' I've had it explained to me but it's hard to follow. How it works is; it keeps 'em from gettin' inbred by makin' close relatives outta bounds when it comes to pickin' a wife.'

Nettie poured a pint of tea for Eric and they sat talking until a wail carried to them from the camp, the keening of high-pitched women's cries.

'He's dead,' Eric said.

'Just like that?'

'Yeah, he asked me to leave so he could die by himself. He hunted the others away as I was leavin' him.'

'That's spooky.'

'That's the way they are Nettie an' maybe they know more'n we do about lots a things. They been here in this country since way, way back, The Dreamtime. Funny though, most tribes don't have a single common word that means dreamtime. The Western Desert Pilbara people call it Manguny and the Cooper Creek tribes in Queensland call it Droonooda. The Tanami Desert people call their whole belief system Jukurrpa.'

'When will you have to take his body?'

'When they got it ready I s'pose. Don't know how long that'll take. I'm sorry this buggers up our plans.'

'Can I stop here until then an' come with you when you do it? I've never been across the border an' I wanna be with you anyhow, whatever you gotta do.'

'He will of been dead a while before I get him there an' they gotta get him ready yet. He'll stink a bit by then, most likely a fair bit more than just a little bit.'

'If you can put up with that I can too an' I ain't goin' back till I spend a bit of time with you because I probably won't see you till next years' races once I go.'

'Yeah, I'm happy for you to come with me if you want to.'

She noticed the blood on the back of his hand as he took his tobacco tin out of his pocket.

'What happened to your hand? You're bleedin'.'

'The old bloke's fingernails dug into me when we shook hands sayin' goodbye.'

'Show me.'

He held his hand out, palm down.

'Jesus he must of give you a fair shake!'

'Yeah, I was surprised how strong because otherwise he was pretty weak. But his fingernails is pretty long, more like big eagle claws.'

'Eric this is really spooky.'

'What is?'

'You got six puncture marks.'

'Yeah he's got five fingers an' a thumb. Didn't you ever notice that when you was workin' here?'

'No, I never had a lot to do with 'im. I knew he had real big hands but how can he have six fingers?'

'He reckons his mother did too. I asked him about it one time.'

'You sure he ain't Kadaicha?'

'No he ain't but his cousin is. He's a 'clever man' in their lingo. You ain't superstitious are you?'

'Course I ain't. I just never seen nothin' like that before.'

(* Kitja (white man) – pronounced Gudia; also sometimes spelt Kartiya or Cudea.)

CHAPTER 2

Yamburra sniffed the air as a light breeze from the east brought the unwelcome scents of yarraman and Kitja to his keen nose.

He was wary of white men and usually avoided them, which was not difficult because he could melt into the landscape like a dragon lizard, but they usually came from downriver to the north in search of their cattle, not from the east.

He trotted up the ridge and studied the eastern view from its crest. Two mounted whites were coming in the distance leading a third yarraman with a pack on its back. He could sense death. They would reach the river soon.

The weather was humid and scattered dark clouds loomed. He would call it to rain and that might discourage the intruders from whatever they intended.

He concentrated his mind on the clouds and intoned his communication to the rain spirit and then trotted back to the river, slinking silently like a dingo. He was unarmed because he shunned weapons, relying instead on his powers. He was naked save for the sacred woven dillybag hung around his neck.

He paused on a sandy beach on the bank of the lazily flowing river just downstream from where high red cliffs pinched its course. Only the trickling of the waterfall broke the brooding silence. During the Wet it became a raging cataract that ate the red rock, and the roaring torrent ran high on the flanking cliffs at this choke point swallowing the gorge, but the floods had passed until next Wet.

The giant spirit crocodile sunned himself on the opposite bank, his slit eyes watching Yamburra with a flat stare. He spoke in greeting to the spirit before lying face-down. He slit his eyes like the crocodile and then with his fingers spread like claws he writhed towards the water leaving his crocodile slide track in the sand.

He paused at the edge of the water to speak to the great reptile and then submerged himself and swam confidently underwater towards it, knowing his power protected him.

He climbed out of the water within yards of the giant reptile and it watched as he passed but made no move towards or away from him. It could have been a stone.

Let the whites come now with their death smell. The spirit would guard this place. He climbed the broken cliff-face to a vantage spot as he wondered about their mission and the feeling of death that accompanied them.

CHAPTER 3

Captain's people had prepared his already emaciated body for burial, pickling the cadaver with coarse salt and folding the knees up onto the chest with the arms between them. Salt was plentiful on the station for stock-lick, corning beef and curing greenhide.

Using greenhide thongs, they had sewn the corpse into a piece of crocodile belly hide which must have been sourced from somewhere to the north. Eric suspected the preparation of the cadaver was a mixture of tribal and white man custom with some innovation for good measure, but he hadn't been privy to the actual process. The use of crocodile hide, rather than tea tree bark was supposedly done to appease the crocodile spirit and seemed slightly out of tradition to him, as did the use of so much salt as preservative. Once they would have let meat ants and crows pick the cadaver bare, or for mummification pickled him in a rock-hole or hollow log using wattle bark tannin and other secret bush ingredients mixed with salt water. The corpse would also have been sun-dried after pickling. The process would have taken much longer in past times.

Brine oozed from the tightly sewn bundle that was compressed to about the size of a small swag. Even wrapped in an old piece of canvas it stank. The packhorse had bailed up about allowing the funereal parcel to be loaded on its back, so Eric had wrapped the stinking bundle in the tarp and the horse had since got used to its grisly load and settled.

He had studied a map of the area before leaving and knew that they had crossed the unmarked border into Western Australia sometime the previous afternoon.

'I reckon we oughta be gettin' close to the river now but them clouds is buildin' up a bit,' he commented. 'Looks like it could rain any minute.'

'Yeah, feels like rain too,' Nettie responded, 'Sticky an' still enough for a storm.'

They crested a rough ridge and saw the river at its foot.

'It's a bigger creek than what I expected,' he said as he took in the lie of the land and spotted the cliffs lining the eastern riverbank to their south. 'Them cliffs is what we're lookin' for I reckon.'

They rode down onto the riverbank out of the breeze and immediately began sweating in the humidity. The sky was darkening rapidly and Nettie shivered involuntarily at the ominous feel of the place.

'I don't like this place, Eric. It's givin' me the bloody heebie-jeebies.'

'Yeah, it's a bit quiet alright. Keep an eye out for blacks. I reckon they mightn't be too friendly here no matter what old Captain said.'

He loosened the Lee Enfield .303 in its scabbard and felt his revolver in its holster.

'There's no birds singin' out neither Eric.'

They heard the trickling sound of a small waterfall and then came to a large rock-hole with a sandy beach. Cliffs loomed high on both sides of the hole and a huge crocodile lay on a rock shelf on the opposite bank.

'That's the biggest croc I ever seen,' Nettie commented.

'Yeah, he's big alright. I reckon this is the spot that Captain told me about. Now I just gotta find a cave up high on this side to stick him in an' the job's done. Shouldn't take too long.'

'Eric, look at the croc-slide on the sand there!' she pointed.

He rode closer. 'That ain't no croc Nettie. I reckon that goori-goori Yamburra made that track to put the wind up us. It ain't any more'n half an hour old.'

'Yeah well if that's what he done it's definitely put the wind up me but it looks like a croc-slide to me just the same.'

'You ever see a croc with six claws?'

'Why did you have to show me that? This place is spooky enough without that bloody Kadaicha business. It's givin' me the creeps.'

'He won't hurt us, or so Captain reckoned.'

'That's alright for 'im he's bloody dead.'

'We won't be here long, just long enough to poke old Captain into one of them holes up there an' we can get goin' again.'

The flood-line on the cliff showed that when the river was in full flood it would be sixty feet deep in the gorge where it was pinched by the cliffs at the top of the falls so Eric knew he would have to find a cave above that flood mark. He unloaded the grizzly bundle from the packhorse and slung it over his shoulder with a rope.

'You hang onto the horses while I find a hole up there for him,' he said.

'Don't take too long. It's goin' to rain in a minute.' She pointed upriver at the white curtain of rain that marched silently towards them blotting out the landscape and creating an even more sombre mood.

'I'll be as quick as I can.'

He kicked his boots off to make the ascent easier and then set off to climb while she hobbled the horses. With that chore done she mounted a nearby ledge where she could watch Eric and keep an eye on the horses at the same time.

The cliff was relatively easy to climb, with deep cracks for footholds and a series of ledges. Eric watched the white veil coming closer and picked out a likely looking cave. He had almost reached it when the rain came down in a tropical downpour, soaking him instantly.

Nettie watched, anxious about Eric's safety. He was perched seventy or eighty feet above her almost blotted out by the rain, with the ungainly pack still on his back. She knew the rock would be slippery even to his bare feet.

'Be careful Eric!' she yelled up to him.

He looked down at her and waved to acknowledge he had heard and then unslung his burden. It slipped neatly into the small, rounded hole in the wall and he pushed it in as far as he could reach before sealing the opening with a stone. Once it was done he looked up and saw that he was closer to the crest than where Nettie waited below. He waved and yelled down. 'I'll go up the top an' come round. You get in outta the rain somewhere till I get there.'

He saw her take a step back on the ledge as she tried to follow his progress and then he sucked in his breath sharply as she slipped and went backwards over the drop into the river.

Nettie landed with a splash and went under, just as he saw the unmistakable bow-wave of a crocodile moving swiftly alongside where she had entered. She broke the surface swimming wildly for the edge, but he knew she had scant chance of out-swimming the reptile as he watched helplessly, expecting her to be taken at any instant.

She reached the edge and ran panic-stricken up the bank, limping noticeably. One leg of her trousers was red with blood but there was no sign of the crocodile anymore.

'Nettie, are you alright?' he called.

'Yeah more fright than anythin'. I landed on top of a bloody great croc an' he got as big a fright as I done an' took off.'

'You're bleedin'.'

'He scratched me with his claws. I'm alright but you be careful up there.'

'I'll be there soon an' I'll have a look. Just get in under cover an' wait.'

Twenty minutes later he inspected the wounds on her calf after washing his hands and splashing Lysol solution on them. There were two deep cuts and a puncture as deep as the length of his finger which he used as a probe. Her face was pale and she shivered slightly from pain and shock.

'Is it hurtin'?' he asked.

'It weren't at first but yeah it's startin' to tune me up a bit now. Specially when you stuck your finger in it.'

'I'll clean it up an' disinfect an' bandage it. I got laudanum for the pain too.'

He tended her as best he could under the circumstances with limited equipment but was concerned that the deep puncture may become septic because it would not drain well. It really needed to be syringed out with a Lysol or saltwater mixture until it was clean, a treatment he often used for deeply wounded horses but he had no syringe.

'Reckon you'll be able to ride?' he asked.

'Too bloody bad if I can't Eric. We're a fair way from anywhere. I got no choice in the matter.' Her words were brave but he could see she was experiencing severe pain by then.

'Here have a swig of laudanum an' then we better get you back home before you get blood poisonin'.'

The light was failing and it was still raining when they mounted up for the return ride. It had taken them the best part of two long days to reach the river from Tomahawk Plains but Eric hoped they could cover the distance in less time than that on this more urgent return trip. In two days' time, Nettie's condition could well be serious.

'We'll keep goin' without stoppin' an' we'll push 'em along till we get there if you reckon you can handle that.'

'Yeah. Just gimme a minute to get a smoke rolled first before we go.'

He reached to get his own tobacco tin out of his pocket but it and his matches were gone.

'I must of lost me tobacco when this bloody horse of mine rooted this mornin'. Gimme yours when you got your smoke made.'

He felt his other shirt pocket to check that the diamond talisman Captain had given him was safe but the button had been torn off the pocket and it too was empty.

A sudden feeling of superstitious dread came over him that Nettie had been hurt simply because he had lost the stone but he tried to push it aside.

A quail had exploded out of the grass underfoot and his horse had shied and bucked, taking him under a low branch that had torn his shirt and scratched his face. That must have been where he had lost the stone but he would have no hope of finding it in the night on their way back.

They lit their smokes and set off into the overcast evening, his main concern being to get her to medical treatment as quickly as possible.

Yamburra had watched everything that had happened and had realised why they had come. The white man had buried Minjurra's body. Without being told he had known of Minjurra's death before these two had come. Yamburra was glad the crocodile had not killed the woman but knew the power of the spirit was strong and that she could yet easily die from her wound. It was beyond his powers to intervene on her behalf because she was white and his spell would have no effect.

* * *

It was a long uncomfortable wet night. Eric set as fast a pace in the unfamiliar country as seemed sensible. At daylight it was still raining and Nettie's condition had deteriorated considerably during the night. By then he had her wrapped in a sodden blanket but she shivered constantly. He kept her drugged with laudanum to alleviate her considerable pain and watched her constantly in case he had to tie her to the saddle to keep her aboard.

He bemoaned the fact that the fledgling Australian Inland Aerial Medical Service, pioneered by the Reverend John Flynn was only based at Cloncurry in Queensland and still had no service in the Northern Territory, which meant that when they arrived back at the Tomahawk Plains homestead, he would have to take Nettie to Darwin in the plane. When the service eventually expanded to the Territory people like them in far-flung areas would feel safer.

In November 1926 an associate of Flynn's, Alfred Traeger, had set up a Morse code connection between Alice Springs and Hermannsburg Mission and by late 1927 he had set up a transmitter and receiver unit powered by a bicycle-pedal-driven generator. These sets were already in use by the AIM Aerial Medical Service in Queensland while Traeger was working on adding a keyboard to make the procedure simpler for those not trained in telegraph. Eric and Ben had arranged at the race visit that they would both get pedal radio sets so that they would be able to communicate with each other.

They arrived back at the homestead well before midday on worn-out horses, ironically just as the rain stopped and the sun came out.

Nettie was cold and stiff and her teeth were tightly clenched so that they had stopped chattering but she had stayed in the saddle without being tied. He lifted her rigid body down and carried her inside.

'I'm gonna give you a hot bath as soon as I can boil some water. You won't mind if I undress you to do that will you?'

She shook her head and tried to speak but her mouth would not open. Her eyes were starting to roll back and he realised with a shock that she was exhibiting the typical lockjaw and other symptoms of tetanus.

Using kerosene as an accelerant he got the copper boiled fairly quickly and had to slit her clothes off with his pocketknife because she was too rigid to undress without difficulty. He was much too concerned about her condition for her nudity to be a distraction.

He washed her and cleaned the now swollen and suppurating wound which was red and angry looking. By the time he had her dried and wrapped in a dry blanket she had stopped shivering constantly but still did so spasmodically. He managed to prize her mouth open to dose her with laudanum and managed to get her to swallow hot sweet tea with great difficulty.

He realised that it was too late in the day to reach Darwin that night but knew he would be able to get as far as Timber Creek before dark. He got the Auster going and taxied up to the house, then carried Nettie out and got her into the spare seat with difficulty. Her body was stiff and resistant.

He landed at Timber Creek before sundown, where he knew that the police sergeant's wife Joan was a nurse. She willingly helped Eric unload Nettie and take her inside. She managed to put a tube up Nettie's nose and fed her gruel that way because by then her jaws were locked solid and her mouth could not be opened. She also provided a dressing-gown instead of the blanket which had been her only cover.

'I don't like her chances Eric. Not many people recover from tetanus but if you can get her to Darwin in the morning they may be able to save her there.'

'I won't wait till mornin' Joan. Sooner I can get her there the better I reckon.'

'You can't fly at night Eric,' Sergeant Fred Smith said. 'I can't allow you to take that risk because I know you aren't endorsed for night flying.'

'But I'll be able to see good enough to take off an' fly as soon as the moon comes up Fred an' it'll be well an' truly daylight by the time I get to Daly River. I gotta land there to get fuel anyhow. That way I'll get her to Darwin as quick as possible. I wish I could get her there quicker but that's the best I can do.'

'You won't make it unless you have a feed and a sleep first. You look pretty buggered to me. I'll refuel your plane for you while you have a feed and a bath and I can lend you clean clothes. Then I want you to get a few hours sleep. I'll wake you when the moon comes up.'

'Thanks Fred. I gotta give her the best chance I can. If she died because I slept too long I'd never forgive meself.'

He landed at Darwin aerodrome before midday the following morning and got a taxi to the hospital, where Nettie was quickly attended by staff and assessed by a doctor.

'She's in a fairly advanced state of tetanus and given what she's already been through she's lucky to still be alive. We've syringed the wound thoroughly with hydrogen peroxide because the bug won't survive in an oxygenated environment and got her in a brace so she can't break her back or neck. We're also medicating her intravenously. That's about all we can do now except hope Mister McDonald. She's unlikely to regain consciousness for quite some time so I suggest you get some rest yourself or we'll have you in here as a patient too,' the doctor told him. 'You look to be at the end of your tether to me.'

'Yeah I know what you're sayin'. I seen horses an' blackfellers die of tetanus an' mostly there ain't too much you can do about it once it sets in. Look, don't start worryin' about me. I just need a sleep, only had a few hours in the last few days.'

'We'll do our best. Now why don't you book into a hotel and get some rest?'

He took a taxi the ten miles or so out to Jack Miller's place where he was welcomed by his old friends. Jack and Ethel both knew Nettie because she and her father had been working at Tomahawk Plains at the time when Jack had been trying to manage the operation from a squatters' chair on the verandah. That was when Eric had arrived on the mail truck to take over from him.

Eric explained what had happened to Nettie and was invited to stay as long as he needed.

That night he revisited the accident in a nightmare. The crocodile was dragging Nettie back into the water and she cried out for him to save her but he was rooted to the spot, unable to move even a muscle. All he could do was watch her terror-stricken plight helplessly, knowing it was his fault because he had lost the diamond.

He woke in a cold sweat, pawing at his pocket in search of the stone. To escape the horror of it he rolled a smoke with shaking fingers and sat on the side of the bed until the nicotine settled his nerves. With his head clearer he made a decision. In the morning he would go to the hospital and see how Nettie was but he was not hopeful there would be any improvement. Then he would fly home and try to find the diamond. He was confident that he could locate the spot where the horse had bucked. That was where he was sure the diamond must be and prayed it would still be there. He could not shake off the superstitious belief that that was the reason Nettie had the accident and that finding the stone was the only way of saving her life now. He had never been the least bit superstitious before but had the strongest conviction that her life depended on him getting the crocodile blood diamond back in his possession.

When he went to the hospital she was still in a deep coma.

'I've opened the deep puncture and drained it and flushed with peroxide but apart from the medication we're using there's little else we can do I'm afraid,' the doctor told him.

'She ain't got much hope has she?'

'Not without a miracle I'm afraid but it's also likely we won't be sure for weeks.'

'I gotta go home for a few days but I'll get back as soon as I can Doctor.'

CHAPTER 4

Eric had no difficulty returning to the spot where his horse had bucked. His bushcraft enabled him to instinctively find his way back anywhere he had been before and he could track as well as any Aborigine.

He located the low branch which had almost torn him off his horse's back as it bucked him into it. The tobacco tin and the tin matchbox were close by in the churned-up ground. He found the leather pouch that had contained the diamond, as well as the metal button off his shirt-pocket. However, search as he might there was no sign of the diamond anywhere in the vicinity.

There were no tracks in the nearby area that would have been left if somebody had found it but then that was extremely unlikely anyway in this remote spot. He knew that not even Aborigines went anywhere without a purpose. Most were supported by the stations and seldom went hunting any more except at the times when they went walkabout around the beginning of the Wet or were on the run from police.

He had faith in his tracking ability but where the diamond could be had him baffled. He was in no doubt, that was where he had lost it and the other evidence proved the assumption. The stone could not be far away although a thorough search among every bunch of grass and under every stick, leaf or piece of bark had revealed nothing.

The horse track was the only set anywhere near the site. He scratched the dirt from each hoof-print in case the diamond had been trampled into the ground by his mount.

He smoked a cigarette and contemplated the mystery while he sat on a log feeling dread and despair. The superstition came strongly again as a crow drawled its mournfully droll cry nearby, reminding him that Minjurra's clansmen were the crow people. In that instant he had the fanciful thought that old Captain was calling him in the same way his own family had always used the curlew call to communicate unobtrusively. It called again right above him but when he looked up there was no sign of the bird.

Captain's playing games with me. I give up old man, where is it? And where the hell are you?

His eyes searched the foliage above him but there was no sign of the glossy black scavenger bird that had made the call. Then it carked again and this time he saw the slightest movement. He strained his eyes to make it out but until it moved once more he was puzzled.

When he finally did clearly see a bird it was not the crow he was looking for that he located but a Great Bowerbird, the master-mimic of the northern bush. A bowerbird could faithfully mimic any sound familiar to it from the cry of a baby to the chop of an axe. It was beautifully camouflaged by its fawn-grey coloured plumage with speckled back and wings. He identified this one as a male by the small mauve-pink crest on the nape of its neck.

Yeah! I bet you stole the bloody thing, you beady-eyed bastard! What the hell have you done with it?

Male bowerbirds collected anything shiny, particularly green or red objects, for their bowers to attract females. In that instant he knew that this bird had stolen the diamond, as it would a shiny piece of broken glass, a brass button, a stark white knucklebone or a brightly coloured piece of cloth or China.

Captain had been speaking to him through the voice of this chameleon bird. The hair prickled on the nape of his neck at the superstitious thought.

The bird watched him with its bright eyes as he pondered how to find its bower. He knew they ranged far and wide and that their bowers were often miles away from where they scavenged their trinkets. Missing jewellery and coins had often been found in bowers miles from any habitation. It could be almost impossible to find.

If the bird had stolen the diamond which was more than likely given its interest in him, the only possible way he could think of was to provide it with another attractive object to interest it and then follow when it took the bait. He could not think of anything he had with him that would tempt the bird. It had to be something shiny or alluring to entice him and yet small enough for the feathered culprit to carry.

Then he thought of the bullets he carried in his saddlebag. Among them were some .22 bullets from when he had ridden out to get a killer. He went slowly to his saddlebag so as not to frighten the bird and returned with a handful of the pea-rifle bullets. Then he carefully prized the lead projectile out of one using his pocketknife and tipped out the gunpowder. The cock-bird still watched with its head held to one side inquisitively.

He lifted the bullet shell to his lips and blew across its neck to produce a high-pitched whistle. The bird cocked its head the other way and he repeated the exercise. Then he flicked the shell away and saw it glint in the bright sunlight. The bird watched it but did not attempt to come down from the tree.

He repeated the procedure until ten shiny brass cases lay about on the ground. He knew the bird was interested but was not about to come down while he was in close proximity.

He retreated to the shady tree where his horse was hobbled and tethered to stop it wandering and confusing tracks. He smoked another cigarette while he waited for the curious thief to take his bait.

It flew down and inspected the brass cases and then it picked one up in its claw and flew off. He gave it a hundred yards lead so as not to frighten it as he followed on his horse.

Half a mile later he lost sight of it but it had been flying on a straight path so he slowed his pace and continued on that course, keeping his eyes peeled for the bower.

He had gone a couple of hundred yards more when he heard the flutter of wings overhead and saw the bird returning for another bullet-shell.

Three more times he followed it until he lost sight again before he finally saw it land on the ground ahead of him.

The bird flew up into a tree and watched him approach its bower which was camouflaged among a thicket of low bushes in a small clearing.

He dismounted and knee-hobbled his mount with a bull strap then crawled into the bushes, taking care not to damage the courtship structure any more than he could help. It was a small tunnel, skillfully constructed from grass and twigs. At either end lay all the bright trinkets the bird had gathered, the bullet-shells among them. Then he saw the diamond catching the rays of the sun. With an exclamation of relief he picked it up and popped it into his mouth before carefully backing out of the bushes.

Sorry bird, the pea-rifle shells will have to do the job of getting a mate for you. I need this one more than you do. What your hen don't know about shouldn't make any difference to your chances anyhow.

His sense of relief left him feeling slightly shaky and it took another cigarette to settle him enough to take the hobble-strap off his horse and mount up.

You're gettin' to be as bloody superstitious as any blackfeller but will it make any difference for Nettie? Is superstition all it is or did old Captain know what he was talkin' about?

He kicked the horse to a trot, feeling cautiously optimistic.

★ ★ ★

When Eric returned to the homestead from his search the next day, the first thing he noticed was two strange horses tethered under the spreading pepperina tree outside the house-yard at Tomahawk plains, one saddled and the other carrying a swag and a pack for provisions. He hitched his mount with them and went over to the house to see who his visitor was.

Nettie's father Len Chambers rose from a chair and came to meet him as he mounted the verandah. 'G'day Eric.'

'You been waitin' here long Len?'

'Couple of hours, just about long enough to read all the magazines I could find. I reckoned you'd turn up directly.'

They shook hands.

'You got my message then Len?'

'No. What message?'

'About Nettie.'

'What about Nettie? I come over to see what's keepin' her. She was due back a few days before I left there from what she told me before I went back after the races.'

'She's had an accident an' she's got tetanus. I asked Fred Smith at Timber Creek Police Station to try an' get a message to you at Wave Hill.'

'Musta come after I left then. How did it happen? Muckin' about with horses I s'pose? Got tagged by a horseshoe nail, not watchin' what she was doin' I'll bet? Nothin' worse'n that for tetanus.'

Eric told him the chain of events from the day of the races until when he had left Nettie in Darwin hospital.

'It don't look too good for her Len an' I blame meself for it. If she'd of gone back to Wave Hill with you it wouldn't of happened.'

'Ain't your fault she decided to stay on here for a bit.'

'Yeah that was my fault too Len.'

'How? You two got somethin' goin'?'

'We nearly did but maybe we never will now. I'm sorry.'

'She's old enough to know what she wants so it ain't your fault if she's keen on you Eric. I got no issue with whatever she does as long as I know what's goin' on. Are you goin' to go back in to see her in hospital?'

'Yeah I'm flyin' back in the mornin'. You want to come with me?'

'I never been in a plane in me life but yeah I will thanks. She's all I got now since her mother cleared out with the other kids.'

CHAPTER 5

As soon as he saw Nettie Eric realised without being told that her condition had improved considerably in the short time he had been away. She no longer looked like a rigid corpse.

He asked the nurse who sat by her bedside what had caused her rapid recovery.

'We're a bit baffled. The day before yesterday when I came on duty there was no change in her condition from the previous day. Then later in the day I noticed her eyelids moving as if she was dreaming. Within a few minutes her respiration and colour improved and within a few hours her pulse and temperature stabilized. It was quite a dramatic thing to watch, given her previous condition and lack of response. The doctor agrees that she's past the worst of it now and should continue to improve. Her jaw isn't locked any more either and the tension has gone out of her muscles.'

'What time in the afternoon was it when she started pickin' up?'

'About one o'clock. Why do you ask?'

'Just wonderin'.'

That was almost exactly the time he had found the diamond. He had heard remarkable stories about Aborigines who had been sung or had the bone pointed at them and were in a critically ill condition before suddenly improving after the spell had been called off from afar. But he was a whitefeller, a Kitja. He had never believed in anything supernatural in his life. If anything his attitude had always been more on the sceptical than receptive side.

His rational mind fought the idea that his finding the diamond could have caused her rapid recovery, but he could not shake the feeling that it had. If Captain's assurance was right and they had inadvertently gone into Yamburra's territory without the protection of the talisman it was possible the Kadaicha had called the crocodile spirit to cause them harm. Yamburra's fresh track had been there in the sand and it was likely he had been watching them the whole time they were at the site.

Previously he had never placed much significance on the fact that old Captain had an extra finger and toe compared to other people, having put it down to a freak of nature or a deformity but it seemed that Yamburra also had the same oddity from his simulated crocodile slide, which suggested either heredity or something supernatural. Surely it was heredity.

He pulled himself from his reverie. 'Has she come to yet?' he asked.

'No. It may be a while before she does regain consciousness but then it could happen at any time. Hers is a very unusual case so anything is possible.'

Eric and Len went outside for a smoke.

'She's a hell of a lot better'n what I expected from what you said Eric.'

'Yeah I reckon so too. I was frightened she might of died while I was away to tell you the truth. It's hard to believe that she's the same girl I left here only four or five days ago.'

'Seems like she'll be alright now by the look of her an' from what they're sayin'. I seen a blackfeller get over tetanus once an' he reckoned the witch-doctor cured 'im but I don't believe in that stuff Eric. One thing I do know is that not too many horses beat it.'

'You hear them stories Len an' you gotta wonder sometimes just the same.'

'I ain't superstitious.'

'I got a job to do in town. You want to stop here with Nettie while I do that?'

'Yeah maybe she might come around an' if she does it'd be good if one of us was here. She's never been in a hospital before so she might get a bit toey about wakin' up in one.'

Eric took a taxi to Chinatown and went to a modest shop that had a sign proclaiming, SUNIL SYNA, Haberdashery & General Merchandise.

The tall grey haired Indian behind the counter recognised him immediately as he entered. 'Eric it has been a long time,' he said with his native accent which he had never lost.

'Sunny it's good to see you.' They shook hands.

Sunil had once been a travelling hawker touring the outback with his camel-drawn covered wagonette, selling his wares at the various settlements, camps and stations. Now with changing times and the rural depression he operated his modest business in town.

They chatted over events of the past few years since they had last met.

'But you didn't just come here to talk Eric. How can I be of assistance?'

'You still muck around with gemstones?'

Eric knew Sunil had been a gem-cutter in India before he had come to this country. Early on when he had been hawking some of the diamonds Captain had sold him he had shown Sunil a parcel but soon after that he got a more reliable and profitable market for them through his uncle Henry McDonald, best known by his alias of Jimmy Henry. Previously he had been selling them too cheaply to a Chinese trader.

'Still a little, why do you ask?'

Eric untied the thong from around his neck and showed Sunil the crocodile diamond. He reacted strangely, glancing around before quickly going to the door and locking it. Then he pulled the blinds.

'What's up Sunny?'

'That's a diamond Eric, a very valuable one. In this town there are many thieves. I have never seen such a magnificent stone.'

'Yeah I reckon it's probably pretty rare from what I've read.'

'Are you asking me to cut that stone for you? It is a perfect crystal and it would be a travesty to ruin it that way. But that is just my humble opinion.'

'No I just wanted to show it to you because I reckoned you'd love to see it. These ones are what I want cut.'

He tipped over a hundred small pink diamonds out on the glass-topped counter from a chamois pouch.

Sunil fetched a portable lamp which he put under the glass top. Then he studied the stones with a loupe.

'They are good stones Eric. Many of them are beautiful quality, the first water as they say in the diamond trade.'

'Can you cut 'em for me?'

'Yes I can but there are so many stones. It will take a long time and it would cost a considerable amount for so many.'

'That don't matter. I only want one of 'em done pretty soon.'

'Which one?'

'You pick the best one for a ring.'

Sunil studied them some more and picked a stone. 'This one is flawless and it should cut into a five or five and a half carat gem which will look quite large on a ring.'

'How long will that take you?'

'Perhaps a week. Perhaps less.' He shrugged eloquently.

'I want you to make the ring to put it on too. That'll take you a bit longer I reckon.'

'I don't work gold Eric but I know a Chinese man who does very good work. You will need to get the size for him to work with and he can be doing that while I cut the stone. May I suggest white gold because it would set the stone off best?'

'Yeah whatever you reckon. I'll get her size an' I'll get you to organise it with him please Sunny.'

'You have not asked the cost.'

'I know you won't cheat me an' whatever it costs don't matter much as long as you do a good job. Cost's the least of me worries.'

'What about the other stones? You said you wanted them cut too.'

'I want a necklace to match the ring but there's no rush for that.'

'They will be beautiful pieces of jewellery and whoever the young lady is, she is very lucky.'

'Yeah she's real lucky just to be alive right now Sunny. A week ago you wouldn't of give two bob for her chances. She got tetanus.'

'Eric you have at least £10,000 worth of stones here without that big one with the garnet inclusion. It is worth at least that much by itself. Do you trust me with all that value?'

'Yeah I trust you but I'll keep this flash one.' He put the blood diamond back in the pouch. 'I need this one with me. It's sort of special. An old blackfeller mate give it to me. It's a long story.'

'Don't forget to measure her finger.'

'I won't forget. I'll be back in a couple of hours.'

Eric had brought the parcel of diamonds with him on a last-minute impulse, buoyed by the superstitious belief that Nettie would recover because he had found the diamond. He had not dared ignore that impulse for fear that doubting the power of the blood stone could reverse that possible recovery. Once he had observed her improvement his optimism had been vindicated.

★ ★ ★

One of the nurses lent Eric a cheap dress ring that fitted Nettie's finger to get the size for the jeweller and when he slipped the new diamond ring on her finger it fitted perfectly.

In the meantime he had taken Len back to Tomahawk Plains to collect his horses so that he could get back to Wave Hill for the muster. Nettie still had not regained consciousness in the days he had been away but her condition had continued to improve nevertheless.

He kissed her gently on the lips and her eyelids fluttered and then opened.

'Is that you Eric?'

He felt a surge of emotion at the sound of her voice. 'Yeah it's me Nettie.'

'Has the rain stopped?'

He realised that her last memory was of riding home in the rain after her accident. The fever had robbed her of everything since then.

'Yeah it stopped a few weeks ago an' you been pretty crook since then. No not pretty crook, real crook actually. Not even the doctor give you much chance of pullin' through.'

'I feel a bit weak an' I can't see properly. Me eyes are all blurry but I knew it was you. Didn't reckon anyone else'd be kissin' me like that.'

'You're in hospital in Darwin Nettie an' you been unconscious for two, goin' on three weeks. You had tetanus an' your eyes rolled back with it. Maybe that's why you're havin' trouble seein' now.'

'I'm tired Eric, real tired.' She fell asleep again almost as soon as she had said it.

Eric told the doctor she had recovered consciousness and asked him about her sight.

'The eye muscles are likely strained from the eyes being rolled back for a long period and it's having the same effect as being cross-eyed until they right themselves. The muscles have been tense for so long that they've stretched. She's obviously not focusing properly yet and that could take time to remedy with exercises but I'm sure they will return to normal in time.'

Later that evening Nettie woke again and was fed her first solid meal since the accident. Eric stayed with her after the nurse left and they talked.

'Len come in with me the other day to see you. He turned up lookin' for you at home when you never got back to Wave Hill.'

'He knows I'm alright then?'

'Not alright like you are now but you had picked up a hell of a lot between when I left you here an' then. It looked pretty much touch-an'-go there for a while an' we was both pretty worried.'

'You flew me in here in the plane?'

'Yeah.'

'Just as well I was out of it otherwise you never woulda got me in that bloody thing.'

'Len had never been in one either but he reckoned it wasn't too bad once he got used to it. Then I flew him back again. He reckons they're alright now.'

She took his hand. 'Thanks Eric, sounds like you saved me life.'

'It was my fault it happened in the first place Nettie an' that you even needed savin'.'

'I done it to meself Eric, it was me own fault for not watchin' what I was doin'. Me boot slipped on the wet rock. I shoulda took notice what I was doin' an' it looks like I blew me chance again.'

'Me an' you, you mean?'

'Yeah I must be jinxed I reckon. I got pissed the night of the races an' now this. You'll start to reckon I'm too much trouble to be bothered with.'

'It don't change anythin'. You couldn't help gettin' hurt. I don't feel no different about you than what I did before.'

'You do care about me don't you Eric?'

'I wouldn't of got that ring made for you if I never cared about you Nettie.'

'What ring?'

'The one you got on your finger.'

She held her hands up but could not focus enough to see the ring. Then she felt it with the fingers of her other hand.

'What's it like?'

'It's a pink diamond on a white gold ring. I got an old Indian bloke to cut the stone an' he got a Chinaman to make the ring for you.'

'A diamond! You're mad Eric. You can't afford a bloody diamond. There's a depression on.'

'It never cost me that much. Old Captain found the diamond in the river near where we buried him.'

'Thank you Eric but why did you do that?'

'Because I want to marry you girl.'

'Do you really wanna marry me?' She asked incredulously. 'We ain't even done no canoodlin' yet. As far as you know I could turn out to be a dud in the sack.'

'We'll have time for that down the track an' I know you ain't a dud anyhow. You're too smart of a woman to be a dud at anythin'. Will you marry me?'

'Yeah I'll marry you Eric, course I will. I always wanted that, ever since I was nothin' much more'n a kid. You'll have to ask Dad first but an' see what he reckons about it.'

'I don't reckon he'll object. He asked me if we had somethin' goin' an' I told him yeah we did.'

'I never had nothin' of me own in me life before this except a few horses an' now I got a diamond. Is it pretty Eric?'

'Yeah I reckon it is anyhow.'

'Here gimme a kiss.'

It was a lingering, gentle kiss.

'I'll try an' make you a good wife Eric. Ain't nothin' I'd rather do than that.'

'I got no doubt about that. I'll do me best to make you happy too.'

She smiled contentedly. 'We both got a bit of learnin' to do yet ay?'

'Nothin' we don't both want to learn. We'll work it out Nettie.'

'Yeah an' have fun doin' it too I reckon.'

CHAPTER 6

Nettie was released from hospital and went to stay with Jack and Ethel Miller while she waited for Eric to come in to collect her. Her vision had improved to the stage she could see reasonably clearly but she could not yet focus well enough to read a newspaper. She had been told to persevere with her exercises.

She gave Jack a hand to break in some colts while she waited because she knew Eric was doing a first round of mustering and would not be able to come in for her until that was done.

They arrived back at the yards one afternoon after taking a couple of colts for a long ride and Eric walked out to meet them.

'I was just sayin' to Jack that you might turn up soon Eric,' she greeted him.

She kissed him and Jack grinned at him. 'You want to give Nettie a hand here Eric? I'll get Ethel to put the billy on.'

'Ethel reckons you oughta give the breakin' in away Jack.'

'Yeah an' then I'd be sittin' around in me bloody slippers drinkin' tea all day. Then see what she'd reckon. That's no good to me Eric, too many dry gullies behind me for that. An' also what Ethel don't say is we make good money outta the few horses I do break. Anyhow, I'd prob'ly seize up like a old wore-out horse if I stopped doin' things. They reckoned I was buggered when you come an' took over from me at Tomahawk but I kept pokin' around an' doin' a bit till I come half good. I'll leave you two talk for a bit anyhow.'

Jack left them and Nettie kissed Eric again, a lot more seriously than just a friendly greeting.

'It's good to see you Eric. I been watchin' out for you ever since they let me outta hospital, lookin' down the road all the time, hangin' for home like a old night-horse.'

'I been thinkin' about you too but we had to finish a round of musterin' first, brandin' cleanskins an' gettin' the bullocks an' spayed cows together from over on Sarah Springs an' down along the Keep River. How's your eyes now?'

'Yeah they're comin' good, not as good as they was yet but they're still gettin' better all the time. When are we goin' home?'

'I'll drop you back at Wave Hill on me way home. You can pick your horses up whenever you're ready.'

'Wave Hill? I thought you reckoned you wanted to marry me!' She exclaimed in a shocked tone.

'Yeah I do but I thought you was needed there for the muster.'

'Bugger Wave Hill Eric, I wanna be with you. Ain't you got a job at Tomahawk Plains for me? I'll even take on the cookin' in the camp if there ain't anythin' else an' Gawd knows how bad of a cook I am.'

'Yeah course I do an' it ain't cookin'. We're behind anyhow because I was muckin' about in here, which means we'll be pretty busy till we got it all done an' got the bullocks an' spayed cows away to Stone Fort. Old lame Simon's doin' the cookin' anyhow an' he can knock up a pretty fair feed.'

'Well that's organised then. I reckoned for a sec there that you musta changed your mind about marryin' me, got cold feet like.'

'No that ain't ever gonna happen. I love you an' if that's what we're doin' we better call at Wave Hill anyhow so that Len knows you're alright an' so's I can ask him can I marry you.'

'Eric I wanna get to know you like normal people in love do an' to do that I gotta be with you. I hope you don't reckon I'm pushin' me way into your life an' I hope you won't take it the wrong way if I ask you somethin' sorta private.'

'What's that?'

'The night of the races I woulda pulled me pants off for you at the drop of a hat an' I wanted to real bad. But maybe it's better if we get to know each other a bit better first. I still want you just the same as I ever done but would you mind if we done that? I been thinkin' about it an' don't want to rush into somethin' just cause I want you in me swag. There's gotta be more to it than that.'

'I'm glad you said that. I been a bit nervous about it too, like the first time you climb on a horse you know is gonna buck fair-dinkum.'

She laughed. 'I like the way you put it, makes me sound like a buckjumpin' young filly.'

'Like the joke about the prostitute you reckon?'

'I never heard that one.'

'Well old mate's askin' her how much she charges an' what he gets for that an' she reckons, 'Gimme a quid an' then you just get on an' bloody well hang on'.'

She laughed. 'Yeah somethin' like that.'

'Well that ain't what I meant Nettie an' we got plenty of time now. I reckoned we'd missed our chance an' you was gonna die on me but luckily that ain't the case anymore.'

'I'm a bit nervous about flyin' in the plane Eric. I hope you don't reckon I'm a squib or I'm gutless.'

'I know you ain't gutless. I seen you throw too many mickies an' ride too many rough horses to think that. Anyhow once you get used to it I'll teach you to fly the plane.'

'Don't hold your breath on that one. But I know I gotta at least get used to flyin' in it now if we're gonna get married. It's a bit like gettin' on that horse you was talkin' about, this flyin'. I reckon we'll hop in the swag together long before I'll learn to fly that bloody thing.'

CHAPTER 7

Len gave his blessing to their engagement when they called to see him and they returned to Tomahawk Plains.

The following day, while they were shoeing Nettie's horses for the next round of mustering they saw a man approaching on foot leading a mule.

'It's Tony Avery,' Nettie said as she shaded her eyes against the glare. Tony was the stockman who Eric had fought at the races, after he had drunkenly punched Nettie in the mouth. Neither he nor Nettie held a grudge over the event because they were both of a mind that grievances were settled on the spot and best forgotten thereafter.

'G'day Tony,' Eric said, as the man arrived and came over to them.

'Eric, Nettie, good to see youse both.'

'What the hell are you doin' walkin' an' leadin' a bloody mule?' Nettie asked. 'I thought you was a gun horseman.'

'Lookin' for a job I s'pose.'

'I thought you was workin' for old man Carson,' Eric said.

Tony gave a cynical laugh. 'Yeah I was.'

'An'?'

'He give me a bloody chop with the whip over nothin' much at all so I got a bit mungery an' give 'im a touch-up. Then he sacked me an' wouldn't pay me the wages that was owin' to me. He give me this bloody mule 'in lieu of wages' he reckoned an' I know why he give me the mongrel now. You'd have to be Lance bloody Skuthorp to ride the bloody thing. It can buck like a bastard, miles too good for me.'

Eric laughed. 'How far you walked Tony?'

''Bout a hundred mile it feels like.'

'You got any problem if I hire Tony Nettie?'

'No Tony's alright except when he's pissed.'

'Alright Tony we could use an extra hand. We got a bit behind with the muster, with one thing an' another. You want to sell me that mule?'

'I'll give you the bastard if you want it Eric.'

'I got a use for him an' I'll give you a tenner for him.'

'What do you want 'im for?' Nettie asked. 'Bloody mules ain't much use in this country, alright as packhorses an' out in the desert or in the rough stuff. They got feet like little anvils, never need shoein'.'

'I got a bloke needs a mount just like that,' Eric replied.

After the death of old Captain his youngest son had returned to Tomahawk Plains. Somehow the bush telegraph had told him it was safe to come home. He had been working in one of the stock camps at Victoria River Downs for a few years and had become too big for his boots in that time.

Since getting back on home ground his cocky attitude had already caused discontent among the young Aboriginal stockmen and he needed to be taken down a peg. He fancied himself as a buckjump rider and like many flash young stockmen was hard on horses and cheeky to boot. He saw himself as better than his peers and the equal of any Kitja he could put it over, which to his mind was most whitefellers.

'Yeah he's just what Johnny needs,' Eric spoke his thoughts aloud.

It was not long after Tony had arrived before the stockmen got back from tailing weaners. They came over to the horse-yards near the saddle shed to unsaddle their horses and Eric called Johnny over.

'Yeah you want somethin' Eric?' Johnny had a slight curl to his lip, in keeping with his overconfident attitude.

'You can hang up a bit they reckon from what I heard round the ridges?'

'No bloody yarraman too good for this blackfeller Eric. I got a bit of a name for meself around 'ere in case you ain't heard.'

'Yeah that's what I heard. I got somethin' for you to have a go at.' He pointed to the mule.

'That's a bloody mule.'

'You won't have a go at him then? Beneath your gun blackfeller dignity ay? Your old man would of rode him before breakfast an' not even spoke about it from what I heard about him but then he was a real man not a Wompoo.'

Eric could see that Johnny had not heard the word 'dignity' before from the frown that had superimposed itself on his face from the mention of the word onwards and deepened at the final gibe which implied incompetence.

'You reckon you can take the piss outta me just because I don't talk flash like you bloody stuck up Kitja cow-cockies.' Johnny spat on the ground and winked at the other stockmen. 'Yeah I'll ride the bastard. Trot 'im out.'

Johnny pulled the saddle off the horse he had been riding and carelessly threw it on the mule's back. It flinched but did not buck it off. He jerked the girth up and the mule cow-kicked, but he was too fast and laughed harshly as he savagely ripped the girth up another hole.

He threw the reins over the mule's neck and was on its back in a flash without touching the stirrups, as neat as anything Eric had seen before. The animal stood with its ears laid back and its tail jammed. He spurred it savagely down both shoulders and it galvanized into action. Everyone climbed the rails to watch.

Eric knew he had got his money's worth. The mule bucked as only a mule can. Johnny spurred it again and let out a whoop. 'Yow-ai! Buck you bastard, buck!' he yelled confidently.

'More gibbit Johnny!' one of the other stockmen yelled, 'More gibbit!'

Half a dozen bucks later he hit the ground hard and only just missed getting kicked in the head. The men on the fence howled with laughter. Eric smiled and winked at Nettie. Tony grinned, obviously pleased that he was not the only one who was unable to stay aboard the fractious animal and also amused to see Johnny taken down a peg.

Johnny caught the mule again and got back on. He lasted no more than three seconds before being thrown into the rails.

He got up with blood running from a cut on his eyebrow.

'He's cranky now,' Nettie whispered to Eric. Rage showed on Johnny's face as the other men jeered him.

He was no more successful at his next attempt and the mule kicked him in the ribs as he hit the ground. He got up slowly and glared at Eric. The other men were quiet then, sensing trouble.

'You're so bloody smart. You ride the mongrel,' he dared Eric.

Eric grinned. 'Thought you was gonna say that. You're only gonna spoil him the way you're goin' anyhow.'

Eric mounted the animal and it went off like a spring suddenly released. It bucked, spun, sucked back, reared and tried to cow-kick Eric's feet out of the irons. He spurred it in long fluid strokes to get the best out of it without hanging on with the hooks because he was a balance rider. He rode it easily with a smile on his face until it finally stopped bucking and stood trembling. He patted its neck before stepping off and it did not even try to kick him. The stockmen cheered him and Johnny's face was contorted with rage. Eric had humiliated him without saying a word.

'Have a go at him now that he's got the gas took outta him Johnny.'

Johnny swung on again and it bucked but this time he rode it to a standstill.

'I knew you'd handle him Johnny. You can take him in your plant, make somethin' worthwhile outta him. He'll be as tough as nails. Handy thing a good mule.'

He knew he had made a fool of Johnny in front of his peers and that it was not yet the end of the matter. He would have to keep his wits about him. One way or another, this showdown had been looming ever since Johnny had returned to Tomahawk Plains anyway. Eric had no intention of letting the flash young man get the better of him and it had to be faced sometime, the sooner the better in his opinion.

He did not have long to wait. Three weeks later they were bronco branding on an open camp. Eric was castrating a big mickey while Johnny held the head and another man the hind leg. Johnny let the head go when Eric was in the middle of the operation. The young bull threw Eric off and hooked him with a sharp horn. His knife slipped and cut his finger deeply. Johnny laughed as he saw the blood welling from Eric's finger but the other men were silent, expecting trouble.

Eric flicked blood from the cut as he bent to pick up the knife. He wiped the blood off the blade and put it back in the pouch deliberately. Then he stepped towards Johnny with his fists bunched and his eyes bleak. Johnny stood his ground and raised his fists.

Without a word Eric chopped him savagely on the nose and felt it break. He had no intention of sparring until he got Johnny's measure. He intended to treat him the way he would a scrub bull or a brumby buck and give him all he had straight up. Johnny's fists flailed but Eric ignored the hits he took as he systematically smashed the man's face.

Johnny had cuts on both cheekbones and both eyebrows. His lips were torn and he spat out a broken tooth.

Eric ripped an upward blow to his solar-plexus and the wind gushed out of him. Then he rained right and left hooks to Johnny's head until he went down.

Eric kicked him gently in the ribs with the toe of his boot. 'You had enough yet Johnny? I got more here if you want it; plenty more actually.'

Johnny nodded. Eric took his hand and helped him to his feet, where he stood unsteadily. His smoky bloodshot dark eyes showed outright enmity and it was almost a tangible thing but Eric didn't want to lose Johnny so he got his own emotions under control and pulled out his tobacco tin. To his mind if he allowed Jacky to walk off camp or if he sacked him he would be the one who lost face and reputation. It could also lead to payback from Johnny in some unexpected form in future. He pasted a couple of cigarette papers on the cut finger to stem the bleeding and stuck one to his lip for the cigarette. Then he palmed and rubbed the makings.

'You'd have to be one of the best men in the Top End Johnny. You ride an' fight like a man. You're old Captain's son alright. Best man I had here on Tomahawk Plains since he died that's for sure.'

Johnny looked at him uncertainly with a question in his eyes.

'Here shake hands Johnny. We're mates again, got him sorted out ay?'

Johnny shook his hand. There was no more fight in him and the hatred had gone out of his eyes. Eric had belted him but he had not humiliated him this time and Johnny knew he easily could have. He had left no doubt who was boss and who was next in line.

'Yeah boss, we mates again ay.'

Equilibrium had been restored without apology. Eric had reestablished his authority and he saw praise in Nettie's eyes as he finished rolling the smoke and fired it.

'Might have a bit of a blow an' a drink of tea once we finish this mick ay Johnny?'

Johnny's look was like that of a faithful dog and Eric hoped it was the beginning of something worthwhile between them. A white man in that country could not afford to be an island like some of them had tried to be in the old days.

Back then many a white boss, head-stockman, manager or squatter had copped a shovel-nosed spear in the back at night for his treatment of Aborigines or at very least woken to an empty mustering camp at a critical time.

Eric had heard the yarns and filed the information away in his mind. He wanted to be thought of as a tough but fair boss, a man with no enemies like Jack Miller had undoubtedly been in his day.

CHAPTER 8

Tomahawk Plains and Sarah Springs were run as one big block, unfenced save for the Bullock Paddock and a few horse paddocks and holding paddocks around the homestead and various mustering camps. The total area was over 4,000 square miles and the country ran right to Queen's Channel of Joseph Bonaparte Gulf to the north-east. Legune Station joined them between there and the Western Australian border and extended north to the coast along the lower reach of the Keep River.

By the time the branding and weaning was done it was time to muster the bullock paddock for the bullocks and spayed cows to go to Stone Fort on the Barkly Tableland where they would be fattened before moving down the chain to Queensland for sale via Eric's other blocks Galloway and Red Hill.

Wyndham meatworks was much closer but prices paid there were considerably lower than in Queensland and they could not fatten stock on Tomahawk Plains like on the other places anyway. This strategy got their sale cattle to the most lucrative market in the best possible condition with the least possible droving, stress and effort.

Eric's father's old wartime friend Bluey Lamont managed Stone Fort for Eric and he brought his crew of men to meet them on the road with the mob after Eric had sent one of the young stockmen ahead to give him notice they were coming.

Eric handed the mob over to Bluey and left Tony in charge of taking the horse plant home while he and Nettie rode ahead with spare mounts for themselves.

'How come you're in a hurry to get home?' Nettie asked.

'Should be a few weeks before the Wet starts with any luck an' we ain't had any time together yet since you been here. I reckon it's time we took a week or so off an' spent it with each other. We might poke along a bit an' get there quick as we can ay?'

In the mustering camps they had rolled their swags out alongside each other and at the homestead they had slept in separate beds. There had been no time for anything but work.

'You're sweet Eric. What you got planned?' she asked.

'I want to go an' get some more diamonds anyhow, before the Wet sets in an' stops me from doin' it.'

'I thought you got the diamonds off old Captain an' when he died that was the end of it.'

'Yeah I did but now he ain't here to get 'em for me anymore I still need the income.'

'You sell 'em?'

'I never told you but Stone Fort, Galloway an' Red Hill got paid for with money from diamonds that old Captain got me. We ain't made any money outta cattle for years now an' I need some more stones to send to Henry 'cause I'm gettin' short of money.'

Nettie had first met Eric's uncle Henry when he had been visiting from Egypt at the time when his son Ben Abdul had been staying at Tomahawk Plains for an extended period getting bush experience.

'He buys 'em off you?'

'No he sells 'em for me in Europe. He's sold four or five lots for me so far.'

'I thought the one you give me was the only one you had.'

'I'll show you somethin'.'

He took the blood diamond out of its pouch and handed it to her.

'That's a bloody diamond? It's huge. An' what about that red bit in the guts of it?'

'Yeah it's a diamond alright. The red bit inside it is a garnet crystal. Old Captain give it to me when he was dyin' to protect me at the crocodile hole.'

'Well I reckon his black-magic buggered up that time, fat lot a good it done me!'

'I ain't so sure. I never been superstitious like I told you but you remember me horse rooted that mornin' when we was on our way over there?'

'Yeah a quail flew up under 'im outta the kangaroo grass an' started 'im goin'.'

'Well I lost me tobacco an' matches an' also this stone but I didn't know I lost it till later after you got hurt. We never had it with us when we got to the river an' then when you got so crook an' it looked like you was dyin' I come back lookin' an' found it. Nobody but me knew what I was doin'. I never mentioned it to no-one but you started pickin' up in Darwin Hospital at exactly the same time as I found it out here.'

'Gotta be a coincidence Eric.'

'Well let's hope it ain't just a coincidence.'

'Why's that?'

'Because the Ord River is where we gotta go to get the diamonds.'

'I ain't sure I wanna do that Eric, not after what happened last time.'

'What do you do when you fall off a horse?'

'Get back on again.'

'Well this is the same. You'll always be scared of the place unless you go back an' face it, get on top of it in your head.'

'Yeah but what about the bloody crocs?'

'I reckon Captain's cousin-in-law the witch-doctor of that mob was the one that made them tracks in the sand to warn us off. Yamburra's his name an' I reckon he called the crocodile spirit onto us.'

'Well that's even worse then.'

'I handled Jacky didn't I?'

'What's that got to do with this?'

'I'll handle Yamburra if he gives us any trouble but I reckon he won't if we got this diamond with us. The red garnet in the middle is the blood of the crocodile spirit, or so Captain reckoned.'

She leaned across and kissed him. 'Let's get some more diamonds.'

CHAPTER 9

Yamburra sensed an intruder. His nostrils flared as his keen eyes swept the environs of the rock-hole, anxious to identify any alien presence.

The spirit crocodile dozed in his normal spot with his eyes shut. A dozen lesser reptiles showed no alarm either. The lazy drawl of a crow came from nearby. Nothing seemed amiss but his scalp crawled nevertheless.

He sniffed the breeze that wafted in from the north-east and smelt the familiar scent of a buck euro.

By then the waterfall had diminished to a low burble late in the dry season. No unusual sound came to his ears but with his instincts honed fine he knew there was an intruder, regardless of any signs or lack of them.

He trotted off downstream for half a mile, pausing regularly to assess his surroundings but still nothing gave the presence of strangers away.

He veered away from the river and jogged to the top of a low ridge. From there he picked up the smell of yarraman. After carefully scanning the area upwind of him he eventually made out a lone rider leading three horses.

He waited patiently, not moving until the rider was close enough to recognise that it was the same white woman who had been injured by the crocodile after the last Wet. At the time he had hoped she would not die and now he felt relief to see that she had not. However a white woman alone in the bush was unusual and he felt alarm that something was not as it should be.

She was coming towards him so he trotted back to the rock hole without pause and it was not long before she approached the river.

He watched, wary of danger, his senses alert.

Then he spotted something that had not been there before he had gone up the ridge. On the sandy bank where he had left his crocodile tracks that previous time a white man's wet clothes hung from a limb. A pair of boots sat nearby with a gunbelt and revolver. He approached with his nerves taut and saw sets of plain footprints leading to and from the clothes down into the water and back out again.

The crocodiles lay on the opposite bank as before seemingly oblivious to any intrusion, still exactly where they had been when he left. Why had they not attacked the man who had entered their waterhole? Where was he now?

Yamburra was as quiet as a puff of smoke as he warily came closer and saw a naked white man basking on a flat rock in the sun like the crocodiles, with his eyes shut and his body still wet.

The man opened his eyes and sat up but showed no surprise or alarm when he saw Yamburra. It was the same man who had come before to bury Minjurra's body.

'Yamburra, guardian of the great crocodile spirit, friend of Minjurra, I greet you.' He spoke the dialect of the crow people which was similar to that of Yamburra's clan.

'You know my name white man. How is this?'

'Minjurra told me I would know you when I saw you.'

'You buried his body in a cave here. Were you and he friends?'

'Yes he called me his son and he gave me this before he died.' He produced the crocodile blood stone from the pouch that he now wore around his neck on a thong.

'I know you did not steal that sacred stone from him white man. It is your passage and protection in my country because you tell the truth.'

'How do you know this wise one?'

'The crocodiles did not harm you when you swam in their river even when the water is lowest and more dangerous than at any other time. They are hungry now they have eaten all the sharks and barramundi and wait for the rains to bring more. They would have killed you if you had stolen that stone from Minjurra.'

'I meant no insult to them or to you but I wished to speak with you and I knew that if I rode up on my yarraman you would be gone like the early morning mist or smoke from a fire.'

'Your woman comes now.'

'Yes she knows I am here.'

'What is your name white man, friend of Minjurra?'

'My name is Eric McDonald and I was conceived at the spring hole in Minjurra's country, the place white men call Sarah Spring.'

'Tell me Eric McDonald, were you watching when I left not long ago?'

'Yes it was I who called like the crow of Minjurra's people.'

'How was it that I did not smell you?'

'I rolled in the dirt of a euro's camp and rubbed the dust into my skin and my hair and my clothes.'

'I knew you were here but you deceived me. You have the cunning of a dingo bitch with pups Eric McDonald. What is it you wish to discuss with me?'

'I want your permission to look for the stones that Minjurra found in this place and for me and my woman to camp here.'

Yamburra smiled. 'You speak directly Eric McDonald, not like the whites who try to trick my people with their lies. I am the only one of my people who may make camp here but upstream of the waterfall you may camp. You can search for your stones here but I warn you again that the crocodiles are hungry and not to tempt them unnecessarily.'

'Minjurra told me you were a man of honour.'

'My father was the brother of his mother.'

The white woman came on her yarraman then, approaching warily and Eric introduced her.

'Yamburra my woman's name is Nettie.'

'Net–tie,' Yamburra pronounced.

'Yamburra I have heard of you,' Nettie responded but her command of the dialect was sketchy.

'How long will you spend here Eric?' Yamburra asked.

'Only so many days this time Yamburra but we will come again.' He held up both hands with fingers extended.

Yamburra was satisfied with that.

'I will leave you now Eric. You are welcome in my country.'

As Yamburra trotted off Eric noticed an amused smile on Nettie's face. 'What's funny?'

'Tell you later. Well you were right when you reckoned you'd handle Yamburra.'

'Yeah as long as we don't upset him we oughta be alright here.'

'You went in the water with them bloody crocs everywhere?'

'Yeah I reckoned the stone would protect me an' I stank like a wallaroo anyhow so I wanted to wash it off of me an' my clothes.'

'You got more blackfeller faith than what I got then that's for sure.'

'If we're gonna camp up past the waterfall we'll have to go around the long way. Them cliffs come right in against it just up there an' we won't get the horses through. We'll go back an' find a way round.'

Eric dressed and they rode back onto the ridge and followed it south until they found a spot where they could get down onto the river again.

Above the waterfall the river widened out and had a wide water-worn rock bottom, with rock-holes gouged into its surface by millennia of monsoon floods. Broken cliffs formed the eastern bank and the western side sloped away more gently in a series of low volcanic hills and breakaway gullies.

The flood-line was lower there than downstream of the fall because the river was wider but still fairly high because of the damming effect of the bottle-neck cliffs downstream. They found an ample cave just above that line which was suitable for their camp. A deep rock-hole was close to the site and slightly south of them was a grassy area between the river and the cliffs where they hobbled out their horses on the sweet grazing.

Eric had brought fishing lines and they went to the rock-hole to try to catch their dinner because the day was drawing to a close.

'What we gonna use for bait?' Nettie asked.

'I never thought of that.'

'Maybe you could use your worm.' She smiled mischievously.

'My worm?'

'The little white one you was wigglin' about back there when you was talkin' to the old goori-goori.' She burst into peals of laughter.

'That's what you was laughin' about before?'

She nodded, not able to speak because she was laughing so much.

'At least I got one, not like some people I could name.'

'Sorry Eric. I just never seen it before an' it just seemed funny to me when I come up an' found you in the raw.'

'I never seen you in the raw yet Nettie.'

She looked at him soberly. 'Maybe it's about time you did or you'll start to reckon it ain't ever gonna happen.'

'Well seein' we ain't got any bait to go fishin' why don't we have a swim in the hole? See what else we can come up with.'

'I'm game.' She began undressing.

They swam and frolicked, chased and teased each other and they both knew the game could have only one conclusion. Their touches became more intimate, provoking, yearning for satisfaction until finally Eric hugged her close and they kissed. Their need became immediate as they sank to their knees on the smooth rock, fondling each other erotically.

They made love on the warm rock and then lay looking up at the sky as they smoked their cigarettes, completely comfortable now in their nudity.

'You still reckon it's a worm?' Eric asked playfully.

She rolled over to face him and kissed him gently.

'If it is, it's what I've needed for a long time Eric. I never woulda expected anythin' to be that good even though it's all I been thinkin' about lately. Thanks for waitin'.'

'At least we got time to waste now if we wanna. I'm glad we waited too Nettie.'

'I love you even more now Eric.'

'What's for dinner, now that we got sidetracked woman?'

'Salt meat an' get to bed early I reckon.'

They laid their swags together for the first time that night and slept comfortable in each other's arms after again satisfying their urges.

Eric woke as daylight came but Nettie was not beside him. He saw her at the waterhole fishing and went to join her.

He stooped to kiss her and saw she had already caught two small barramundi.

'What you usin' for bait?'

'I found a few little grey barra frogs under the rocks.'

He squatted down behind her and cupped her breasts. It felt nice the way the nipples tightened and the skin puckered at his touch. She made no move to discourage him.

'You'll scare the fish,' she admonished playfully.

'Two fish is enough.' He nuzzled her neck.

'What you want for breakfast, fish or nooky?'

'Both but nooky first.'

Later they explored the riverbed, finding gravel in many niches and grooves carved into the rock by water. Eric had brought a coarse kitchen sieve and he used it to screen the gravel. Amongst the water-worn sand and gravel were a number of small diamonds and at the bottom of the sediment in one hole he found a large cubic black crystal diamond.

'That don't look like a diamond to me,' Nettie said when he showed her.

'Yeah it's what they call Bort but it is a diamond an' maybe it's an omen too.'

'Omen? You're soundin' more like a bloody goori-goori all the time.'

'Old Captain's clan is the crow people an' it was his crow call that helped me find the diamond when it got lost. If the stone he give me is the crocodile blood diamond this one's the crow diamond. Maybe it'll help us to find more of 'em.'

She shook her head but did not reply.

By lunchtime they had filled a tobacco tin with small diamonds. They fished for their meal and ate and then whiled the afternoon away swimming and luxuriating in each other's company.

They watched the shadows spearing out across the riverbed toward them like fugitive one-dimensional spirit beings as the sun set behind a rocky knoll to the west. The scene had an almost spiritual atmosphere.

'I'm happy Eric an' I'm glad you made me come back here an' face up to me fears.'

'I never been this happy before in me life neither Nettie.'

'It wouldn't a happened if you never got around old Yamburra. You're just like a blackfeller sometimes the way you know how to manage 'em.'

'I told you I got black blood.'

'Yeah but I got more'n you because mine's a generation closer than yours. Me mother was half-caste an' me grandfather was Afghan on her side. That's where I get the colour of me eyes from, the Afghan.'

'Nobody else got them greeny-brown eyes like yours Nettie. I like 'em an' you're real pretty.'

'You wouldn't know what colour they is. You spend all your time lookin' at me everywhere else except me eyes.'

'Guilty your honour but you're no better you know. You don't mind gettin' an eyeful or a handful neither.'

Their ten days passed too quickly but by the time they left they had filled a sizable glass jar with marketable diamonds, including a couple of pinks, one small green one and well over two dozen large good-quality stones.

As they were riding out they encountered Yamburra and Eric showed him the black stone.

'It is a crow stone Eric. It will bring you good fortune.'

Yamburra showed them his own diamond which had the same garnet inclusion as his but was as large as a pullets' egg, a truly magnificent stone.

They reluctantly rode towards home, each a little loath to leave their idyll behind.

'You reckon I might have a baby outta this Eric?'

'I dunno, maybe. We been doin' what you gotta do to make one.'

'I hope so. Do you mind if I do?'

'Sounds alright to me. Ain't that why people get married?'

'I don't reckon I ever been this happy before Eric.'

'I know I ain't Nettie. I reckon we're good together, sort of like it was meant to happen.'

CHAPTER 10

By race time the following year Nettie was obviously pregnant, her little belly already filling her shirt. Eric forbade her from riding despite her protests and Len, who had arrived a week earlier, backed him up. Len had been delighted when he arrived to find his daughter was expecting.

They had ordered pedal-wireless sets for each of the places and organised men to erect sixty-feet-tall aerial towers which would enable regular contact between their properties. That was still in the process of happening. Eric was learning Morse code in preparation and would feel happier once it was operational, especially with Nettie pregnant if he had to call on help for her birth from Joan Smith at Timber Creek or a midwife somewhere.

At the race-meeting they both came in for a fair amount of ribbing from friends, although there was no apparent disapproval regarding the out-of-wedlock gestation there on the frontier.

'Looks like the Tomahawk Plains races started somethin'. Hope it ain't catchin',' Bluey observed laconically.

Tony Avery got raging drunk again but stayed peaceful this time. The daughter of a head-stockman from one of the Victoria River Downs stock camps had her eye on him and he had his on her.

Nettie drank lemonade and had stopped smoking until after the baby was born.

Len Chambers beat Eric for the cup riding one of Nettie's horses. Tony's new girlfriend won the ladies race on a VRD plant horse.

The main topic of conversation was the depression that gripped the land like a physical thing. Cattle prices had been low for ten years already and the banks had little sentiment for those who could not service their debts.

'This country's buggered,' one man said.

'I seen it all before. It'll come good again, you'll see,' Jack Miller countered.

'Yeah, if we can last that bloody long,' someone replied, 'Can't see it happenin' in my time Jack. Cattle are just about worthless, couldn't even give stores away. Maybe worth somethin' if you can fatten 'em but how many can do that an' then get 'em to market? Walk 'emselves poor on the road gettin' there an' that's if you can afford the drovin'.'

'Might be alright if you're Lord bloody Vestey or someone like him,' another retorted, 'but somehow or other I missed out on that silver spoon.'

'Don't know that even Vestey's makin' money outta cattle. He's got a few other irons in the fire an' not all that legal neither,' another responded.

They all had stories of bagmen or swaggies humping their blueys in search of work. Many of the bagmen were city men from the south, sorely out of their depth and way out of their environment. Having no concept of northern heat and distance they often perished on the long dry stages in unfamiliar country. Everyone agreed it was a sad state of affairs but none had a solution to the quandary.

A few weeks after the races a Chinaman and his young daughter turned up carrying cigarette swags and little else, both barefoot and footsore. They had walked from Halls Creek over the border.

Nettie talked to Eric about hiring them.

'Look we can't take everyone on that walks in,' was his answer. 'We just can't afford it Nettie.'

Nettie gave the pair a meal and Eric joined them as they ate. 'I can't offer you a job but if you wanna stop here an' grow a vegetable garden down by the creek we'll buy your stuff off of you.'

The man was effusively grateful because he said the girl could not keep going much further the way her feet were and her only chance of work in Darwin would be as a prostitute if she could not get domestic work as a housemaid on a station before they reached the port.

Tommy and Lily Tan set up camp on the creekbank and within weeks had ground cultivated and fenced ready for seed that Eric ordered.

Nettie gave birth to twins, Len and Lily, on 15th September 1930. Lily Tan and one of the Aboriginal women from the camp assisted her and the birth was uncomplicated.

Eric presented Nettie with the elaborate diamond necklace that he had collected from Sunil Syna when they had last gone to Darwin.

'I'm gonna need a packhorse to cart me bloody diamonds around if you keep this up Eric,' Nettie joked.

'I tried to give 'em to old Eliza at our family reunion when I was twenty-one. She told me to keep 'em for me girl. Well that's what I done. You're the only girl I ever had.'

'You've had 'em all that time? I love you Eric an' it ain't because of the diamonds. I just do an' the babies you give me are better than anythin' else. I wish I could meet Eliza.'

'I doubt if you ever will, she's ninety now. An' yeah I love you too.'

Eliza the family matriarch was Eric's great-grandmother and had once been a drover and bushranger, posing as a man and going by the alias Elijah Henry in her heyday.

He had written telling his parents that he and Nettie were engaged, and that Nettie was pregnant. He had told them the pedal-wireless had been installed and said they would be waiting for a Morse transmission from Kalgoorlie at ten pm on the last night of the month.

They had finally made radio contact a few weeks before the birth, at which time Sarah had messaged Eric that on 24th July an expedition had left Alice Springs, or Stuart as it was still sometimes called, to search for gold in the south-west of Centralia. 'A man named Harry Lasseter claims to have found a miles long gold reef in that Petermann Range area. Do you remember hearing about him?'

'No.'

'Taffy reckons Lasseter got wind of the reef Taffy was mining there at the time he rescued us when we were on the run from the police and now Lasseter is claiming he found it.'

'Well good luck to them as long as Taffy's mate Evan is not still mining there.'

'I will let you know how they get on.'

There had not been any more news of the expedition and after the twins were born Eric telegraphed his parents with the news. 'Twins Len and Lily born 15 September. Nettie reckons they are better than foals and both look like me. She is smiling a fair bit.'

After a pause the answer came. 'Ben says it must run in the family because we have twins and now you do too. Tell Nettie we are so pleased for both of you and remind her that I told her the morning after the races that she would get another chance with you. When are you planning to get married?'

'When we get around to it is about our best guess.'

'Do not wait until we are too old to make the trip. Love to you all.'

'Love back. We will try to get it organised.'

'Over and out from us Eric.'

'Yes ditto.'

CHAPTER 11

Nettie missed the next muster, being housebound with rearing the twins. She loved being a mother but missed the stockwork she had done ever since she had been not much more than a child.

Early in May they read in a newspaper that the prospector Lasseter had perished out in the Centralian desert after a mysterious chain of events. It seemed the expedition had not found the fabulous reef, the quest for which had apparently entranced depression-ridden Australia. Gold often had that effect on people, especially in hard times.

Towards the end of the year's cattle-work when they were mustering and tailing the bullocks to go to Stone Fort, Eric was working from home instead of staying in the mustering camp.

The twins were a year old by then and he sat on the verandah nursing both of them. He enjoyed fatherhood but realised he had missed a good part of their growth while he was in the camp with the ringers.

Nettie brought drinks out for them both and he thought she looked happy. 'You remember you reckoned you'd teach me to fly the plane one day?' she asked.

'Yeah you changed your mind about it?'

'I've missed not bein' in the camp this year. I know it can't be helped seein' I got the kids but I been thinkin' if I could fly the plane, next muster I could fly out an' spot cattle for you. That'd probably save a lot of ridin' an' I'd be doin' somethin' useful instead a just lookin' after kids.'

'Who'd look after the kids while you was out bein' an aviator?'

'Lily's here helpin' with 'em a fair bit anyhow an' she wouldn't mind.'

'You really wanna do it? You ain't just sayin' it because you reckon that's what I want you to do?'

'Yeah I do Eric. I wanna work with you even if I can't be in the camp while the kids are young an' I got used to the idea of flyin' now anyhow.'

'What you say makes sense you know. I never thought of usin' the plane for musterin' but it's a good idea.'

'You'll teach me to fly it then?'

'Yeah when I get back from the drovin' trip ay.'

True to his word Eric began teaching Nettie the fundamentals of flying, first explaining the principles of wing-stall, aerodynamics and the reason aeroplanes stayed in the air at all.

To demonstrate what he was telling her, he made paper planes and they experimented with various settings for rudder and flaps. Nettie grasped the concept quickly and they laughed a lot at the aerobatics they could get the models to perform.

If one of the paper planes landed within reach of children's hands it usually spelt doom for the plane. The little ones enjoyed the game too, as much as the adults if not more.

Next he taught her to service the plane, to fuel and check it over for damage and grease the wheel hubs. He showed her how to remove the sparkplugs and clean and adjust the point gap. They also dismantled the magneto, greased the cam and cleaned and set the points.

She learnt to start the engine by swinging the propeller. Then she would taxi along the strip practicing steering and becoming familiar with the operation of the flaps.

They went up for a flight with Nettie sitting on Eric's lap to observe what he did because the passenger seat was behind the pilot's seat. He had the seat pushed right back to give them enough space in the small cockpit.

'Don't you get any ideas while we're up here,' she joked.

'You just give me one.'

'Wait till we're on the ground Eric ay.'

When they levelled out at about 1,000 feet he handed the controls over to her and slid back so that she sat between his knees and could work unimpeded.

She learnt to turn and climb and descend following his directions.

'Alright take her home,' he said in her ear after half an hour of instruction.

She flew back and lined the strip up and then he slid forward and took over for the landing. Then he slid back again and let her taxi back to the hangar, idle down and shut down.

She turned and kissed him. 'That was great once you stop bein' scared. You can get any ideas you want now we're on the ground.'

Within a month Nettie was flying solo. She found it exhilarating and gradually gained confidence as she learnt the limits of both the aircraft and her own ability.

By the beginning of the next muster, she was a capable pilot and they found the plane saved the horsemen considerable time by scouting ahead and directing men where they were needed, rather than having to cover country where there were no cattle.

She experimented and found she could muster scattered mobs together and turn them towards the riders by flying low and wheeling them with the plane. Because the machine was foreign to bush cattle and was noisier than a horse, she had to learn stockwork all over again so as not to run them too hard and overheat them in the process. Learning what altitude and distance from the mob encouraged the cattle to settle best took time and patience. She also learnt to use the shadow of the plane to wheel wayward beasts rather than stir the mob up by flying lower.

'You're a bloody genius,' Eric told her as she flew him home one evening. He had taken to going home with her every second night so he could spend time with his family and it was a happy time for all of them. He realised that to spend the other night in camp with the men also helped to keep harmony in the operation. Men respected a boss who camped and worked with them.

'Why am I a genius?'

'You invented the idea of usin' the plane for musterin'. We'll finish a month earlier than usual this year an' that's all because of you. I weren't too sure about it at first because I reckoned you'd just stir the cattle up with it but you got a real feel for doin' it this way now.'

She smiled as she brought the plane in and landed smoothly. Lily and the twins waited at the hangar because they had heard her coming.

They now kept fuel at the mustering camp so she could refuel at lunch time, thus saving time and distance. At first she had been going back to the homestead to fuel the machine to get through the day and also to check on the twins until they settled into the routine.

They had developed regular wireless contact with Eric's parents in Kalgoorlie at eleven o'clock each Saturday night when long-distance communication was best and inquisitive eyes were mostly otherwise engaged. Reliable wireless contact over that distance often depended on weather and solar activity and was not always a certainty.

During the year they had upgraded to the new keyboard versions of the Traegar transceivers on all their places which made communication easier again and Nettie had learnt to type and use the set because she was the one at home while he was in the mustering camp.

She suggested they should have a wireless set in the plane to communicate with a base station.

'It'll come before too long the way everythin' is gettin' mechanised. We're gonna see lots of new gadgets like radio telephone I reckon,' Eric said.

CHAPTER 12

The Tomahawk Plains homestead was badly damaged in a cyclone at New Year but no-one was injured. Eric realised it had not withstood the storm because much of the bush timber frame was badly weakened by termites, a fact which had not been apparent until the event had exposed the damage.

They shifted to the hangar once the cyclone was over and set up camp there until a new building could be erected. It was a pretty basic camp but it kept the rain out, although with children to rear it was inconvenient. The plane was left exposed to the elements for the remainder of the Wet and it deteriorated as a result.

Eric had received payment for the diamonds he and Nettie had got at the Ord River. He had also sent a second shipment away, for which he was still awaiting payment.

'As soon as the Wet's over I'm gonna get a carpenter to get stuck into buildin' a new house for us. I'll trade the old Auster in on a new Tiger Moth too. It's gettin' on in years anyhow,' Eric said. 'Father used it for a fair while before he give it to me.'

'Yeah well you'll be too busy with the muster to worry about buildin' anythin' yourself so I reckon that's a good idea. I reckon the new plane's a good idea too. This one's had a bit of a rough life.'

'I'm gonna get the new house built outta stone so the white ants can't eat it again. There's good flat sandstone slabs on some of the ridges here an' we'll get a cement floor too. The only timber will be the ceilin' an' the frame for the roof an' we'll treat that with arsenic to beat the ants.'

'Won't that be dangerous?'

'No not up in the ceilin' under the roof.'

The new house was ready to move into by the time their next baby Nathan arrived on 20th October 1932, just after the twins' second birthday. The building was a sturdy affair with rough sandstone walls two feet thick, concrete foundations and floor. The ceiling was sawn timber and the roof was galvanized iron. They decided it would not blow down in a cyclone, burn in a fire or be susceptible to termite attack. A charcoal room which was far superior to the old Coolgardie safe was constructed on the verandah as a cool-room for keeping foodstuffs fresh longer.

Eric bought the new DH 82 Tiger Moth plane and they were both happy that it was more suitable for their needs than the old Auster had been. It had a 120 horsepower Gypsy III engine and was capable of very low flying speed which suited mustering. It required only a short strip for landing and take-off, was very maneuverable and of simple but robust construction.

With the depression continuing and cattle prices staying low they depended on income from the diamonds which Eric got regularly from the Kimberley.

There had been some local excitement when the renegade Aborigine Nemarluk, from the Daly River region well north-east of them, had been captured along with a number of his murderous band on Legune Station not far from their northern boundary. They had killed the Japanese crew of the shark lugger Ouida in August 1931 near the mouth of the Fitzmaurice River and had been fugitives for quite some time. The captives were taken to Fannie Bay Gaol at Darwin but Namarluk escaped and was on the run again for six months before being recaptured early in 1934, in the same area as previously.

They kept regular wireless contact with Eric's parents at Kalgoorlie and it seemed they too were weathering the depression better than most. They had upgraded their mine infrastructure prior to the crash and were now putting out more gold than ever before, much of which they sold through Eric's Uncle Henry on the European black-market.

Just before the twins' sixth birthday Nettie was waiting for the regular communication on their radio transceiver late on a Saturday night.

'Kalgoorlie base to Tomahawk Plains,' Sarah's message came.

'Tomahawk Plains receiving,' she sent back.

'I've got bad news for Eric. Ben had his back broken in a mine cave-in and the doctor has doubts he will live. If Eric can get away and come down I would like to see him and he will probably want to see his father too if he is not going to pull through.'

'I'll get Eric to reply once we talk about it Sarah.'

Nettie gave Eric the message.

'Jesus that ain't too good is it? I never would of expected that. I often reckon we'll be gettin' a message that old Eliza has died. Yeah tell Mother I'll leave first thing in the mornin', should be there in two days I reckon.'

Nettie returned to the set and messaged, 'Eric will leave early tomorrow morning and should be there in two days. We are both thinking about you and hoping Ben will come out of it all right.'

'Thank you Nettie. We shall be waiting to see him. Over and out.'

'Yes over and out Sarah.'

Eric shut the set down after she sent the message and Nettie hugged him. 'I'm sorry Eric.'

'You don't mind if I go do you?'

'No you gotta go, otherwise he might die an' you wouldn't a seen 'im.'

He left at daylight the next morning and Nettie wished she could have gone with him but with three children and the place to look after that was not really an option even if the plane could have carried them all.

Eric arrived home ten days after leaving.

'How's Ben Eric?' Nettie asked.

'Not too good. They still don't know if he'll pull through.'

'How did it happen? He don't work underground in the mines anymore does he?'

'No. There was a cave-in down in one of the drives late at night an' he went an' took charge of the rescue. One bloke was killed an' one was trapped by the leg. He got the rest of 'em out an' was cuttin' the bloke's leg off with his pocketknife when the roof come down on him.'

'Is he conscious?'

'He come to for a minute one night when I was sittin' with him, just opened his eyes for a bit an' then drifted off again.'

'Did he know you?'

'Yeah I think he did.'

'How's Sarah handlin' it?'

'Not bad considerin' but she was pretty upset when it happened I reckon. Lucky that Gordy's there to help her run the show. He's pretty handy with the mine work.'

'You shoulda stopped down there longer.'

'No point Nettie. He might or mightn't survive an' he could hang on for months before there's any change so the doctor reckons. Nothin' anyone can do now, just wait an' see I reckon.'

They kept regular contact with Sarah but it was six months before Ben could leave the hospital and even then the doctors said that he would never walk again. That was a considerably better outcome than could easily have been the case.

'I got him a wheelchair and he says he will not need it for long. I have serious doubts about that but you know what Ben is like. If he says he will do something he usually does,' Sarah messaged them.

'Tell him good day and we'll get down when we can get away,' Eric replied.

'He would like that if you have the time.'

CHAPTER 13

The world was gripped by economic depression and there had been political unrest in Europe as the Nazi regime in Germany led by Adolf Hitler flexed its might and threatened neighbouring countries.

For the past few years there had been talk of war again and the newspapers said it was inevitable. Then Germany, the Free City of Danzig, Russia and a small Slovak contingent joined forces to invade Poland. Germany started the invasion before their other allies on 1st September and the news that Britain and France had declared war on Germany came over the pedal-wireless.

'We'll be in it soon too I reckon,' Eric said.

'You won't have to go though Eric, will you?' Nettie asked nervously.

'Yeah I reckon I gotta go Nettie, like Father an' Bluey joined up for the last one.'

'But farmers an' graziers an' stockmen an' drovers an' meatworkers never had to go. They never got called up. Protected industry or somethin' they called it.'

'It's our duty though the way I look at it.'

Then a message came over the pedal-wireless that Australia had declared war on Germany the previous day, 3rd September, 1939.

'Well, looks like that's it Nettie. I'm gonna enlist in the Air Force. I'd rather do that than be a footslogger an' there ain't no Light Horse cavalry like it was no more.'

'When will you do that?' She knew he had made up his mind and accepted that she would not be able to dissuade him from his decision.

'I'll go to Darwin in the next week or two an' join up. Then I'll probably have to wait a while before I gotta go.'

The twins were nine and Nat was seven. Eric was torn between loyalty to his family and his country but knew he would never be able to hold his head up if he did not enlist.

They flew into Darwin the following week for him to join up, expecting that he would have to wait some time for a posting but when he did enlist he found that a sense of urgency prevailed. He was told to report to the aerodrome at eight am the next day, when he would be flown south for training.

Now that their impending separation was thrust on them at such short notice, they realised there was so much to discuss and so little time in which to do so. They attended to urgent business then booked into a hotel for the night but neither of them was relaxed and they just lay in each other's arms talking until the sun rose.

Nettie went with him to the aerodrome to see him off, feeling very apprehensive about the future.

'You better get one of them new short-wave radios while you're in town so you'll be able to hear what's goin' on,' Eric suggested, 'an' I hear there's a new Traeger radio telephone out so you can talk instead of typin' a message. You better organise one for yourself an' tell the others to get 'em too.'

'I'm gonna miss you like hell Eric. We're all gonna miss you like hell.'

'Yeah an' I'll miss you all too. I'll write an' let you know how you can contact me. You gonna be alright by yourself lookin' after everythin' here at home?'

'Yeah I'll be alright Eric. I just hope you will too an' that you'll come back to us at the end of it.'

'I will Nettie.' He gave her a wink and a confident smile.

They heard a loud-speaker announcement giving five minutes for Eric to board his flight.

'You better have a sleep before you fly home,' he told her.

'Yeah I will. Just hold me now Eric. We been together ten year now you know.'

They kissed then, a long kiss, as they both agonised over their impending separation.

'I gotta go now. I love you all. Look after yourself.'

'Come home safe please Eric.'

He boarded the plane and a few minutes later it took off. She watched as it flew out over the sea before turning south-east.

Eric had a window seat and he could see Nettie still standing where he had left her as they passed back over the strip. She looked tiny and lonely standing there, her face turned up as she watched.

She had a big job in front of her raising their family and running Tomahawk Plains but he knew she was strong. That was part of why he loved her.

The pang of their sudden separation was almost a physical cramp in his stomach, which made him realise just how inseparable and dependant they had become. It was not something that either of them could have articulated easily but it was patently obvious to him as Darwin fell astern of the plane.

CHAPTER 14

'Bandits two o'clock!' the urgent call crackled on the radio.

It was Eric's first daytime mission with his Spitfire squadron. Previously all their sorties had been at night and provided they did not get caught in the German searchlights and hit by ack-ack fire their chances of survival had been good. This time they were flying as fighter-support for a daytime bombing raid on a German rail yard. Their drop tanks which extended fuel range to 1,100 miles made raids into Germany possible.

The evil looking Ju 87 Stuka fighter-bombers came at them out of the sun and they were caught napping. Already in the first few seconds of the engagement two Spitfires trailed smoke and he saw first one and then the other pilot abandon their stricken craft. Their parachutes blossomed and he felt reassured by the fact they were alive and with luck would survive even if it was in an enemy prison camp.

The ensuing dogfight was fast and furious for the next twenty minutes. Three Stukas had gone down in that time.

Eric glanced at his fuel-gauge and knew they would have to break off the engagement in the next ten or so minutes. Then he spotted the ugly black shape of a bandit in his rearview mirror and slammed his foot on the rudder as he pulled the throttle full on at the same time. The Spitfire responded like a good camp-horse and the burst of fire from the Stuka went wide.

He tried to manoeuvre into position to attack the bandit but the Stuka was fast and evasive. Twice he fired short machinegun bursts to no effect as the enemy crossed his sights.

He came up behind it and hit the gun-button again. Shiny metal flew off the tail of the enemy plane before it dived suddenly to avoid him, while at the same time another Stuka below him swung upward in an evasive move from a separate skirmish oblivious of his presence.

He dipped his nose, watching the gunsight as it swung towards his quarry. It seemed to be on a collision course with the other Stuka and he expected they would hit each other. His sight came on the target and he fired all his guns. The whole plane shuddered with the recoil. For an instant he had both planes in his sights as his machinegun fire chewed at them. They both rapidly began trailing smoke as he followed the first one and kept up his fire. It was burning fiercely and he lost sight of the other one.

His radio crackled. 'Break off engagement, mission accomplished. Alright boys head for home.'

He saw the cockpit of the Stuka slide back and he stopped firing to let the enemy pilot parachute to safety.

They had lost three of their number and had downed five of the enemy. In that chance second it seemed he had scored two of them.

That night in the canteen they all drank to the pilot who had not parachuted to safety that day. Someone proposed a toast to Eric's two kills on his first real encounter with the enemy. The atmosphere was light-hearted in spite of the deadly nature of their work. They were there to kill Germans and Eric felt good about his first blood.

'Mail call!' came a shout.

There was a letter from Nettie, and Eric left the canteen and took it to his room to open.

Dearest Eric,

Things are good here. I hope they are for you too.

I said in my last letter I was worried I wouldn't have enough fuel for the plane to do the muster because of petrol rationing. Well, both Jack and Bluey sent me their ration coupons. They both told the authorities they had motor vehicles and nobody checked up. So far I've had enough petrol as long as I'm careful.

Lenny is in the camp and Lily wanted to go too but I wouldn't let her. It would be different if you were there to keep an eye on her. She flies out with me each day and then musters with the men and has to be content with that. The muster is going well and we'll be finished in about a month.

There are no white men of any worth so I've had to put Johnny in charge as head-stockman. I was worried he'd cause trouble without you to keep him in line but he's been good. He's taken the twins under his wing and Lenny in particular is thriving and loving every minute of it. I think the responsibility is doing him good. You'd be so proud of him and he's a real little man now.

We're all proud of you too. I pray for you every night even though you know I've never been religious. Times like this make you think about things though and maybe there is something in it.

I talked to Ben on the radio last night while Sarah pedalled for him. They've got one of the new Traeger radio telephone sets. He sounded pretty cheerful. They're both proud of you too and send their love. They've built a swimming pool and Ben's learning to swim with just his arms and he still reckons he's going to walk again. Maybe he will too, if being stubborn is what it takes.

The kids' lessons have had to go by the wayside till after the muster and they love that of course. I sometimes wonder if I'll manage to get Lenny interested again now he thinks he's grown up. He's never been what you'd call a good student and as you know I'm barely educated myself. I reckon he's probably a bit like you were at the same age.

I'm glad you like what you're doing. Those Spitfires sound like they'd be good to have but I can't imagine flying at that speed. I don't know how I'd manage without our little plane. The only time I've been on a horse since you left is when we're drafting cattle. I always get on a horse for that.

The kids send their love. Lenny hopes the war will last long enough so that he can come and fly with you! I wish it was over now.

Jack and Bluey said to say hullo to you and so did Tommy and Lily.

We all miss you Eric and I love you so much.

Nettie. XXXX

P.S. Come home soon! XXX

Eric read the letter again. He always marvelled at how articulate Nettie was in her letters, although like him she had very little schooling. They were both readers and he knew he had learnt more by reading than he ever had at school.

Her letters always made him feel homesick for her and the kids and Tomahawk Plains.

CHAPTER 15

When Eric heard the news that Australia was at war with Japan, following simultaneous attacks on Pearl Harbour, Kota Bharu, Singapore, Thailand and Guam he realised that Australia was now directly threatened by the new enemy. He applied to be transferred home to fight against the Japanese. Prior to that he had been quite content to be fighting to protect the British Empire but he saw this new development as a personal threat to his homeland.

His CO said he would do what he could but was loath to recommend the transfer because every pilot they had was needed in England as the war was now at a critical stage.

He wrote to Nettie telling her that he had applied to be sent home but did not like his chances of it happening in the short term.

She received the letter towards the end of January and she also had been quite apprehensive about the talk that the Japanese would invade Australia. What will I do if they do invade? What can I do to protect what we have?

She listened avidly to the news broadcasts on short-wave Radio Australia and was glad Eric had told her to buy the set. It meant that at least news was not a month old when she got it like it had often been in the past. The pedal-wireless had been a boon but this was revolutionary.

The Wet looked as if it may finish early and she was getting organised for the muster when fine weather did come. She got the horses in and they started breaking in some colts to put into the plant for the muster.

The Traeger radio broke down and she decided they could not afford to be without it in those uncertain times. She flew to Darwin, taking it in for repair. She had been too busy to write to Eric before she left but decided to stay with Jack and Ethel while the wireless was being fixed and assumed she would get time to write then.

As she came in for her landing at Darwin after skirting a new military aerodrome that had been constructed a few miles south of the town she could see the civil airfield was also a hive of activity compared to their last visit. She realised she should have anticipated that change given the war footing but it had not occurred to her.

She landed and taxied over to refuel. Two military policemen drove up in a funny looking little vehicle.

'Did you just land that plane?' one of them asked.

'Yeah, why? What's wrong with that?'

'You'll have to come with us.'

'Can I get me plane fuelled first?'

'Have you got coupons?'

'Yeah.'

He instructed a man to fuel the plane and he took the relevant number of coupons from Nettie.

'He'll fix it up and park it when he's finished. You come with us.'

She got into the back of the small vehicle which had open sides and a canvas canopy. They took her to a new corrugated-iron igloo shaped building which had not been there when she had come in with Eric when he enlisted over two years earlier. The airfield had obviously been used by the military while building the new one. She was escorted into a waiting room and one of them stayed with her while the other one left.

Half an hour passed and she was getting annoyed because she did not have the time to waste. She wanted to get the radio repaired and get home as soon as possible.

The other MP returned and ushered her into an office and left her standing there. A man worked on some papers at a desk but he did not look up.

'Ay!' she called out and he looked up sharply.

'I'll be with you in a minute!' he snapped in an irritated tone. She could see he was an officer.

He finished what he was doing and looked up. 'I'm told you just flew a light plane in and landed without authorisation.'

'Didn't know I needed it.'

'Your name?'

'Annette McDonald,' she lied.

'Where from?'

'Tomahawk Plains, over near the West Australia border past Timber Creek.'

'Do you have a licence to fly that plane?'

''Course I have,' she lied again.

'Can I see it please?'

'I ain't got it with me.'

'You know you're supposed to have it on you whenever you're flying.'

'I forgot it.'

'It doesn't matter. It's irrelevant right now because I'm going to have to requisition your aircraft anyway. All private planes are needed for the war effort.'

'But I need it to run the place.'

'I can't help that Missus McDonald. I'm afraid it's not negotiable. I'll give you a requisition order so you can be compensated for the aircraft.'

'But how will I get home?'

'That's not my problem either Missus McDonald.'

Nettie got the requisition order and the MPs took her back to the plane to get her duffle bag and the radio, before dropping her at the gate which was guarded by a soldier. The perimeter of the airfield was encircled by barb-wire entanglement. She saw high posts with floodlights pointing inward and outward and searchlights that pointed skyward.

She was fuming as she walked towards town carrying her duffle bag and the heavy radio. She should have realised Darwin would have been crawling with military personnel and should have landed on the road near Jack's place instead. She put the radio in for repair at the same shop where she had originally bought it but was told it could take months to get parts for it because of military preference. That was something she had not even considered. Then she took a taxi out to Jack's place where she was warmly greeted. She told them what had happened.

'How will you get home now?' Jack asked.

'I dunno Jack. I'll work somethin' out.'

They talked the afternoon away before a thought came to her. 'Jack can I borrow a horse an' a pair of pliers an' a pair of leather gloves?'

'Yeah of course you can. What do you want 'em for?'

'I'm gonna shake me plane back off them bastards.'

'You'll never do it Nettie. The place is guarded an' there's barbwire fences to get through. You won't even get in there, let alone get the plane an' manage to take off before they get a hold of you.'

'Yeah I know that Jack. That's why I want the pliers an' gloves to cut the fence. Once I'm in there I got a fair chance of gettin' off the ground before anyone comes along. Once I'm in the air I'm gone, too late to argue about it then.'

'Guards patrol the fence at night.'

'Yeah I reckoned they would but they can't be everywhere at once.'

'It's too risky Nettie. They might shoot you. The military ain't like the police you know.'

'I ain't got much choice because I need the plane. I can't run the place without it now that Eric ain't here an' I only got blackfellers to do it with. I know they're pretty handy men but the plane makes it all possible for me.'

'There must be a better way.'

'No me mind's made up Jack.'

She arranged that she would leave the borrowed horse with her nurse friend at the hospital and Jack could pick it up from there the next day.

The airfield was brightly floodlit as she approached it and her heart sank for a moment before she realised it would make her task easier if she had the light to work by, as well as to watch out for guards.

She sneaked along outside the wire until she located the plane which was parked close inside the fence. She began cutting the wires while she watched out for the guards. It was slow work because the wire was so tangled and she lost count of how many strands she cut and pushed aside with her gloved hands.

She pretty quickly realised that the guard patrolled about every half hour. Each time he came along she lay still and hoped he did not spot her.

It was taking much longer to cut her way through the wire than she had expected and she realised it would be after daylight before she gained access to the field. She decided to stick to her plan anyway. It was the only way she would be able to get the plane back.

As the first daylight lightened the sky she rubbed dust into her hair, face, hands and clothes and kept working.

It was after sunrise when she cut the last wire. She had lost track of the time in her hurry and was startled by the crunch of boots on gravel nearby. She lay still, with her pulse racing and her face pressed against the ground.

The guard stopped, not ten feet from her and she fought the urge to run as she wondered whether he had seen her because his footsteps had stopped. She slowly turned her head to look and saw he had his back to her and was having a leak. She almost sighed with relief. He buttoned his fly and resumed his patrol without seeing her.

She crawled on her belly to the plane and again her heart sank. One wheel was chained to a steel post that was cemented into the ground and the chain was padlocked. She would have to break the lock but she knew there was nothing strong enough in the plane toolbox to do it and Jack's pliers would not be up to the job either.

She remembered seeing a pile of rubbish near the hospital with steel bars and other construction waste.

She reversed out through her hole in the wire, pulling it together behind her as she went so it would not be noticed. Once she was a hundred yards clear of the fence she stood up and walked briskly and jogged between walks all the way back to the rubbish pile.

By then the sun was well and truly up and she cursed the delay but knew she had to stay calm. Eventually she found a steel bar strong enough with which to twist the padlock and set off on the two or more mile journey back to the airfield.

She waited for the guard to pass and then wriggled to the fence and crawled through it again. Then she surveyed the area before crawling to the plane.

The bar fit through the loop of the lock but she skinned her knuckles on her first attempt. She put all her strength into twisting the lock but had to wind up the chain to some extent which made the task more difficult and weakened the pressure she was able to exert. There was no direct purchase possible.

She still had not managed to get it broken when she saw the guard was coming on his boring rounds once more. Again she crawled back out through the perimeter wire to wait. Again he passed without taking much notice of anything. As she went back in she heard vehicles moving about down near the hangars and buildings where she had been taken the previous day. Orders were being shouted casually as the days' activity got underway and she began to realise that military procedure was not as tight as she had supposed. It was around smoko time and they were just getting started.

By maneuvering the chain until the lock was against the post she was able to apply more pressure on it. It broke suddenly and she sat down hard on her behind.

There was nobody near as she climbed into the plane, switched the ignition on and set the throttle. The guard seemed to have stopped patrolling now the day was busy again. She climbed down and dragged the plane around so that it pointed towards the strip.

She swung the propeller. Then, as the engine fired to life, she climbed in hurriedly and throttled up more than normally to warm the motor quickly in case she was spotted.

Suddenly she heard a distant explosion over the noise of the motor and then another. A huge column of black smoke billowed up from the direction of the harbour. A siren started wailing and she could see men running down near the terminal buildings.

More explosions followed and they seemed to be closer. She decided she could not wait any longer although still nobody seemed to have noticed her as she taxied out on to the strip. Her pulse was racing from the tension and her mouth was dry but she was committed.

Come on old girl, let's get this behind us, she mentally cajoled the plane.

She wiped the sweat of her tension out of her eyes as she revved the motor and moved off down the strip. Planes were flying straight towards her and she saw red circles under their wings.

Bloody hell! They're Jap planes!

She was almost at full groundspeed when she saw a Japanese plane coming in low at right angles to her. She saw flashes of flame from its guns and gouts of dust kicked up by the bullets that tracked across the strip towards her.

There was the sound of bullets tearing through the fuselage behind the cockpit and then the enemy plane went over her with a roar which drowned the sound of the Tiger Moth.

She wiggled the rudder and the flaps and found they still worked so she used the flaps and shot into the air. Then, when she was airborne she saw a string of bombs exploding as the blasts marched inexorably along the strip towards her. When she was about 100 feet off the ground one exploded almost right below her and the concussion of it made her plane buck violently as it was thrown off-course and it also showered her with debris.

She kept the throttle wide-open and could see Japanese planes everywhere. The hospital was on fire and she saw explosions rock the buildings there. Great palls of black fuel-smoke boiled into the sky down by the harbour and the air seemed full of enemy planes.

She did not know how she escaped further attack as she detoured around the RAAF airfield where some USAF fighters were being overwhelmed by Japanese attackers in a one-sided dogfight. Eventually it was all behind her and she set course for home. She heaved a sigh of relief and realised her shirt was wet with sweat and her pulse was racing. The sky behind her was filled with columns of smoke and she knew just how lucky she had been.

She refueled at Daly River and continued. It was late afternoon when she landed at Tomahawk Plains and stowed the plane in the hangar. By then she was exhausted from lack of sleep and tension and adrenalin overload.

The children came out to meet her and she told them what had happened.

'If Dad was here he'd have shot them down,' Lenny said.

The mail truck had called while she had been away and she eagerly sorted through the pile of mail. There was no letter from Eric but there was an official looking brown package crossed in red ink which signified that it was a registered parcel. It had the letters OHMS stamped on it and it was addressed to Mrs. E. McDonald, Tomahawk Plains Station, via Timber Creek, NT, Australia.

She rolled and lit a cigarette then took the parcel out to the verandah and sat in a squatters' chair. There were two sealed letters and a slim wooden case inside the parcel. One of the letters was addressed to her in Eric's handwriting and she smiled as she opened it.

Dearest Nettie,

Still no word about my transfer. I might have to jump ship if something doesn't happen soon. To make matters worse, I got made squadron leader the other day and that will make it even harder to get away.

Recently they started giving us Benzedrine pills. They keep you going and you don't get tired. They work best if you take them three at a time and wash them down with rum. Just as well too because we've been flying at least two missions a day. I flew three yesterday and we're off again in a couple of hours.

The Huns have been giving us a bashing lately. They've got oxygen cylinders in their cockpits so they can breathe at high altitude and we don't. That means we can't go above 18,000 feet without risking blacking out but they can go to 25,000 feet and ambush us from above. Even 18,000 feet is pretty much borderline for most because it starts to affect your judgment and you're struggling for breath. Because our Spitfires have two-stage superchargers they can fly higher than us pilots' lungs can handle and also higher than any of the German planes but we really should have oxygen like the Germans do. If we did we'd be the ones doing the ambushing. We've heard that we're to get oxygen soon which will be a godsend, can't be too soon.

There are only three of us original members of the squadron left now and I've got 15 kills to my name.

Some blokes can't cope with the strain. A Kiwi cove, Jim McTavish, cracked up the other day. We were going on a raid and he got to his plane and bailed up and wouldn't get in it. Nervous breakdown they called it but we call it shell-shock. He was sent home.

Some of the young replacements are Kiwis and there's a fair bit of rivalry between us Aussies and them. There are also a few Canadians flying with us. Apparently there are a lot of them over here.

I'd better get some sleep my love. We're off again before daylight and I'm a bit buggered.

Love to you all,

Always,

Eric. XXXX

Poor Eric, she thought. She hoped he did not crack up like some of the others even though she dearly wanted him to come home.

She opened the other official envelope and read.

Dear Mrs. McDonald,

It is my unfortunate duty to inform you that your husband, Squadron Leader Eric Ranald McDonald, is reported as missing in action, believed killed.

My department extends its sympathy to you and your family.

He was recently awarded the Distinguished Service Order as well as the Flying Cross. I enclose these decorations as well as a letter found addressed to you in his quarters.

In due course you will be sent his personal effects.

I remain,

Yours faithfully, the signature was a scrawl.

Under Secretary of War.

Nettie felt numb with the shock and the impersonal finality of it. In a few minutes she had read the last letter Eric would ever write to her and now this bombshell.

Oh God, no! It can't be true. How Eric? How?

How is it that they can't tell me what happened? Surely they know.

CHAPTER 16

Eric was in the canteen at four am. He ate some scrambled egg and swigged a mug of strong black tea before washing three Benzedrine tablets down with a double shot of neat rum. He put a handful of the tablets in his pocket, thinking the day was bound to be a long narrow one like they often were. The other pilots of his squadron gathered there and most repeated his ritual.

He called for quiet.

'What's the job boss?' Trevor Jones one of the few remaining original members of the squadron asked.

'Fuel-dump an' I'll give you the coordinates before we leave. Your two outside guns are armed with incendiaries so save 'em for the target. If we get into a scrap just use the others. Any questions?'

There were none. They had all done it many times before and trusted their leader.

When all the pilots were in their planes warming up their engines Eric went around handing each of them their sealed orders. It was a security precaution they usually followed in a bid to thwart Nazi spies.

They were almost to their Berlin target when the sun rose and it promised to be a clear day. The channel crossing had been achieved at extremely low altitude and so far they had not encountered any enemy resistance.

Eric led the first wave into the attack and still there were no enemy planes to hamper them. He skimmed low over the buildings and ack-ack and heavy machinegun fire opened up as he made his approach.

The large steel tanks loomed in front of him and he hit the gun-button. The armour-piercing incendiaries punched through the steel plate and there was an eruption of flame as he pulled hard on the flaps, climbing steeply to give back-up cover to the next wave of attack. The tank he had hit exploded behind him and he saw the other Spitfires going into the pall of smoke and fire.

'Bandits nine o'clock!' the radio crackled and then, 'Bandits twelve o'clock!'

He scanned the sky and saw a squadron of Messerschmitt BF 109 fighters at nine o'clock and a squadron of Stuka fighter-bombers at twelve o'clock.

'Devil section stay on strike,' he called into his microphone. 'Angel section engage and cover. I reckoned the picnic was too good to last.'

He swung back towards the fuel-dump and lined up a row of tanks which were barely visible in the firestorm. He hit the gun-button as he went into the smoke and fired blindly until he came out the other side of the pall.

The sky was alive with enemy planes and he saw a Spitfire explode as it hit the ground. Two others trailed smoke and they were now heavily outnumbered by the Huns who preyed like a pack of baying hounds.

'Break contact. Make your own way home boys,' he called as he flew straight at a clump of Stukas which were stalking the wounded Spitfires. He still had incendiaries left and the Germans did not see him coming out of the smoke.

His guns hammered and he grinned as first one then two and then three Stukas burst into flames as he raked them with gunfire.

He put the plane into a tight turn, deliberately stalling the wing. The turn was fast and he had the altitude as he came at them again but this time they were ready for him. He flew straight at them and then opened up with all his guns at once and could feel the plane shuddering from the recoil.

One Stuka exploded, two peeled off, one up and one down but the remaining one kept coming on collision-course.

C'mon Fritz, let's see how good your nerves are.

Both planes held their fire and both were at maximum speed, the gap diminishing at almost a quarter of a mile per second. At about half a mile from contact he hit the gun-buttons again and held for about a second before taking evasive action. The Stuka's fuel tank exploded and in that second he realised he had left it a fraction too late to pull out.

His Spitfire was hurled sideways by the collision and he saw a considerable section of the tip of his port wing disintegrate as it took the tail off the stricken Stuka.

Even at full power he could barely hold altitude in the turn as he swung for home like a broken-winged bird. It handled like a dray. The fuel needle was down to a quarter and he was all but out of ammunition. He knew it would be touch-and-go but luckily no enemy planes followed as he lumbered across the channel alone, watching the fuel gauge sink towards empty and the choppy grey sea close underneath waiting like a hungry predator to claim him.

He took the shortest route but the fuel gauge was showing empty when he crossed the English coast well off-course for his base.

The engine temperature was in the red like the tachometer had been all the way just to keep the craft airborne. He spotted an airfield and came straight in on a vacant runway without calling for permission to land because his radio had been dead since his prang. The supercharged Merlin backfired as it starved for fuel. He was coming in too fast but knew the engine would stall if he backed off the throttle and he had little faith it would glide far in its present condition once it had no motor to keep it airborne.

The wheels would not go down when he activated the mechanism so he slammed the throttle shut and pulled full flaps just before he touched down in a belly landing at over 100 miles an hour.

The noise was deafening as the Spitfire slewed along the strip trailing debris off the fuselage. Then he was off the edge of the tarmac on the grass still travelling fast. A Blitz truck loomed up in his vision and then he lost consciousness as he collided with it.

He regained his senses as he was being loaded into an ambulance.

'Here I'm alright,' he protested. He had a cut on his forehead but knew he was still intact. 'Put me down, I can walk.'

An officer helped him to his feet and he was somewhat groggy but knew he was still speeding from the Benzedrine pills which made pain merely academic and would enable him to manage unassisted.

'Where am I?' he asked.

'You bloody Aussies are all crazy,' the man said.

'Jesus! The old crate done well to just bloody well get me here. I was outta fuel an' had no bloody wheels. How in the name of Christ was I supposed to do it any other way? If I had of backed off the throttle she would of just pranged straight into the ground.'

'You came in much too fast.'

'Couldn't be helped. I tried to judge it an' that was the best I could manage. Sorry old chap but too bloody bad!' He added the last with an exaggerated English accent.

'No need to get smart Squadron Leader. By the way my phone has been running hot. Intelligence is looking for you, if you're Squadron Leader Eric McDonald?'

'Yeah that's me ay. Who's after me?'

'Colonel Henry, he said his name was.'

'Good old Jimmy.'

'You know him then?'

'You could say that. When's he comin' to pick me up?'

'He'll have a car here for you soon. By the way, the button must have been stuck on your radio microphone and your language left a bit to be desired.'

'You could hear me?'

'Everyone in England could hear you and most likely Germany too.'

'I thought it was on the blink.'

'You should be more careful Squadron Leader in more ways than one. You have what could be called a cavalier attitude to procedure.'

He fought back a retort realising no good would come of it. He had survived and that was enough. The amphetamine was inclined to cause aggression and he was well aware of that fact.

The staff-car came and collected him. Then as they were driving out he noticed vehicles congregating at his wrecked plane and wondered what they were doing. The very next second, his crippled plane suddenly exploded in a sheet of flame that engulfed it and the Blitz truck with which it had collided. He knew the fuel tanks had been empty and was instantly suspicious.

What the bloody hell are they up to?

CHAPTER 17

The car turned into the driveway of a large country estate and Eric could see horses grazing on either side of the avenue of ancient trees. It was quite a shock to see such a tranquil scene after the events of his day thus far.

Presently they came to a high fence surrounding a large mansion, with a gate guarded by armed soldiers. The driver identified himself and they continued up the driveway flanked by an escort of six big staghounds which trotted beside the car.

At the grand mansion at the head of the drive a soldier opened the door for Eric and stepped back to salute him. A uniformed butler came down the steps to welcome him as the car drove off again.

'Colonel Henry is expecting you Squadron Leader.'

The wide entrance doors opened into a grand reception lobby of huge proportions. The walls were hung with large old oil paintings and tapestries, medieval weapons, animal skins and mounted trophy heads. It was like stepping into a long-gone era.

They went through the room and up a flight of stairs to a large oak door. The butler knocked and opened the door then stood aside for Eric to enter.

Henry was sitting in an office chair with his back to the room looking out a window behind the huge desk.

'Shut the door Eric and come over here.'

Henry rose as Eric approached and took his hand in a firm grip.

'This your place Henry?' Eric asked.

'Yes, not bad is it?'

Eric had recently contacted his uncle to see if he could use his influence to help him get transferred back to Australia and expected that was the reason for his mysterious extraction from the airfield.

'Have you managed to get anywhere with my transfer Henry?'

'That's not the reason you're here Eric. Well it is and it isn't.'

'How do you mean?'

'Let's have a drink first. Whisky?'

'No, rum if you got it an' a beer if you ain't, thanks.'

Henry went to a bar and poured the drinks. 'Ice?' he asked.

Eric shook his head. 'As it comes outta the bottle thanks Henry.'

They went out through French doors onto a wide balcony verandah which afforded a view right out to the road where they had turned into the estate.

'I had this verandah put on after I bought the place. These bloody Poms don't know how to build sensible houses. The rest of this place is a couple of hundred years old but a proper house needs a verandah.'

'How long have you had it?'

'Twenty years I suppose.'

'So you ain't ever plannin' on goin' home to live?'

'I've always intended to but something always seems to stop it happening.'

'Why am I really here Henry?'

Henry looked around. 'Walls have ears Eric. Let's take a walk. Want another drink to take with you?'

'Please.' Eric popped three Benzedrine pills into his mouth and swallowed the last of his rum before Henry took his glass.

'You don't want to overdo those things Eric.'

'The Bennies?'

'Yes too many aren't good for you even if they do the job of keeping you focused.'

Eric shrugged. 'Yeah they help you to do the job. They're pretty good for that. Keep you sharp too like you said.'

They walked down the paddock towards a mob of horses. 'I'll show you a nice foal Eric.'

'What's the story Henry? Why have you really brought me here?'

'Do you still want a transfer home?'

'Yeah?'

'You aren't going to like what I'm going to tell you. I think I can get you the transfer but it has a price tag. This is probably the only way I can wangle it.'

'I owe you anyhow in lots of ways. You practically been keepin' me financially afloat for years now sellin' the diamonds for me.'

'You do a job for me and I'll do all I can to arrange your transfer.'

'I'll do it.'

'Don't you at least want to know what it is before you commit yourself?'

'If you're askin' me to do it I will Henry. That's good enough for me. What is it?'

'You've got to rob a bank.'

'Yeah where? That shouldn't be too hard.'

'Germany.'

'Yeah that's a bit different ain't it?'

'And that's the good part.'

'What's the bad part?'

'You were just killed today or presumed killed in our jargon.'

'You mean I gotta disappear?'

'Sort of and the part you're not going to like is that Nettie will be notified you're missing believed dead.'

'That ain't negotiable Henry?'

'Sorry Eric. It's not because she's considered untrustworthy but absolute secrecy is critical and anything put in writing can be intercepted.'

Eric knew both he and his father owed a lot to Henry. Henry was his father's younger brother who had absconded from or deserted the Australian Light Horse, depending on how it was viewed, during the First World War in Egypt. Since then he had gone under the aliases of Jimmy Henry or El Jimma bin Henry depending on the situation. He had been involved in British Intelligence since the First World War. Apart from selling Eric's diamonds he was also a partner in the Kalgoorlie mines and sold some of their gold on the black-market in Europe.

'I don't like that part of course Henry but yeah I'll do it.'

'Good man. The bank is in Berlin and it's where most of the high-ranking Gestapo officers deposit their ill-gotten gains to be transferred to their Swiss bank accounts. It won't be easy but with our family history I'm sure you'll manage it.'

'Who gets the money?'

'We get the money. The British Government gets any documents and other records, of Nazi corrupt activities and genocide of the Jews.'

'That's the deal?'

'Yes but not officially of course. These black ops are always unofficial. That's how it's done in our game.'

'How much money are we talkin' about Henry?'

'It varies all the time of course depending on transfers but I estimate at least the equivalent of £1,000,000 Sterling.'

Eric whistled. Henry went on, 'The expenses at this end come out of our pockets, except where we use military people and equipment. You and I will share the costs which will be minimal because most of it is in my system anyway and we'll split the take fifty-fifty. Are you happy with that?'

'Yeah, more than happy.'

'You'll earn it I assure you. By the way how many Hun planes did you kill today?'

'Five.'

'I heard six.'

'No five. Why?'

'Just need to know for the official records. That takes your score up to twenty then?'

'Yeah that's right.' Eric was surprised how much Henry knew about him.

'Also by the way you've been decorated with the DSO and Flying Cross.'

'I don't deserve that.'

'Bullshit Eric.'

'Where am I goin' to stop while we're organizin' this robbery?'

'Here of course. Not even Churchill comes here without my say-so, especially now but I won't elaborate on what I just said. You'll be here for quite a while because you have to learn to speak German and French as fluently and with as close to the right accents as possible before you're ready for the job. I'm not prepared to send you in before you're equipped to pull it off with as much safety as can be had in such a rushed transaction.'

'When do I start?' Eric wondered about Henry's oblique reference to Churchill but did not pursue the subject.

'Tomorrow and you'll need a good sleep for a start. Your record shows you've averaged seventy hours a week on duty for the past two years.'

'Why was my plane burnt after I crash-landed?'

'You had your radio on all the way home so anyone who was listening knows you were still alive until you came in to land. You crashed and burnt on landing Eric.'

'I thought you reckoned missin', believed dead.'

'The plane and the body were both too badly burnt for identification to be definite. It was a very fierce fire.'

'What about a body though? There wasn't one.'

'A body was substituted Eric. There'll be photographs in tomorrow's papers.'

Eric knew there was no turning back.

★ ★ ★

The next morning Henry briefed Eric in minute detail regarding the location of the bank and its security arrangements, staff, guards and also regular depositors of interest. It took all morning.

'Now I want you to come up with a preliminary plan and we'll discuss it but I want your ideas.'

'How soon do you want it?'

'Tomorrow morning. Plans are always better slept on.'

'Why do we need to come up with a plan straight away?'

'Any plan will require you to know certain things and arrangements will need to be made. Over the next week we'll thrash out the primary plan and at least two backup plans in case things should go awry.'

'You reckon the deposits are transferred to a Swiss bank?'

'Yes but don't even consider robbing a Swiss bank. You'd have more chance of getting away with assassinating Hitler or the Pope.'

'Do you have undercover people in Germany or France?'

'Yes of course. I have one very useful agent in Paris in the French Resistance movement. It would be easiest to get in through France but we've also got agents in Germany if we choose that entry point.'

'Who's your French agent?'

'Odette Duval. She's the leader of an extremely active group in Paris.'

'You trust her?'

'You learn never to totally trust anybody in this game Eric but yes she is dependable and is one of our best spies. She's also the mistress of a high-ranking German officer who's based in Paris and who supplies us with a considerable amount of information through her, although of course he doesn't know that.'

Over the next week they thrashed out the basic plans.

'Now it's time for you to begin your training. From now on no-one will speak to you in English except to teach you. You'll live as a Frenchman or a German in every way.'

'We've still got bits of the plans to work out.'

'We'll obviously speak English for that.'

Eric had never undergone such rigorous training in his life. There were two cottages on the grounds, one decorated as a French house and the other as German. Each day he moved from one to the other. While in one only French was spoken and French food eaten, French wine drunk, French newspapers magazines and books read and French gramophone records played. The wireless was tuned to a Paris radio station.

Similarly, it was the same in the German house where schnapps or German beer was drunk instead of wine and the broadcasts came from Berlin.

At night he watched moving pictures in Henry's small theatre. There were official German war-correspondent films, Nazi propaganda films, footage of Hitler's speeches and rallies as well as ordinary films in German and French.

He and his tutors dressed in appropriate fashion and his teachers comprised a whole cast of characters including men, women and pets. Eric was required to change roles himself from a German officer to a French freedom fighter or school teacher, a Nazi Party official or a farm labourer.

He learnt to change his accent from that of a common peasant or labourer to that of a diplomat or society person. He learnt the slang and the swear words, the religion and the legends that went with the identities. He realised he was being trained to think on his feet, to adapt strategy on the spur of the moment and to be ready for any contingency.

Many of his tutors had been actors pre-war. Some were French or German by birth. He was virtually being crash trained as an actor except that he knew that the stakes were much higher than the response of any audience could ever matter.

He studied the dossiers of each of the people with whom he was likely to come in contact and the details of the files were comprehensive. He read the one on Odette Duval carefully.

ODETTE BRIGITTE DUVAL: born 3-5-1916.

RELIGION: Roman Catholic (lapsed).

EDUCATION: primary and secondary at various Paris schools.

TERTIARY EDUCATION: SORBONNE UNIVERSITY 1933-36, degree in Arts, majoring in politics. CAMBRIDGE UNIVERSITY 1937-39, PHD in political science.

POLITICAL AFFILIATIONS: Member Nazi Party since 1935. Member Communist Party 1937-39. Known political activist.

PHYSICAL DESCRIPTION: Natural blonde, 5'7"tall, weight 9 stone, seven pounds, measurements 36"-23"-36". Eyes - blue/grey; Complexion - fair.

IDENTIFICATION MARKS: Moles, left cheek, right breast, inside right thigh. Birthmark, small port wine coloured patch (1/2" diameter) in hair above right ear. Scars, ¾" under chin, 1" left knee.

INTERESTS: classical music, politics.

SPORT: unarmed combat, fencing, swimming, ballet dancing.

LANGUAGES: French, English, German, Italian, Dutch, Spanish.

Accent: educated.

DEPORTMENT: Erect, athletic, lithe.

NATURE: Flirtatious, moody, bordering on fanatical, self-confident, natural leader, sexually active (partners various).

IQ: 140.

RECRUITED: 1933 by agent Fingal O'Malley, at Sorbonne University.

SERVICE: 1933 – current.

OTHER DETAILS: Leader (Colonel) French Resistance Unit (Paris), mistress of General Dieter Mueller.

There were pages of further information detailing her missions, achievements and vital information supplied by her.

GENERAL DIETER MUELLER (Gestapo), born Benjamin Levi, Berlin 1896.

IDENTIFICATION MARKS: scar left shoulder (result of removal of Star of David tattoo), scar left cheek (sustained in duelling contest), scar right shoulder (bullet wound).

Henry came in at this point.

'That Dieter Mueller is a powerful man but as you can see he has a major weakness, his Jewish birth. This is my personal file and nobody else knows that fact. During the First World War I posed as a Jewish Rabbi at one stage while I spied in Jerusalem. This young German officer came to pray and he confessed to me that even at that time Jews were despised in Germany and he had changed his name to cover his heritage but he told me he had the Star of David tattooed on his shoulder. I sympathised with him and assured him that as long as he was a Jew in his heart the rest didn't matter. I cut the tattoo off.'

'How'd you know about the mole inside her thigh Henry?'

'O'Malley put it in his report,' Henry said dryly.

The endless study went on and gradually Eric reckoned he was even beginning to think in French or German.

He also began lessons in basic Swiss as well as the sign language of the deaf and dumb in case he had to pose as a deaf-mute.

He learnt the Catholic rosary and the prayers of the Calvinist Church.

It was constant, sixteen hours a day, seven days a week. He lost track of reality and was gradually becoming addicted to Benzedrine.

He was constantly interrogated by actors posing as Nazis or English. He learnt to lie effortlessly, to fake emotions, to cry, to make false confessions and most of all to be personally emotionless while performing a role.

One day Henry turned up and handed him a letter. He recognised the writing on the envelope as Jack Miller's uneducated hand and saw it had been re-addressed.

Dear Eric,

I thought I better write. Nettie was here the night before the first Jap attack on Darwin. The army took the plane off her and she went to steal it back the next day. I lent her a horse and it got killed at the hospital in the air-raid. There were a lot of unidentified bodies there from what we heard. The hospital and the aerodrome got bombed and there was a lot of damage everywhere in town and the port. Hundreds of people got killed.

Nettie never came back here. I been trying to contact her on the new radio for over a week but there's no answer. I don't want to worry you Eric but we're concerned about your kids if she never got home. I thought you should know the score.

Regards, Jack.

'Sorry Eric,' Henry said.

'You read it first?'

'Yes that's my job. Look I'll make enquiries and she may be quite alright.'

'If she is alright an' you make enquiries it could get 'em onto her if she did manage to steal the plane an' get away Henry.'

'What if she's not alright Eric? What if your kids are there alone?'

'I said I'd do the bloody job Henry an' I'll bloody well do it!'

'You're getting emotional.'

'Ain't you ever been emotional?'

Henry's eyes grew cold. 'Yes Eric I've been very emotional at times in my life but in retrospect you realise it makes you vulnerable. I'll send Ben Abdul out to Tomahawk Plains if I possibly can and that way we'll know the score without alerting any authorities. If she's alright he can stay and help her for a while and if she's not there are your kids and the place to consider.'

'Thanks Henry. I just wish I could go. I love that girl.'

'I had a girl like her once too Eric.' Henry didn't elaborate but Eric knew the grisly truth about her kidnapping and gruesome murder.

'Yeah I know.'

CHAPTER 18

Nettie knew she could not afford to cave in to her grief because she had a family and a place for which she was responsible. She also knew it was extremely likely the military authorities would be after her for stealing the plane and she was under no illusion that she had not committed a serious offence. Now more than ever before she needed the plane and she had no regret about what she had done.

She told the children what had happened because they had to know that Eric was probably dead. In her heart she still hoped that by some chance the authorities were wrong, that he had run out of fuel or that he had been captured by the Germans but she knew the chances were slim.

As a subterfuge she organised the Aboriginal stockmen, as well as Tommy and Lily and her own children and between them all they dismantled the hangar, moved it down past the cattle-yards where it would be less noticeable and then, reassembled it there. They made doors for it and she padlocked them as an extra precaution.

Two days after they had finished the job an RAAF light plane landed on the strip and two officers came over to the house. She had no doubts regarding the purpose of their visit and did not go to meet them but came to the verandah apprehensively, knowing her handling of the situation could have considerable bearing on her ability to keep running Tomahawk Plains as she had been.

'Are you Missus McDonald?' one of them asked as they reached where she waited.

'Yeah?'

'Your aeroplane, a Tiger Moth was requisitioned at Darwin a week ago.'

'Yeah, that's right.'

'Where is it now Missus McDonald?'

'What do you mean, where is it?'

'As you're probably aware Darwin was bombed by the Japanese and a number of planes were damaged or destroyed. Yours wasn't one of them and it's missing.'

'Yeah, I heard about the air-raid but I was gone by then.'

'And the plane?'

'I don't know nothin' about it. Last I know is it got took off me by the military.'

'That was a week ago and you are now approximately 500 miles from Darwin. How did you get here?'

'I bloody walked.'

The man looked annoyed. 'Missus McDonald, this is a serious matter and we have to know the truth.'

'I got a lift.'

'Who gave you a lift?'

'The flyin' doctor.'

Recently the Royal Flying Doctor Service of Australia, which had grown out of the Doctor Aerial Service, had come to the Northern Territory and was based at Alice Springs to also service South Australia from there. She gambled that the officer would not see through her lie.

'Their plane wasn't in Darwin at the time.'

'I got a lift with a bloke in a car as far as Katherine an' they was there.'

'What was his name?'

'Bob or somethin' I think he said.'

'What sort of car was it?'

'A bloody motor car! They all look the same to me.'

She could see they were not sure whether to believe her or not and she wished she could contact the flying doctor to get him to verify her story. She would just have to hope they did not check too thoroughly.

'Look its bad enough losin' the bloody plane without gettin' blamed for it goin' missin' too. I'll show you where the hangar was. We pulled it down because it's no use without the plane an' we needed the corrugated iron for somethin' useful.'

She showed the men the remaining posts of the hangar and the empty petrol tins they had left there. That allayed their suspicion somewhat and they seemed satisfied, even slightly embarrassed. They apologised and left soon after.

In the following week she heard on the short-wave radio that Broome and Wyndham had also been attacked. Then a sloop, HMAS Yarra, was sunk south of Java and nearly a week later the Australian forces in Java surrendered to the Japanese.

The likelihood of a Japanese invasion was then a reality and she decided to move the children to Kalgoorlie where they would be safe. However, she was concerned how four of them could fit in the two-seat plane. The only way she could see to do it would be for Nat to sit on her lap and the twins to share the back seat. It would be a long uncomfortable flight but she had little choice. No commercial flight or transport was available.

The plane was fueled and all the spare cans of petrol were strapped onto the wings. She hoped to be able to get fuel at Halls Creek at least.

With a stated payload of only 535 pounds the little craft was overloaded. The trip was slow and uncomfortable. She was not able to get fuel at Halls Creek as she had expected but landed at a station and begged fuel there. The journey took three days and they slept on the bare ground under the wings at night because there had been no space or carrying capacity for swags.

Ben and Sarah had not been expecting them but were nevertheless extremely relieved when they arrived because there had been no contact between them since the radio had broken down. They too feared the Japanese would invade and tried to persuade Nettie to stay with them also.

'No I gotta get back. What'll happen to the place with nobody there lookin' after it?'

She had shown them the letters from Eric and the War Department.

'I owe it to Eric to keep runnin' the place Sarah. You understand that don't you? It'd just go to wrack an' ruin with nobody there an' the cattle would either go wild or get shook by someone. There's people would do that to us cause they reckon we could afford it.'

'Yes I do, Nettie, and I'd probably do the same as you, but if something happens to you the kids won't have any parents.'

'Well I suppose that's war Sarah. I'll just take me chances like plenty more have gotta do anyhow.'

'Yes but not plenty more women Nettie. We've heard that most women and children have been evacuated from the Territory and sent south for their safety. Unofficially there's talk of a Brisbane Line on the map, which means that if there's an invasion an east-west line across Australia at that point will be where Australia is defended, not at the northern coast. It appears the Government isn't confident of defending the country.'

'Well we ain't like the big company places that got managers an' staff. There's just me an' a few blackfellers to run Tomahawk Plains an' Sarah Springs. But I will admit I'm lucky I got a good cooperative blackfeller for head-stockman. Since Eric give Johnny a floggin' he's been real good, no trouble at all.'

Sarah was amazed at the strength and courage of the girl. She admired her and hoped for her sake as much as theirs that Eric would be found alive.

Nettie spent a week with them before returning home.

★   ★   ★

Less than a month after Nettie had returned to Tomahawk Plains an army Blitz truck turned up at the homestead, heavily loaded with drums of fuel and supplies.

The two men in charge of the vehicle introduced themselves as Slim Connors and Alf Thomas and said they were members of a highly secret branch of the army, the North Australia Observer Unit, or as they had already been nicknamed the Nackeroos or Curtin's Cowboys.

'What do you want here?' she asked warily, still concerned the authorities would discover she had the plane hidden.

'We're heading for our base and we don't know where we are,' Slim said. They were both young and shirtless and they were both freshly sunburnt.

'Well where's your base then?'

'It's supposed to be a secret.'

'Well how the bloody hell can I help you if you won't tell me where it is?'

They both looked at each other and shrugged. Then they laughed, realising it was a ridiculous situation. They likely also realised that they would never be able to do their job without the cooperation of the people who lived in the Top End.

'Look I ain't about to send a message to the Japs about whatever it is you're doin'. The radio is broke down even if I wanted to. You already let the cat outta the bag anyhow so you might as well tell me where it is you're lookin' for. If it ain't too far away I might be able to put you on the right track.'

She invited them in for a cup of tea and they told her their story. The NAOU had been formed to watch the whole northern coast from Broome to the Gulf of Carpentaria. Their brief was to report any Japanese sea or air movements because it was believed an invasion was imminent.

In theory they were supposed to have been recruits who had bush experience and ability as horsemen but as it turned out quite a few of the volunteers had neither of those qualifications.

They had a few Blitz trucks and small vehicles that they called Jeeps, radio transmitters, some horses and not much else it seemed from what they told her. They explained that the name Jeep came from GP or General Purpose Vehicle.

'How about planes?' Nettie asked. Already a vague plan was forming in her mind.

'We're supposed to be able to call on a few if they're available but that's pretty unlikely. We really should be allocated our own but the army doesn't seem to want to give us any more equipment or backup than they've got to. We're already beginning to think the whole show was cooked up in a hurry and that nobody really knows what they're doing.'

'Where's your headquarters then?'

'On the Ord River, at Ivanhoe Station.'

'Yeah I got an idea where it is.' She knew Ivanhoe Station was one of the Durack family properties and that it was downstream from the crocodile hole where she had been wounded and where she and Eric had consummated their love. A tear slipped down her cheek and she brushed it away. 'You got a map?'

Alf fetched a map from the truck. Nettie had become familiar with maps since she had been flying. She showed them where they were and roughly the route they would have to take to get to Ivanhoe.

'There's an old road as far as Sarah Springs if you can follow it. Nobody lives there now but the mail used to go that far once. After that it's cross-country to the best of my knowledge but if you can find it there's a old packhorse an' wagon track goes through to Wyndham from the spring. Ain't used much though, pretty washed out an' hard to follow I'd reckon, at least the bits I've seen are.'

The two men looked worried.

'Don't you reckon you can find your way?'

'We probably can eventually but we're already overdue because we took a wrong turn somewhere after we left Timber Creek.'

'Where did you come from?'

'Katherine's our base headquarters and that's where D Company is stationed. We're B Company.'

'Will you be comin' back from Ivanhoe once you get there?'

'Yes we've got to make a few trips. There are others behind us bringing horses somewhere.'

'Sounds like they might get there before you then. How long before you'll be comin' back past here?'

'We've just got to unload and then we'll be coming straight back for another load.'

'I'll come with you an' show you the way then. Gimme half an hour an' I'll be ready.'

She had been tempted to fly one of them over and pick a route from the air but decided not to risk showing the plane. She was also low on fuel, although she knew they carried 44-gallon drums. She told Tommy and Johnny what she was doing.

'When I get back we're gonna have to get a move on with the muster. We're already late startin'.'

'You want me an' the boys to start musterin' Missus?' Johnny asked.

'Yeah good idea Johnny. Get started over on the north end a Sarah Springs an' we'll work our way back here. I'll catch up with you soon as I can.'

'Alright Missus, don't you worry.'

She set off with the two army men and found them good company. They camped at a creek northwest of Sarah Springs that night and found their headquarters the next afternoon. The going had been rough in some hilly country but they had no trouble negotiating the terrain in the four-wheel-drive truck which had good ground clearance. Some of the way Nettie had managed to follow the old road that had sometimes been traversed by drovers' wagonettes but had mostly found it simpler and quicker to pick her own track.

An officer at the headquarters introduced himself as Lieutenant John Holley. He was grateful for her help and seemed embarrassed that his men had needed assistance.

'Look it ain't no trouble. You're all new here an' I been here in this country all me life.'

'I'm beginning to think we may have to rely on people like you more than we ought to have to but we've got a big area to cover. B Company is responsible for all the country from the Victoria River to the Ord River and all the East Kimberley to Cambridge Gulf and Wyndham. There is a small camp at Timber creek and they service that Victoria River mouth to the Fitzmaurice River area with packhorses from there but we're the main unit. We'll be taking the area west from Joseph Bonaparte Gulf on this side of the Victoria River.'

'Well at least the Wet's over now.'

'I just wish we had at least one plane. It would make our task feasible but the way we are it doesn't even seem possible,' he lamented.

She decided to take a gamble. 'Look I got a plane.'

'Have you? I thought all the private planes had been requisitioned.'

'Yeah mine was too but I got it back off 'em. I shook it actually so don't let on I got it an' I'll try an' help you all I can. I won't give it to you because I need it but if you keep me supplied with fuel I'll help as much as I got time for. That won't be all the time because I got a cattle station to run as well an' we're just startin' our muster.'

'Your husband's away at the war Missus McDonald?'

She nodded and fought back tears but he noticed.

'Is he dead?'

'Missin' believed killed I been told. He's a fighter pilot over in England, Spitfires.'

'I'm sorry.'

'Ain't your fault but it give me a fair bloody kick in the guts when I got the letter, knocked the gas right outta me for a bit.'

'It must be terrible. You've made a very generous offer and officially I can't accept. Technically I should report you to my commander but of course I won't. We'll gladly keep you supplied with fuel and be grateful for any help you can give us thanks. It will make my job so much easier and I hope having better access to fuel will help you too.'

'Yeah you don't mind if I use some of it musterin'?'

'Of course not. You can be looking out for Japs while you're at it, doing some of our work for us.'

'Our secret then?'

'Yes our secret. What the big brass doesn't know won't hurt them.'

CHAPTER 19

No word had come of Nettie. Eric had prepared himself for the worst and had thrown himself into the mission with a zeal that even impressed Henry.

He had been resident at Henry's estate for four months and everything was ready. The mission was organised. Security had been high and very few people were involved. Even those who were part of it were on a need-to-know basis.

By then Eric could easily slip from one identity to another, from one language to another and had been endlessly tested by mock interrogations. He felt confident even though he had never been on the ground in Europe. However, he did know Germany and France reasonably well from the air.

Henry had insisted he wean himself from his Benzedrine habit, saying that no agent could afford to be dependant on anything except his inner resources. Eric knew he was right because after half a lifetime of espionage Henry was still alive as proof of his own advice.

He crossed the channel by submarine and was paddled ashore in a rubber dinghy to a dark beach, after a brief exchange of the password in Morse code by torchlight with the agent who met him. They shook hands and exchanged the verbal passwords and then the dinghy was gone in the dark. Operation Curlew was a reality.

The man's name was Marcel, and he had a truck waiting nearby, an old pre-war contraption. They got underway and Marcel handed him a bottle after taking a swig himself. It was a rough red peasant wine.

'Tres bien, merci,' Eric thanked him. The wine was just what he needed after the foul stale air in the submarine. He took another swallow, wiped the neck on his sleeve and handed it back.

He asked Marcel what their cover story was if they were stopped by the enemy.

'It is not if we are stopped, it is when we are stopped,' Marcel replied. 'We are doing concrete work on the shore defences. We've been visiting an inn after work and the time passed.'

'I am Pierre Leblanc, a labourer from Paris,' Eric said in French.

'You look like him too,' Marcel replied with a smile, 'but best leave the talking to me when we're stopped.'

Eric's longish hair was unkempt and a bushy moustache adorned his lip. He had not shaved for a week and he wore the typical attire and beret of a peasant.

They were stopped by a German roadblock. Troopers came to either side of the truck and demanded in guttural peasant German to see their identification papers. Eric fumbled in his coat pocket and handed the man his papers. The guard shone his torch on the well-worn fake documents and then on Eric's face to check the likeness of the photograph.

'What are you doing out on the road at this time of night? You know there is a curfew.'

Eric shrugged as if he did not understand much German and handed the man the bottle of wine which was almost empty.

Marcel told the Germans their story. 'Pierre and I have had a hard day at work and it was already past the curfew time before we finished. We called at an inn and it is now later than we realised,' he explained in halting German, 'but then we were late before we even went to the inn, so?' He shrugged eloquently.

The two Germans conferred between themselves as Eric and Marcel waited anxiously for their verdict.

They were allowed to continue and subsequently avoided two more checkpoints by detouring off the main thoroughfare. It was almost one o'clock by the time Marcel dropped Eric off outside a squat brick house in a Paris suburb.

'I will leave you now because I must be back at work at six o'clock,' Marcel said.

Eric thanked him and the truck drove off. Then he went to the door of the house and knocked. An old woman opened it almost immediately.

'I am Pierre Leblanc,' he told her.

'Come in, my mistress is expecting you.'

He noticed the house was decorated in modern style, belying its rather drab exterior appearance. The maid escorted him to a sitting room and left.

The door opened and from her file photograph he recognised the handsome blonde woman in her mid-twenties who entered. She wore an expensive silk dressing gown.

'Pierre it's good to see you. I am Odette.' She kissed his cheek and he was somewhat taken aback by the familiarity.

'Do you want some supper Pierre? I have kept some warm for you,' she asked.

'Thank you. I'm hungry.'

While he ate she told him their cover story was that they were friends who had known each other when they were young. He had been evicted from the flat he had rented to make room for the family who owned it and he was staying with her until he could find other lodgings.

'When do you want to go to Berlin?' she asked. She had obviously been briefed to that extent.

'It will take a few days to organise my trip,' he told her. He trusted she would only have been told what she needed to know.

'You are welcome until then but I shall not be here tomorrow night. My lover General Mueller will be in town for the night but the maid will look after you in my absence.'

'May I use your telephone to make my arrangements while I am here?'

'Only for social calls. My phone is not tapped but I do not quite trust that and prefer not to use it for business unless that is totally necessary. If you want to talk business I can take you to a safe telephone you can use. The phones are all tapped here, you realise.'

He knew Henry trusted this woman to a reasonable extent and he did not want to move around the city any more than was necessary so decided to enlist her help.

'Does General Mueller trust you?' he asked.

'Implicitly, I make sure of that.' Her tone was suggestive. He was already aware of the cleft between her ample breasts where the gown had parted slightly. He remembered Henry's dossier on her and realised it was likely accurate.

'Would he be suspicious if you used his telephone?'

'I have my own key to his apartment and I can go there whenever I wish. It would be no trouble to use his phone and I know it's not tapped because he is the head of Gestapo in Paris.'

'I want to arrange to pick up a plane, a BF 109 or a Stuka, to fly to Berlin. I am Squadron Leader Erich Von Lukenbach. I have been on leave in Paris and need to get back to Berlin urgently because I have overstayed my leave.'

'I can arrange that. When do you want it?'

'Early the day after tomorrow, which means not much more than twenty-four hours away but you'll have to let me know fairly quickly so I can arrange things at the Berlin end.'

'I shall go to Mueller's apartment at midday tomorrow to prepare myself for him. He is a passionate man you know and he likes me to be ready when he arrives. I will make the call and ring Claudette, my maid, telling her the time to have a meal ready. That will be the time your plane will be available for you to collect.'

'I'll use your phone to make my arrangements but don't worry it will be in the nature of a social call.'

'Just don't talk too long on a long-distance call because the Gestapo becomes suspicious easily.'

'No it won't take long.'

'Is that all? I need to get to bed otherwise I will be haggard tomorrow night.'

'Yes that's all thanks Odette. Where will I sleep?'

'With me of course. It would look suspicious if you didn't and I'm curious about you anyway.'

He could not follow why it would be suspicious if they did not sleep together and thought the opposite would be the case. Besides, he had never slept with any woman but the mother of his children and the thought of sleeping with Odette made him feel disloyal to Nettie, even if it was likely she was dead. On the other hand, if Nettie was still alive she had probably been told he was dead so had no reason to write any more. This move of Odette's was one he had not expected and did not welcome but realistically he needed her cooperation.

Although he was naïve to the ways of sophisticated females he had heard that some women became aggressive if rejected and he did not need that complication if the plan was to be successful.

'But won't you be even more haggard if we spend the night together?' he suggested hopefully.

'That is different. Sex makes my skin glow with health. See how smooth it is.' She pulled the gown open a little more.

'I'm not a good lover. I have problems,' he said.

'Well then you need Odette's guidance. I will teach you to enjoy sex. It is like food and should be enjoyed daily. Also, I haven't had any for two whole days now so I am beginning to feel unwanted.'

'I'm tired from my trip.' He was running out of excuses.

'I assure you that you won't be too tired for what I offer you.'

He had never realised a woman could be so overtly sexual. He thought he could try to feign sleep as soon as he got into bed but already he was responding to her overt manner and doubted that would work. She would see right through any excuse he gave and may take offence.

She was sitting opposite him and she uncrossed her legs, letting her gown fall open as she did. 'You do not find me attractive then?' Her voice had an edge to it that warned him to be careful how he answered.

'You are a beautiful woman Odette.'

'Well indulge my desire. I shall not disappoint you.' She stroked her own breast and her tongue slid across her lip provocatively. 'Come to bed with me now.'

'I need a bath first.' Perhaps if he took a long time bathing she would fall asleep.

'I will bath you then. Come.' She took his hand as he gazed at her exposed body.

She ran a bath for him and undressed him before slipping out of her own gown. Naked she was even more beautiful and enticing than he had expected.

She caressed and titillated him as she bathed him while he cursed his own lack of self-control as he responded to her experienced hands. Then she dried him with a big soft towel and led him to her bedroom. He could see the imprint her body had left on the silk sheets from where she had lain while she waited for him to arrive. She lay down in the centre of the bed.

'Am I beautiful Pierre?'

He nodded, not trusting himself to speak because by then he was lusting for what she so obviously offered him. It had been over two years since he had last made love with Nettie and the disloyalty of his own excitement shocked him.

She drew her knees up and let them fall apart. 'Do you like what you see?' she purred, content in the knowledge he would not refuse anything she asked.

He sat rigidly on the edge of the bed, fighting both her allure and his better judgment. On the one hand he urgently wanted to savour her pleasures while on the other he despised his weakness. This was the one aspect of Operation Curlew for which he had not been trained.

She switched out the lamp. He somehow felt less vulnerable in the dark as he tried to justify what he knew he was about to do as necessary to the success of his mission.

She pulled him to her and he responded as she knew he would. She had more than woven her erotic spell. He instinctively knew he had no choice if his goal were to be achieved and that she would be a dangerous enemy if thwarted.

You're a beautiful bitch and you just don't care how guilty you make me feel. It's all about you. You don't even care about me personally, except as another notch on your bedpost.

Then he was introduced to a velvet fantasy world, like nothing he had ever experienced before.

* * *

Eric rang the telephone exchange and asked for the Berlin number which he had memorised and it took 20 minutes to make the connection. He was glad Odette had left. Finally a woman answered in German, 'Hello?'

'Aimee, it is Pierre.'

'Pierre my brother, is something wrong?'

'Our mother is ill and she is asking for you. Can you come and see her?' He spoke in French.

'I will have to ask Gunter. I will put him on to speak to you and you can arrange something with him.' She went off the line and there was a pause.

'Pierre, Aimee says her mother is ill. How urgent is it?' The man answered in awkward French with a distinct German accent.

'She is to have an operation at nine am tomorrow and I'm not sure she will survive it Gunter.'

'It is urgent then and I will arrange it if I can.'

He gave the man Odette's phone number. 'Ring me here so I will know to meet her.'

The operator's voice cut in, 'Do you wish to extend the call?'

'No thank you. Let me know Gunter.' He hung up. He had told Gunter the time and everything else was irrelevant. Odette had already verified the time he could collect the plane and he had only supplied the phone number in case the Berlin team had to notify him of any obstacle to the plan at that end.

He arranged for a taxi to collect him at four-thirty am the next morning and when it arrived he slipped into the rear seat, wearing the uniform of a Luftwaffe officer. 'To the air base,' he instructed the driver curtly.

The plane was ready for him as arranged and there were no nasty surprises. He had trained in all sorts of German aircraft in England so had no difficulty handling the Stuka which had been made available.

Air traffic was heavy as he landed at Berlin after calling for clearance. He was glad there was plenty of activity because he would be less likely to be noticed.

He taxied over to a refuel area and cut the ignition. Maintenance men approached and saluted him. He returned the salute casually as he stepped down.

'Have the plane fueled. I will need it to be ready in four hours' time.' He spoke with an arrogant German accent.

He was blocked at the gate and asked for the daily password after showing his identification.

'I slept in and did not have time to get it before I left.'

The guard seemed unsatisfied with his explanation. 'Come with me,' he instructed.

Alarm bells jangled in Eric's mind. He knew his excuse was a common one which would normally be accepted in this busy environment. The guard's demeanor also told him he had been expected. He had been casual and friendly up until he had seen Eric's papers which were impeccable forgeries and would stand up to any scrutiny. The false identity was already on record in German files so the only explanation was that he had been exposed by someone. That someone could only be Odette. The nape of his neck prickled at the thought that not only had she had her way with him but that she could also be a traitor.

He followed the man and noticed other guards watching him as they went, which reinforced his perception that they were forewarned about him. They entered a building into a long corridor while he controlled his urge to run.

He spotted a sign TOILETTEN. 'Can you wait a minute? I need a piss,' he asked the guard.

'Be quick then. I'll wait.'

He knew there would be lockers containing protective clothing in that facility. He selected overalls with a hood from the standard locker and pulled them on over his uniform in a cubicle. As he came out of the cubicle there was a group of airmen at the urinal. He took his time washing his hands and left with them. As they came out into the passage he made sure he was hidden among them from the guard who was waiting nearby.

He glanced back and saw the guard hurry into the toilet to look for him. Eric walked briskly and took the first turn in the hall. There was an exit ahead and he ran to it.

He heard running footsteps as he went out the door. A service buggy was passing, heading towards the hangars where he had left the plane so he hopped on the trailer and sat with his back to the building as the buggy took him away.

He dismounted at the hangars and discarded the overalls before going to where the plane was parked. He told the maintenance chief that his orders had been changed and that he was leaving immediately.

He taxied out onto the runway and called for clearance for takeoff. Clearance came quickly which told him he had not yet been reported to Air Control and that was a slight relief. He took off a minute later, having no choice but to abort the rendezvous with Gunter, who by arrangement would only wait fifteen minutes with his truckload of men disguised as German soldiers before they too aborted the mission. Without any way of alerting Gunter there was no other alternative.

He would have to reorganise and let subsequent events dictate his next move. Luckily his training had prepared him for this eventuality.

He was barely airborne when the radio crackled, 'Code red, security breach!' The identification number of his plane came next. Then a squadron of planes was commanded to pursue him and shoot him down. He heaved a sigh of relief that he had not overreacted and aborted unnecessarily.

He opened the throttle and set a course for Paris while watching for pursuit. He could tell from their radio communication that the hunters were not far behind.

At 5,000 feet the sky was clear but he saw clouds off to his portside at about 10,000 feet so he swung the plane hard and climbed towards them. Just before he entered the cloud formation he looked back to see at least five BF 109s in close formation on the course he had been following, with others trailing close behind them. He knew he would have to act quickly. As soon as he was obscured from view by cloud he dropped the nose of the plane at a steep angle and bailed out, leaving the throttle at full setting.

He resisted the urge to open the parachute as the ground rushed up to meet him, his eyes watering from the speed of his fall. He waited until he saw the explosion as his plane hit the ground four or five miles from where he was falling.

At about 500 feet he pulled the ripcord and the parachute opened lazily, before snapping tight and jerking him hard as it took the air only 100 feet from the ground.

He looked up quickly but could not see his pursuers and then had to concentrate on his landing. He came down in lightly wooded forest, guiding his path by pulling the chute ropes so as to avoid being hung up in a tree or worse still being impaled by one.

CHAPTER 20

The muster was finished and Nettie had sent the bullocks and spayed cows off to Stone Fort with Johnny in charge. He had lived up to her faith in him and had proved to be reliable through the muster, for which she was grateful. More and more of her time was taken up by her activity with the Nackeroos and being able to rely on him made her job so much easier.

John Holley had provided her with a new radio so she could keep communications open with them. It was the latest in technology, an AWA Tele-radio that had its own battery so that it could be left switched on all the time. She was also supplied with a portable generator to charge the battery. She had called Bluey on it and asked him to meet Johnny with the mob. It was a lot simpler to use than the old pedal-wireless had been and even an improvement on the updated radio telephone version which she no longer had anyway.

Tomahawk Plains had gradually become a staging post and minor depot for the Nackeroos. Because of that she saw a lot of them and had become quite friendly with John. He always called for a cup of tea and a chat as he passed through, and he always brought bread and newspapers on his return from Katherine. She had never before in her life had so much contact with the outside world.

John gave her a Tommy-gun for her protection and taught her to load and fire it, as well as the service procedure. She always carried it in the plane as she ferried mail and supplies to their observation posts on the coast where she landed on the beaches. Mounted Nackeroos serviced the ones she could not reach because of the terrain.

The Wet arrived unexpectedly and she had been ground-bound for a few days while it was too dangerous to fly. The creek was running a banker and she knew the Keep River would also be in flood. There would be no Nackeroo vehicles through for a while until there was a break in the weather.

She was sitting on the verandah watching the rain fall in sheets when she saw a figure slogging towards her on foot with sticky clay mud clumped on his boots. John Holley arrived, wet, cold and exhausted, having walked for three days in the mud with little but a single one-day ration pack to eat in that time. He told her he had bogged his Jeep hopelessly before abandoning it.

'You look totally buggered John. Come in an' have a hot bath while I cook you a feed. Fried corn meat and eggs suit you?'

'Sounds like heaven Nettie. Can I also borrow some gear to wear till I wash and dry these?'

'Yeah Eric's clothes oughta fit you. You hop in the bath an' I'll leave 'em outside the door for you.'

After a bath warmed by the chip heater followed by a substantial meal he pushed his plate back as she handed him a mug of hot tea. 'That feels better,' he said. 'You wouldn't believe just how much better.'

'You looked pretty second-hand when you got here but you look like a new man now, even if you are still exhausted.'

'I'm knackered Nettie. My legs nearly gave out from dragging big clods of black soil. If I'd had more rations with me I'd have returned to the Jeep and waited it out.'

'There's a bed made up on the verandah. You ain't goin' nowhere in this rain so you can have a good camp.'

He slept for eighteen hours and then woke hungry again. They sat at the kitchen table eating a late breakfast.

'You don't seem your usual self John,' she observed.

'No I've had a bit on my mind of late.'

'Gettin' bogged down in your work I s'pose?'

'Yes I suppose so but it's not just that.'

She thought he had lost weight since she had last seen him and he also looked somewhat haggard and beaten.

'What is it John?'

'My wife left me Nettie. She just wrote and told me out of the blue that she was going off with a Yank officer and wouldn't be coming back.'

'Hell, that musta been a shock.'

'It was and I never dreamt anything like that would happen because we were always really close. I always trusted her like that.'

'How long since you last seen her?'

'Over a year.'

'An' when did you find out?'

'About a month ago and I haven't eaten a decent meal since then until now. I've got an appetite now though so I must be improving. Just having someone you can talk to helps Nettie.'

The rain continued for days but there was no need to go anywhere. The only ground-travel that would have been possible was on horseback but she offered to fly him back to his base if he needed to be there.

'No, it's too dangerous in this weather Nettie and there'll be nothing moving there either. I'll give them a call on your radio so they know where I am and then I might as well enjoy the spell and your company. You are good company you know.'

'So are you John. I get a bit lonely sometimes with the kids away in Kalgoorlie an' no other whites except you Nackeroos around. I was actually feelin' a bit blue meself when I seen you sloggin' down the road in the rain. It's alright when you're busy but pretty bloody ordinary when you ain't an' you got too much time to think.'

Two weeks later he was still there as the rain continued and the creek rose, inundating the Aboriginal camp and Tommy's vegetable garden.

She lay sleepless watching the lightning out the open door of her bedroom one particularly humid night. She often could not sleep soundly since she had received the news about Eric and had not been busy enough to need much rest anyway. There was a knock on the open door.

'Are you awake Nettie?' John asked quietly.

'Yeah I'm awake. Hang on a minute.'

She pulled a dressing gown on over her pyjamas and went out to the verandah where he waited.

'I couldn't sleep neither,' she said. 'C'mon I'll make us a pot of tea.'

They went to the kitchen, where she lit a lamp stoked up the stove and put the kettle on.

When they were drinking their brew she asked, 'What's botherin' you John?'

He looked away. 'Nothing Nettie.'

She took his hand as he looked at her. She could see indecision in his eyes.

'What is it John? You never knocked on me door for nothin'.'

'No, forget it Nettie. It was a stupid idea anyway.'

'You wanted to come to bed with me?' she guessed.

He looked embarrassed. 'Yes I did but it seems a terrible thing now. It seemed more sensible then.'

'Do you still want to sleep with me?'

'Yes I do I have to confess Nettie and I'm sorry because I have no right to feel this way but I do find you very attractive. You don't know if your husband is alive or dead and even if he is dead it would be like walking on his grave.'

'If I wasn't in love with Eric I would sleep with you but I am an' I won't. I'm sorry to have to turn you down 'cause I know it weren't easy for you to make that move. I do find you attractive too but I can't sleep with you.'

'I understand Nettie and like I said it was a stupid idea. I'm sorry.'

'It weren't a stupid idea. If I never felt the way I do I'd love to do it. Now we better go back to our own beds before I change me mind an' do somethin' I'll regret later.'

The rain stopped the next morning and a couple of days later they rode back to his bogged Jeep on a couple of half-draught bronco horses. They pulled the vehicle out of the bog and he continued on his way while she rode home.

Neither of them had mentioned the matter again in that time.

CHAPTER 21

Eric moved silently on the deep pile carpet, his eyes fixed on the sleeping figures in the bed.

He paused to look at them. General Mueller was a big man slightly past his prime and Odette looked lush and beautiful in the diffused light that came through the window from the street.

Eric was dressed in the fashion of a high-ranking Gestapo official, rumpled navy double breasted suit and heavy dark overcoat, with a black fedora pulled low over his eyes.

He shook Mueller's shoulder and the man opened his eyes. Then Mueller reacted suddenly and whipped a Luger pistol out from under his pillow.

'I wouldn't do that if I were you Herr Mueller.' Eric then gave the current Gestapo password, only used in emergencies between high-ranking officials. 'The leopard has changed its spots.'

Mueller sat up and Odette woke and focused on Eric. He saw recognition in her eyes and hoped she would not give his identity away.

'Who are you?' Mueller asked warily.

'Otto Reiss, Gestapo.' He handed Mueller his papers and switched his torch on so he could read them. 'However, you are unlikely to have heard of me General. My work is mostly of a clandestine nature.'

He handed a sheaf of loose photographs to the man and shone the torch on his own face so Mueller got a good look at him. One faked photograph showed Eric at a dinner table talking to Adolf Hitler. Eva Braun, Hitler's mistress, sat between them. Another showed him among a group of Gestapo officials and Mueller recognised most of them. The last one showed Hitler pinning a medal on Eric's chest. The pictures were expertly forged and would pass any scrutiny.

'What do you want that is so urgent that it compels you come to my private bedside Herr Reiss?'

Eric pointed to Odette. 'Get the whore out of here first Mueller!'

So far Odette had not given any sign she recognised Eric after she had first shown it in her eyes but as she slipped out of the bed naked he could see she was angered by his intrusion and probably also by his reference to her status. It was obvious that she was likely to give him away at any moment. After her treachery which had almost got him killed he cared little what she thought but he could not afford to allow her to identify him to Mueller if his plan was to be successful.

He snatched the pistol from Mueller's hand before either of them could move and shot her in the forehead. She only had an instant to realise her predicament before she went over backwards, hardly making a sound as she fell on the soft carpet.

'You crazy bastard!' Mueller yelled.

'Keep your voice down!' Eric's voice was like ice and he had the pistol pointed at Mueller's head.

He heard running footsteps in the hall outside the apartment and then banging on the door as guards came to investigate the shot.

'Get rid of them!' Eric hissed.

Mueller pulled on a silk dressing gown and went to the door, while Eric watched him carefully. He seemed to be taking the turn of events too casually and Eric tensed, ready to defend himself if necessary.

Mueller opened the door and motioned the two guards into the room. He switched on a torch and shone it on the girl's corpse. 'Get rid of it,' he ordered.

The guards did not seem surprised by the instruction and left a minute later carrying Odette's bleeding body. Eric locked the door behind them.

'You had better have a good explanation for this Herr Reiss. I don't care how important you are,' Mueller said, his voice sounding outraged and dangerous.

'The woman was a spy,' Eric answered.

'I know she was a spy! She worked for me dummkopf!'

'Did you know she also worked for British Intelligence?'

Mueller eyed him coldly. 'I don't believe you.'

'It was she who leaked the cipher that the U boats used and it was also she who actually assassinated the Gestapo agent Black Wolf. She has been spying for the British since 1933. Their master spy Fingal O'Malley recruited her and I had him disposed of last year.'

Mueller looked doubtful but did not voice his thoughts.

'She was a beautiful whore who thought her body gave her immunity,' Eric went on. 'She used it to get information all the time. Did you know she seduced a British spy only three nights ago? She sent him to his death yesterday. Many men other than you have played in that garden Mueller.'

'How do you know these things?'

'I had her too. I used her in the same way she used others. Everyone had her but she had you duped all this time. Was it love on your part or just reckless lust that made you so foolish?'

'What is it you want? You didn't just come here to kill her.'

'No you are right. That was only the beginning Benjamin Levi.'

The man sucked in a sudden breath and his face paled noticeably.

'Oh I know all about you Benjamin Levi.' He prodded Mueller's shoulder. 'You have a scar where a Jewish Rabbi removed your Star of David tattoo during the first war.'

Mueller slumped and Eric knew he had him where he wanted him. 'What do you require of me?' he asked weakly.

'First, I want to reassure you I won't give the fact of your Jewish birth away to the Reich. That is, as long as you cooperate and don't get any ideas about double-crossing me. If you kill me or betray me Hitler will know your secret in hours. You may even thank me in the long run for what I'm going to ask you to do, even though it will go against your better judgement in the short term perhaps.'

★　★　★

The small convoy pulled up outside the Deutsche Bank in Berlin. Eric and

General Mueller rode in a Mercedes Benz staff car with two trucks following, one tarped over, the other loaded with fake Nazi storm troopers. Next in the cavalcade came an armoured vehicle with one 20 mm cannon and two machineguns. The convoy drew almost no attention.

'Let's go Mueller,' Eric said.

Over the past week they had arranged to collect the shipment to go to the Swiss bank and they planned to escort it all the way. It had taken that long to clear the operation through the German security system.

They were escorted to the manager's office, where they showed their papers.

'Is the shipment ready Herr Gottlieb?' Mueller asked.

'Yes Herr General, it is as we arranged. There are eighteen strongboxes of currency and other valuables and six strongboxes of documents for safe keeping.'

'Good. The sooner those documents are safe the better because if they were to fall into the wrong hands there would be serious ramifications for many high-ranking people.'

'You sign the papers General, while I get the loading organised,' Eric told Mueller.

The loading went smoothly and the little convoy was soon underway. Eric was relieved because Mueller had been hard to convince in the first instance that the operation could succeed and in the second that they would both come out of it very rich men. The plan he had outlined to Mueller was that once they were near the Swiss border the truck loaded with documents would continue to Switzerland while they took the second one with the valuables to Spain.

'I've arranged false identity papers for you and also safe passage to South America. Once you're there you'll never need to fear the Gestapo will catch up with you and I estimate your share will amount to at least 20,000,000 Deutschmark. You'll be able to live like a king in safety for the rest of your life, whereas, I'm afraid the alternative is the gas chamber or firing squad if you stay here. As I've explained I will also be a rich man and it's only stealing money that's already been stolen anyway.'

'I only agreed because the documents will be safely deposited in the

Swiss bank. I know you believe me when I say that I am a loyal Nazi in spite of my Jewish birth and I am grateful to you for giving me this chance of survival Herr Reiss.'

'Yes the documents will be safe and they are much more important to the Reich than the money.'

He hoped they would manage to fool Mueller when the convoy changed course because he wanted to capture him alive if possible.

All the troops in the convoy were recruits of British Intelligence, some of them Special Forces commandoes.

So far so good, he thought as he winked at Mueller, who had no sense of humour that he had yet been able to ascertain. Mueller still believed Eric was a Gestapo official and the success of the mission depended on that pretence being maintained.

CHAPTER 22

Henry was fretting and feeling guilty that he had not been able to send Ben Abdul to Tomahawk Plains as he had told Eric he would. Ben Abdul was closely involved in the war in North Africa, in charge of a Special Air Services covert operation there and could not be spared from that responsibility even for a short time. Erwin Rommel's Afrika Korps was sorely testing Allied resistance in that theatre of war.

Ben Abdul's SAS operation was a critical part of that defence. In collaboration with Bedouin desert tribesmen they struck at enemy airfields and stole Stukas, as well as destroying many other planes and attacking enemy convoys. The Stukas they appropriated and repainted in RAF livery were dual purpose machines which had far longer fuel range than Spitfires. Rommel had put a bounty on his squadron leader's head, which Ben Abdul saw as a compliment to himself and his squad because it meant they were a real thorn in the side of the German desert campaign.

Henry had not told Eric, thinking the news could upset him at a critical stage of the preparation for Operation Curlew. Eric had suggested the name and Henry had readily agreed. The curlew call was the clandestine communication his family had used for generations so the name was a natural fit.

He also fretted because it was two weeks since Eric had left for France and they had expected the operation would take no more than ten days to complete. The longer it took the higher the risk, particularly for Eric. He desperately hoped he had not sent Eric to his death. In his own long espionage career Henry had to admit he had not been involved in a more audacious operation.

He had resisted the urge to make enquiries through his German agents, knowing that to do so could draw Nazi attention and jeopardise Eric's safety. Odette was reported missing and the situation smelt fishy. It was possible that security had been breached.

His radio operator knocked on his office door. 'We've just picked up a call sir.'

'Yes?'

'Very faint, probably aircraft radio, one of the German channels, code 13 ...'

'Get to the message, damn it man! I'm not a bloody mind reader.'

''Curlew calling'. That's it sir.'

'Did you get a fix on it?'

'No it was too short, didn't give us time.'

'Alright keep listening and keep me informed. It's vitally important. Good work.'

Half an hour later the operator called him to the radio room. It was hard to make out what was happening. The exchange was all in German and seemed to consist of communication between members of a Luftwaffe squadron but it was confusing because they seemed to be hunting one of their own bombers.

Then Henry recognised Eric's voice, swearing at them in German.

'Get a fix on them! Quickly! It's critical!' he ordered the radio operator.

It occurred to him that Eric was on his way home in a stolen German plane and was being harried by a Luftwaffe fighter squadron. He grabbed the phone and called RAF radar surveillance and then Operations.

'I need two squadrons of fighters to stand by,' he told the Operations Commander. 'One of our people is inbound in a stolen German bomber and he's having trouble with a fighter squadron of theirs. As soon as we've got a fix on them you can go.'

The radio operator was on the phone to another base. He came off and reported. 'It seems to be over Holland and heading this way sir.'

Henry rang Operations Command back and was told there would be two squadrons of Spitfires airborne in ten minutes.

'Tell them to protect that bomber. It must get through at all costs. Do you understand? Priority over all else right now.'

'Yes sir, understood.'

'Well get it happening, man!'

★ ★ ★

'Come in Curlew, come in,' Henry called on the German frequency.

He had monitored the radio reception until he thought Eric was close enough to contact and now he heard a babble of German voices as a number of pilots answered him at once in a slanging match.

'Come in Curlew,' he repeated.

He heard static and then machinegun fire which continued for quite a while on an open channel. Then Eric's voice came on the air. 'Curlew receivin'. Come in Brolga.'

'Can you give me your position Curlew?'

'Sorry Brolga, I'm a bit busy right now. Hang on.' He heard another long burst of fire and then Eric came back on.

'Yeah, sorry about that Brolga. These blockheads just won't take no for an answer an' this bloody microphone jams open half the time unless I'm careful.'

'Where are you Curlew?'

'Over Holland somewhere but I ain't too sure where.'

'How about Operation Curlew?'

'Yeah thumbs up but not enough sleep. You know what holidays in Germany are like at this time of year.'

'We've got two squadrons of Spitfires coming to give you backup Curlew, if you can hang out till then.'

'Jesus, don't tell me I gotta fight 'em too. They'll reckon I'm a bloody Kraut. I'm in a bloody Junkers JU 52, three engine job.'

'Don't worry they know your identity and they're on this channel too.'

'Righto Brolga, got that thanks, might just make all the difference.'

There followed another long burst of fire and then Henry thought he could hear bullets tearing into metal.

'Hope them boys get here soon Brolga. It's sorta gettin' a bit hairy.'

'They'll be there soon. Good luck Curlew.'

Then he heard Eric switch to German. There had been no German radio interference while their exchange took place. 'You hear that squareheads? Hope you're ready for a fight or are you all just schweinhunds? Come on and have a go, last try at me before you run for home with your tails between your legs!'

He continued to taunt his hunters, his broadcasts broken by machinegun fire.

'Back again Brolga. I can see your boys comin'. Hang on, me mate's playin' up here.'

Then he heard the calls of the RAF pilots as they went into battle and he could tell from the calls that a furious dogfight was rapidly developing.

Eric did not come back on air and the minutes ticked by. Then a call came from an RAF pilot, 'Come in Brolga, Ace of Spades calling.'

'Brolga receiving.'

'Curlew has gone quiet and he seems to be changing course.'

'What's your situation?'

'Five of ours down, seven of theirs and they're breaking off the contact now. We're mopping up.'

'Leave it and get close to Curlew. Report what you see.'

Minutes passed with radio silence. 'Ace of Spades to Brolga.'

'Come in Ace of Spades.'

'I'm alongside the Junkers and I can't see anyone in the cockpit. The kite's sustained major damage, one engine is out and it's flying erratically in circles. It must be on auto pilot that's been altered by the dead motor.'

'Which side are you on Ace of Spades, port or starboard?'

'Portside sir.'

'Go starboard and take a look.'

'Receive that Brolga.' There was another pause before the pilot came back on.

'Starboard now Brolga. The side door's open and two men are fighting.'

'Fighting?'

'Fist-fighting sir.'

'Describe them please.'

'One in Gestapo uniform, the other plainclothes. They both look like Krauts.'

Eric had obviously kidnapped someone. He had said his mate was playing up. He must have had his prisoner tied up or unconscious and he had got free. Eric was fighting for his life in a plane that was flying itself in circles over enemy territory.

'The plainclothes one's down and the other one is dragging a crate towards the door.' Then, 'He's thrown it out. Looks like an ammo box.'

Henry waited.

'There goes another box.'

The prisoner must have got the better of Eric and was jettisoning the spoils of the robbery. Why did you disobey orders, Eric?

'He's still throwing boxes out and the starboard engine is trailing smoke, looks like it's been damaged too.'

Henry fretted that Eric had obviously pulled off the robbery and now they were losing the booty. He was tempted to order the other man shot to stop him throwing the boxes out but he could not be sure it was not Eric disposing of them for some reason. Because of his indecision and the fact that accurate shooting from a speeding fighter was not a chance worth taking Henry waited.

'The other one's up and they're scrapping again.'

Then, 'One's half out the door and it looks as if the other one's trying to drag him back in.'

'How's that other engine?'

'It's still going. He's got him back inside now and they're at it again.'

'How far are you from home Ace of Spades?'

'Mid-channel Brolga. The fight's stopped now and I've lost sight of both of them.'

He waited again.

'The Junkers is coming around, trying to straighten up. The starboard motor's still going but it's obviously sick. Looks like someone's at the controls now.'

Eric's voice came back on then. 'I got one dead engine an' one sick one. The gauges are on empty, must be a fuel leak. Otherwise I ain't got a worry in the world.'

'Do you have a parachute Curlew?'

'Yeah somewhere but I ain't got time to look for it. Oh hell, the second engine just died.'

'Curlew find a parachute and abandon ship. That's an order.'

'Negative Brolga, only a couple of mile to the coast now. I'll put her down on the beach if I can make it on one gutless engine.'

'Your call Curlew but be careful.'

'Yeah Brolga. Come round you piece of Kraut junk. I'm losin' altitude, not enough power now. Looks like we ain't gonna make it, flat out keepin' altitude.'

'Good luck Curlew. You do what you think is best.'

CHAPTER 23

Eric was fighting to keep the stricken Junkers airborne. He was tantalizingly close to the English coast but knew he could not hope to reach the beach for a landing in the wounded craft.

Mueller was tied to the copilot's seat and would drown when the plane sank. Over the past twenty-four hours he had been increasingly difficult to manage and more than once Eric had been tempted to shoot him but he had got him so far and did not plan to lose him at this late juncture. Besides, he knew he could not deliberately let the man drown. He fought the heavy controls as he struggled one-handed with the knot that held Mueller, not helped by a shrapnel wound to his own shoulder.

'Can you swim Mueller?'

Mueller nodded. 'You are an unusual man, whoever you are. You could have let me drown.'

'We both still could drown old mate. This is it. Hang on to your hat!'

The doomed bomber planed along the surface of the sea for a moment and it seemed it would be a perfect water ditching. Then suddenly the nose dragged. Eric saw a wave of dark water coming up the windscreen and then the plane buried the nose and capsized. He lost consciousness as his head slammed into the instrument panel.

He was vaguely aware of someone pulling at him but it was not real. It was a dream. He could hear waves breaking and someone was talking but it did not make sense. He was tired and desperately wanted to sleep but the voice nagged at him, preventing it. He wanted to tell whoever it was to leave him alone but he had no voice.

A wave broke over the rubber dinghy and Eric choked as water went down his throat. He fought himself upright and vomited, coughing weakly. His eyes focused on the other man through the watery blood and waves of pain that blurred his vision.

'Mueller,' he croaked.

'What is your name Englishman?'

'No, not English.' He tried to think clearly but his faculties were incapable of the task.

'Keep talking to me. You've got to keep talking,' Mueller said.

'Australian.' He got it out.

'You are Austrian?'

'No Australian, Aussie.'

'You are a good pilot, regardless of your nationality.'

Eric smiled weakly. 'You reckon?'

'What will they do to me?'

'Who?'

Eric's memory after that point was hazy.

CHAPTER 24

Once Eric's medical condition had improved to the point he was out of danger, Henry had him moved to his country estate where he was gradually tended back to health by a personal nurse.

He looked up as Henry entered the room. 'You better leave us alone,' he told the nurse.

'You seem a lot brighter this morning,' Henry commented. Until then Eric had been heavily sedated and Henry had still not been able to piece the complete story together.

'Yeah, first time anythin' has made sense since I dunno when.'

'Your prisoner Mueller saved your life, you know?'

'I remember bein' in a rubber boat an' I remember him talkin' to me. He was worried about what would happen to him. He tried to jump outta the plane in an attempt to kill himself before we ditched.'

'And you saved him?'

'Yeah I wanted to get him back alive because he's as important as any of the documents I reckon. Have you found 'em?'

'Yes, what was left. Divers recovered your remaining cargo from the plane.'

'Where's Mueller now?'

'He's being interrogated but is proving very difficult to crack.'

'Did you try bein' the Rabbi? I used that angle on him to blackmail him into doin' the robbery.'

'No! I never thought of that but it could possibly work.'

'I killed Odette Henry. She was a double-agent, a traitor. She almost got me killed by the Krauts when I went to Berlin for the first attempt.'

'I wondered how she disappeared.'

'Gestapo got rid of her body after I shot her.'

'How did you know she was a double-agent?'

'I found her difficult to trust an' then she dobbed me in to the Nazis when I flew to Berlin. They nearly got me there an' I had no choice but to abort the original plan.'

'As I told you Eric, you never totally trust anyone in this business.'

'How long since I crashed the Junkers Henry?'

'Over three months Eric. They didn't think you were going to make it for a long time. You sustained quite serious head injuries.'

'The money? How much did we get?'

'A lot but nowhere near as much as there would have been. We got nine boxes full of valuables and six of documents.'

'We got all the documents then but there was eighteen boxes of money an' stuff so we lost half of 'em.'

'You did bloody well Eric and I'm proud of you.'

'Even after losin' half of the boxes?'

'I'd be happy if all our operations were as successful as Operation Curlew Eric. Now you're going to recover here and then you'll be sent home.'

'To fight the Japs?'

'We'll see about that when the time comes.'

'Any word of Nettie, Henry?'

'I wasn't able to send Ben Abdul as I promised. I can't tell you anything for sure but I've managed to find out that some civilian woman is involved in an undercover operation in that area of the Northern Territory. Officially that's not the case and officially she doesn't exist but there are vague rumours. I just hope I'm not getting your hopes up over nothing though Eric because it may not be her.'

'That's enough for now Henry. I could see Nettie doin' that sorta thing. If there was anythin' goin' on in our area she'd be in it for sure. She'd reckon it was her duty.'

CHAPTER 25

Nettie was riding around checking cattle. She realised that aeroplanes would never replace horse-work altogether because she could check for tracks and see the condition of the stock better on the ground. Each method had advantages and disadvantages.

She boiled her quart and had lunch at Sarah Springs near Eric's parents' old hut at the spring. A Jeep came into view and she saw it was John Holley driving so she walked out and stopped him.

'Nettie,' he acknowledged her curtly.

'John you ain't called in for months an' months an' I seen you go past lots a times. What have I done to upset you?'

'I thought you wouldn't want to see me after I made such a fool of myself. To tell the truth I've been too embarrassed to call in.'

'Don't be bloody silly John. I missed you. Just because I knocked you back don't mean I don't care about you or like you. I thought we was mates.'

'You're right Nettie, we are mates and I rely heavily on your help. I'm sorry for being so self-involved or aloof or whatever.'

'You headin' to Katherine?'

'Yes, want anything brought back?'

'I need a drum a oil for an oil change for the plane an' some new sparkplugs if you can get 'em thanks John.'

'I'll see what I can do.'

'When you comin' back?'

'I want to be back by Christmas and that's only a week away so I'll have to keep moving.'

On impulse Nettie said, 'Want to spend Christmas with me on your way back? We can both be lonely together an' maybe get on the drink.'

'I can't think of anything I'd rather do thanks Nettie. A bender might be just what the doctor ordered.'

'Good I'll see you then, won't hold you up now.'

The following day she did her rounds of the coast-watch outposts which she helped to service. She had managed to get some beer on the black-market through the Nackeroo drivers and had a moderate supply of bags of straw-wrapped bottles for each of the three outposts she visited regularly. Christmas in the bush or the mangroves with only the sand-flies, mosquitoes and crocodiles for company would not be much fun she reckoned.

She took spare fuel with her so she would not have to come home between calls. Each group of men wanted her to have a Christmas drink with them but she declined. 'No, save it for Christmas Day. I don't drink when I'm flyin' anyhow.'

Most of the men gave her letters to post for them and she thought it must be a lonely existence for those of them who were used to city life. Some had tropical ulcers which had begun as sand-fly bites. Their diet was often deficient in fresh meat so she always took some fresh-killed or salted corn beef for them as well as fruit and vegetables from Tommy's garden and eggs from their fowls.

She was flying home in the afternoon, having left there at daylight. It looked stormy again which was only to be expected at that time of year.

She habitually checked the country as she travelled as well as watching the sky for enemy aircraft because she was always aware of the possibility of encountering Japanese boats on the coast or planes overland as she flew.

Something caught her eye and she concentrated on the spot. Then she saw the glint of sunlight on metal or glass again. It was moving quite fast and she saw it was a plane but dared not take the chance it was friendly because she knew what a slow-moving target she made. She dropped down among the trees and swung towards some rough hills, aiming to get out of sight behind them and hope she was not spotted.

She stayed low between the hills for half an hour before heading for home.

When she arrived she reported the sighting on the radio and was told there were no friendly planes in the area that day. It was most likely a Jap plane she had spotted and the thought that she had been so close to it made her skin crawl.

★　★　★

Nettie was restless once she had finished her chores and there was nothing else left to do in preparation. It was Christmas Eve and she did not expect John until late in the day. She had prepared food for Christmas lunch and had bottles of beer cooling, still wrapped in straw in wet bags under the rainwater tank-stand.

She looked at herself in the mirror as she brushed her teeth, noticing how long her hair had grown. She had been too busy to think of such vain things as haircuts but in the humid weather it was annoying her so she decided on the spur of the moment to cut it. She began by thinning it with a sharp butcher's knife like she would a horse's tail and hacking the ends back with the knife. Then she worked at the laborious task of trimming it with scissors backhand, while watching what she did in the mirror. It was a very awkward procedure but once she had started she was committed.

Finally it was done and she was satisfied with the result. It barely reached her collar and already felt more comfortable. Her skin was itchy where the trimmings had fallen down the neck of her shirt and stuck to her with sweat. It was a brooding still day and clouds were building for a storm.

She had decided to wear a dress when John came that evening. It would feel like a special occasion if she did, even if she was 1,000 miles from her children and would probably never see Eric again. At least she would feel like it was Christmas if she dressed for the occasion.

She carried the dress to the bathroom on a hanger and turned the tap on to run a bath.

She undressed and, in the mirror, noticed crow's feet beginning at the corners of her eyes. She had never been vain but she studied herself critically. Her face was already beginning to show lines even though she was only thirty-seven. Her breasts were still firm even after nursing three children and her belly was still flat and muscular. Her skin was beginning to age on her arms and in the sunburnt vee of her shirtfront.

She decided she would use the scented soap she had been given for Christmas years earlier before the war had irreversibly changed their lives. It was not in the bathroom cupboard and she realised it was in her bedroom so she ran naked to get it. There was nobody to see her so it did not matter.

As she lazed in the bath she thought of John and realised she was more than a little excited about his impending visit. Am I beginning to fall in love with him? The thought confused her because she still loved Eric, even though he had begun to pale into the realm of dreams and the past.

She remembered how disappointed she had been when John had stopped calling and she was not sure she would turn him down again if she got another chance. However, she knew he was unlikely to make another move because he was too much a gentleman. She wondered if she dared make the advance herself. She often craved the intimacy of a man's body since Eric had gone and wondered whether that was a normal response to her loneliness or whether it meant she was promiscuous by nature.

As she daydreamt she became aware of the drone of a motor in the distance. She thought that it would be John coming and she was almost tempted to stay in the bath and let him find her there. No, that would be too blatant. That really would be promiscuous.

The sound was nearing rapidly and it had a high-pitched whine like a fighter plane. It must be an enemy aircraft! She got out hurriedly and knew there was no time to dry herself so she pulled her dress on over her wet body before running to the kitchen to grab her Tommy-gun. The dress clung to her uncomfortably and she tried to straighten it as she ran barefoot along the verandah. The plane flew low over the roof, its engine screaming and she expected it would start strafing the house at any second.

She ran outside and saw it was banking to come back. She knew the Tommy-gun was no match for aircraft machineguns but hoped she could hit the pilot before he got her. The idea of hiding never occurred to her as she reacted spontaneously to the adrenaline rush.

CHAPTER 26

Eric had flown the Spitfire from England in long stages using auxiliary tanks and was now in familiar country. He would soon find out whether Nettie was alive or dead after all the agony of uncertainty. He was excited and tense at the same time. The tension built exponentially as he got closer to home and the moment of truth. He swallowed to relieve the typical dry mouth caused by anxiety.

Familiar landmarks flashed past under the speeding plane and he saw Tomahawk Plains cattle grazing below.

The house appeared quite suddenly and he dropped altitude, flying low over the Aborigine's camp. They ran for cover and he saw no young men among them.

He passed the windmill on the creekbank and noticed the hangar was gone from where it had been. Then he went low over the roof of the house level with the tank-stand but saw no movement there. He banked and came round for another look. His heart sank. Apart from the Aborigines the place seemed deserted.

The strip was too short to land on but he realised that if he used the race-course clay-pan he would be able to slow down enough before he reached rough ground. He came around again and touched-down, braking hard with full flaps. The dust kicked up by the propeller almost obscured his vision. Then he was bumping over the Flinders and Mitchell grass as he taxied up to the house.

A woman in a blue dress was running towards the plane and he realised she carried an automatic weapon. Can it be Nettie? I've hardly ever seen her in a dress. It must be someone else but who can it be if it's not her? Oh Christ, please let it be her.

CHAPTER 27

Nettie realised it was not a Japanese plane when it levelled out over the strip and she could see the red white and blue circles under its wings. It was a Spitfire! She had been taught to recognise all the planes, allied and enemy alike, during her time with the Nackeroos.

She suddenly had the unrealistic feeling it was Eric, even though that was almost an impossibility. She felt weak and her pulse raced at the thought that he may still be alive and coming to her. Then she realised it was more likely a coast-watch plane needing fuel and steeled herself for the fact it was not him. Eric was dead and she had to get used to that idea.

She felt light-headed and breathless with excitement and apprehension as she ran out to meet it, while it taxied up towards the house and stopped 100 yards away. The cockpit opened and a man climbed down onto the wing. Is it Eric? Please let it be him.

She came to a breathless stop as he jumped down onto the ground and she realised with a shock that it really was Eric. He looked much older than the young man she remembered. His face was pale and had hardened somehow. He had a long scar across his forehead.

'Nettie!' he cried and limped towards her. They embraced shyly, as she realised with a shock they were like strangers. It was an odd feeling that almost disoriented her.

She had imagined their reunion a thousand times over during the period they had been separated but it had never been like that. She was unprepared for the reality of the moment and groped for a response.

'Eric they told me you was dead,' she said awkwardly.

'I know an' I thought you was too. Jack wrote an' told me he thought you was killed in that first air raid on Darwin.'

She realised that was the reason she had not heard from Jack for ages after the event. Her radio had been out of action in Darwin and Jack had probably been trying to contact her. In fact the Traeger radio was still in Darwin. Then later when Jack had contacted her on the AWA set it was after she had been told Eric was dead. In the interim he had most likely written to Eric.

'Oh Jesus Eric, this is a hell of a bloody shock for me.'

'I know an' I'm sorry. I didn't know if you was alive or dead an' then Henry found out there was a woman helpin' with some secret military work in this area. I had to come an' find out one way or the other.'

'Where have you just come from?' She was beginning to gather her wits.

'I flew from England as soon as they let me fly again. I been outta circulation for the last six months or more all up.'

'What happened to you Eric? You been hurt. You got that scar on your face an' you're limpin'.'

'I got wounded an' crashed a plane in the sea. Then I was out to it for a long time after that. Brain damage they reckon.'

He climbed back up and retrieved his kitbag from the cockpit and then they walked back to the house, both still awkward in each other's company.

'Where's the kids?' he asked.

'They been in Kalgoorlie with Ben an' Sarah since just after the Japs bombed Darwin. I reckoned they was gonna invade so I flew the kids down there where they'd be safe.'

'An' you been here by yourself ever since, all that time?'

'Yeah.'

'You must of had a hard time.'

'No I been too busy with runnin' the place … that an' helpin' the Nackeroos.'

'The Nackeroos?'

'Yeah, they're a commando sorta outfit watchin' the coast for Jap activity an' they're seriously undermanned an' under-equipped. I been helpin' out with the plane because they ain't got any of their own.'

'But I didn't see the plane an' the hangar's gone.'

'I shifted the hangar because I ain't supposed to still have the plane. They requisitioned it in Darwin an' I stole it back in the middle of the first air-raid. They don't know I got it.'

'Where are the men? I flew over the camp an' only seen the young ones an' old ones there.'

'They took the bullocks an' spayed cows to meet Bluey an' they oughta be back any day now. Do you want a cool beer? I managed to get some on the black-market.'

She opened a bottle and poured them a glass each. Eric raised his glass. 'To us Nettie, us an' the future.'

'Yeah Eric; to us.'

She got them a meal and brought it out to the verandah. It was too hot indoors and there was not a breath of breeze. She had not eaten all day but only picked at her food. Her mind was still reeling.

'Ain't you hungry?' he asked.

'No too hot,' she lied on impulse.

She heard the sound of a motor coming and realised with a shock that in her tense state she had forgotten about John's impending arrival.

The Jeep pulled up at the gate and John got out. She went out to meet him, verging on panic as she wondered what Eric would think if John stayed as they had arranged. She would have to ask him if he minded a change of plans. With the insecurity he already felt it troubled her to do so but it could not be helped. For him to stay would not be wise or diplomatic in the strained circumstances.

'Good day Nettie. Who's here with the plane?'

'It's Eric John. He just turned up an' I had no idea he was comin'. I didn't even know he was still alive. Nobody told me nothin'. They coulda at least done that because they knew all along he weren't dead, the bastards.'

'Are you alright? You look pretty flustered, almost as if you'd seen a ghost.'

She knew she did not look happy like she would normally be expected to look. In fact she felt terrible.

'Yeah I'm alright John but it was a hell of a shock just the same, pretty much the same thing as seein' a ghost.'

'Look Nettie I won't stay. I'd only be in the way and it wouldn't look good either, wouldn't be proper.'

'You don't mind?'

'Of course not and I should really be in camp anyway. This idea was self-indulgence on my part.'

She knew he lied and that he was disappointed. In her own way she also was.

'Come in an' meet Eric anyhow while you're here,' she said.

The two men shook hands when Nettie introduced them and she was acutely conscious of Eric's immediate unspoken hostility towards John. She suddenly remembered that she wore no underclothes. She had just pulled the dress on in her hurry. Eric would probably have noticed already. In fact he had to have noticed because the dress still was not sitting properly. What the hell must he be thinking?

She poured them all beers and John raised his glass. 'Happy Christmas Nettie and Eric. At least you've both got your Christmas present.'

'Yeah happy Christmas John.' She was now acutely aware of her appearance and embarrassed by what it suggested, taking particular care not to expose too much of herself as she sat down.

John finished his beer quickly and said, 'I'd better keep going thanks. It looks like rain.'

'Yeah don't get stuck on the road,' Nettie replied and could not help remembering the last time when he was bogged.

She walked out to the Jeep with him, feeling awkward and apologetic. He unloaded the drum of oil and box of spark plugs she had requested.

'Don't say anything Nettie. It can't be helped and it wouldn't be right if I intruded on your privacy. You don't gatecrash someone's honeymoon.'

She nodded. At least he seemed to understand. He reached into the glove-box of the vehicle and handed her a tiny package. 'Happy Christmas Nettie,' he said apologetically.

She guiltily slipped the gift into her pocket as she waved goodbye. Then she went back inside. Eric was watching her intently and she could not quite meet his gaze.

It rained a few hours later, a wild storm with thunder and lightning. They went to bed and made love urgently but impersonally. Afterwards Nettie lay unfulfilled and moody while Eric slept.

He was restless in his sleep, tossing and turning. She knew it was not easy for him either. He had said nothing about John's visit and she wished he had brought it up so it could be out in the open.

Eric was talking in his sleep in a foreign language, possibly French she thought. She realised they were strangers now and would have to get to know each other again. It was not going to be easy. She could no longer recognise the man with whom she had fallen in love and whose children she had carried.

She got up and made tea and then sat on the verandah watching the storm, feeling empty and detached. She hoped John had got across the black soil country before the rain caught him.

Eric was supposed to report at Darwin after three days but the rain prevented him from taking off. The whole ten days while it continued raining was a strained time for both of them.

Mostly after they made love Eric went to sleep while Nettie sat on the verandah smoking cigarettes and drinking tea. She was desperately unhappy.

'What's up Nettie?' Eric spoke suddenly, startling her from her reverie. She had not heard him approach.

'Couldn't sleep. What about you?'

'Nettie we gotta talk. This ain't no good.'

'What you wanna talk about Eric?'

'You bloody well know what about. You been seein' that John feller ain't you?'

'He's a friend Eric, that's all. An' of course I been seein' 'im, he's the Nackeroo CO.'

'He's more'n that an' you know it. You gotta tell me an' I don't want no bloody lies. You're hidin' somethin' from me.'

She was silent for what felt like ages while she gathered her thoughts, knowing this was make or break time for their relationship, possibly their whole future. They had to clear the air or she would break down. Eric had also been irritable and uncommunicative.

'I'll tell you the whole story Eric but you gotta listen an' not butt in. Then you can think what you like.'

'Alright Nettie but remember I love you an' you're the mother of me kids. I don't want to lose you an' I'll do whatever it takes to hang onto you.'

She told him how she had met John and about the friendship that had gradually evolved between them.

'His wife ran off with a Yank officer an' he was broken-hearted. I found out about it when he got caught here after he bogged 'is Jeep over near Sarah Springs an' walked here in the rain.' She paused and steeled herself.

'He couldn't go nowhere till it fined up enough to get his Jeep outta the bog so I give 'im a bed on the verandah. He knocked on me bedroom door one night an' I got up an' we talked for a fair while. He wanted to sleep with me but nothin' happened Eric, I swear to you it never. All we done was sit in the kitchen an' talk.'

Eric looked as if he was about to interrupt and she put her hand up to stop him.

'The day you met 'im was the first time he's been here since then. I run into 'im over at Sarah Springs a week before Christmas an' invited 'im to spend Christmas here on his way back from Katherine. He arrived on Christmas Eve expectin' to stop here but you was here so he reckoned he'd keep goin'.' She looked at Eric. 'That's the whole story an' I swear I told you the truth. I never left nothin' out. There's never been nothin' like what you're thinkin' between us.'

He looked doubtful. 'Maybe, but I still reckon you ain't told me the whole story Nettie.'

'What do you mean?'

'I turned up outta the blue. You was expectin' him not me an' you was all dressed up an' you wasn't wearin' anythin' under your dress. What am I supposed to think Nettie? I reckon you was plannin' to get that dress off pretty quick. I hardly ever even seen you in a dress an' yet it looks like you wear one for him. Tell me the truth.'

'I dunno Eric. I was havin' a bath when I heard the plane an' I thought it was a Jap one. I just pulled on the dress an' grabbed the gun. I never had time to worry about underclothes or even to dry meself.'

'Did you think you was gonna shoot it out with a fighter plane with a Tommy-gun?'

'It was just instinct. Yeah I probably woulda give it a go.'

'Then you would of been dead.'

'Maybe I'd be happier than I am now if I was bloody dead!'

'You're in love with this John ain't you?'

She paused. 'No I don't think so but I woulda probably slept with 'im if you never turned up. I won't pretend it mightn't a happened. I'm glad I never did though because I couldn't live with that now that I know you're still alive.'

Eric was silent and his face was pale.

'Jesus Eric, I never stopped hopin' you'd turn up alive but I never knew if you was or not. I was by meself an' there was lots of times I nearly give up hope but I never stopped lovin' you. I told John that when he wanted to sleep with me. I still love you an' I want to be happy with you again but you're different too, like a stranger. What's happened to you? I don't know you anymore. We used to be able to talk to each other.'

'I believe you Nettie an' I can't pretend I'm happy that you would of ended up in the cot with him. I understand though. I was the same an' I never knew whether you was alive or dead either.' He paused and Nettie took his hand.

'All the time I was over there I never went with another woman till I was in France on that undercover operation. I let you down Nettie. Can you forgive that? I slept with another woman. But before that I never was even tempted to, even when other blokes went off chasin' skirt.'

'I don't wanna know any more about it Eric. I know how easy it could happen. I ain't gonna tell you that I ain't hurt but at least we both know

now an' I still love you.'

'Do you Nettie?'

'Yeah Eric. Now do you wanna make love like we really do love each other? I wanted you for that long an' so far you ain't given yourself to me. I guess I ain't neither. It's been more like war than love.'

He kissed her then, a long slow kiss.

'I'm sorry it's been like that. It ain't how I wanted it to be neither. I just feel that protective about you, like you're made of glass or somethin' but that ain't how it comes out.'

He took her hand and led her to their bedroom.

★ ★ ★

Nettie did not wake early the next morning and Eric let her sleep. He had risen at first light, to see that the weather had cleared and the day promised to be another hot one. Before he had left England it had been cold and bleak and now he was finding the Southern Hemisphere heat and humidity oppressive. In spite of that it was good to be home in the familiar Australian bush after the alien landscape of England and Europe.

He felt strongly patriotic about this land which now faced invasion by the Japanese, and was keen to contribute to its defence.

The last ten days since he had arrived home had been a hell of emotional turmoil for him, consumed by jealousy as he had been about Nettie's relationship with the Nackeroo officer. Also there had also been his own recurrent guilt, as Odette had insinuated herself into their bed in spite of his determination to forget her and his total lack of respect for her memory.

He was relieved that they had finally got it out in the open during the night. Otherwise he would have gone off again with nothing resolved, leaving them both anxious and possibly resentful towards each other.

After it had been talked through, they had made love just like they had in their early days together and for the first time since coming home he had felt relaxed and fulfilled afterwards.

He tiptoed to the bedroom door and stood admiring Nettie as she slept. It was too hot for covers on the bed and she slept naked and relaxed, with a soft smile on her face. He had no doubt he loved her and felt good about that. The sight of her naked body left no possibility that anybody else could ever replace her and he did not feel guilty about feasting his gaze on her or the response it engendered in him.

For the past ten days, Odette had forced her way into his dreams but now he knew she had finally lost the contest. She would never be the unwelcome third person in their bed again.

He went to the kitchen and made tea then carried the pints to their bedroom. Nettie stretched like a cat as he put the mugs down on a bedside table, her eyes still closed. He stooped and kissed her breast and her eyes opened as she arched her back to give him better access.

'That's nice Eric. Do it again.'

They forgot about the tea. Much later they lay in each other's arms sweating and totally sated, sharing a cigarette.

'Thank you Eric,' she said softly as she nibbled his lip gently.

'For what?'

'For comin' home, for lovin' me an' for gettin' our tension outta the way before you went off again. I couldn't a gone on much longer like we was. It was startin' to do me head in. You wasn't the man I remember an' I was startin' not to want you to be 'im.'

'Me neither. I was feelin' guilty about what I done an' lookin' for you to be guilty of somethin' too so I didn't need to feel so bad. I'm sorry about that. It weren't fair to you.'

'I never done nothin' wrong with someone else but in me own way I was just as guilty for thinkin' about doin' it Eric. Let's always trust each other from now on.'

'Yeah nobody else could ever replace you for me. I love you.'

'I'm the same Eric. Please don't hold it against John because of what I probably woulda done if you never turned up. He was always a perfect gentleman an' he's a good, decent bloke.'

'I won't Nettie. I been a bloody fool.'

'No you just been jealous an' you had good reason to be. If you wasn't jealous it woulda meant you didn't care an' I don't know that I coulda coped with that. For a moment when you told me you slept with another woman, I coulda killed 'er I was that bloody jealous.'

'I did kill her Nettie.'

She stared at him shocked, a question in her eyes.

'She was a whore but that was her better side. She was a double agent, a spy for the Germans an' she nearly got me killed. She's gone now Nettie an' you never need to fear her turnin' up again, not even in me mind anymore.'

'I'm sorry. That musta been a hard thing to do.'

'No I never even liked her from the beginnin' an' I never liked meself much neither for lettin' her seduce me into doin' somethin' I never wanted to do. I know I can't blame her entirely. I was weak enough to let her have her way. But when it came down to it she was just a dangerous enemy.'

'Let's not talk about 'er. I see the sun's out. If it's fine enough I'll take some meat an' fresh vegetables to the Nackeroos today. You can come with me an' see what war work I do while you're off killin' Germans. It ain't quite as excitin' but that's what I do when you ain't here.'

It felt good being flown by her and he realised she had become an excellent pilot. A couple of their landings were in tricky places on eroded beaches but she handled them nonchalantly and flew confidently.

It was obvious how well regarded she was by the men they visited and he could understand why. They lived in lonely, deprived circumstances away from their families and the rest of the world. It was easy to see just how boring and depressing their work was for the most part and he could understand that her visits would be bright spots in their otherwise uncomfortable and somewhat miserable existence.

'I'm proud of you Nettie,' he told her that evening, as they drank cool beers on the verandah.

'Why?'

'For what you're doin' with the Nackeroos. It's just as important as anythin' I done in the war.'

'You reckon?' She glowed at his praise. 'How long before you'll have to go?'

'It'll be another couple of days before the black soil will be dry enough for me to take off without gettin' bogged I reckon. Or that's what I'll tell 'em when I report in. The truth of the matter is that I got this hot little woman I wanna spend a bit more time with.'

She laughed. 'We can go an' have a look around Tomahawk Plains tomorrow then if you'd like to do that? An' in the meantime you can keep this little woman hot all night if you want.'

'You can fly me round for the rest of me life Nettie an' I'll take you up on that other offer too.'

They had three happy days together until the ground dried enough for the Spitfire to take off.

'You gotta go in the mornin',' Nettie said quietly on their last night.

'I wish I never. I could of got a discharge if I had of wanted to but I couldn't do that while the war's still on Nettie. I wouldn't feel right comin' home an' stoppin' here when all them other poor bastards are still out there dyin' to protect our country.'

'I'm glad you never Eric because you'd only feel guilty if you wasn't out there with 'em. That's what you're like.'

'Yeah I know. Do you mind?'

'I'm doin' the same thing in me own way. Yeah, I do mind that we'll be apart again after the good time we just had but no I don't mind that you gotta do it.'

'I trust you with the Nackeroos Nettie.'

'Thanks Eric, I'm glad you said that 'cause I can't stop now till I ain't needed no more.'

'Can I bum some of your fuel in the mornin'?'

'Yeah, you ain't got enough to get to Darwin?'

'Yeah I have but I'd like to take you for a spin before I go if you'd like that?'

'I'd love it.'

Eric piloted for the take-off and took it up to 1,000 feet with Nettie sitting on his lap in the single seat.

'Righto she's yours now,' he told her.

She took the controls nervously. The plane was much more responsive than the Tiger Moth and it felt incredibly powerful as she climbed and turned.

'How fast are we goin'?' she asked.

'About 200. Open her up.'

'How fast can it go?'

'Just over 360 mile-an-hour flat-out.'

She opened the throttle to full setting and the acceleration was awesome. She grinned at Eric.

'Do a few turns,' he said.

The G force on the turns excited her as she felt the adrenalin rush. She spent ten minutes putting the plane through its paces before he tapped her on the shoulder.

'Better head for home now.'

'You'll have to land. It's too fast for me.'

He took the controls and put the plane into a steep climb, the V12 Rolls Royce Merlin howling under full throttle. Suddenly he did a loop backwards. Halfway through it he swung hard to port and pressed the gun-buttons. The gunfire thundered over the noise of the engine. Then he did a complete roll and looked at Nettie. She grinned broadly.

They landed and he taxied up to the new hangar to top up with enough fuel for his trip to Darwin.

'What do you reckon?' he asked her.

'I nearly wet meself I was that excited Eric. I love it. It's the best thing I ever done. Bloody hell it's fast.'

'Better than sex?'

She cuffed him playfully. 'No, nothin's better than sex with you. Speakin' of which, do you reckon we got time for a quick one before you go? That flight sittin' on your lap got me in the mood.'

Half an hour later he was gone and she stood watching the plane disappearing in the distance as she cried. She cried in loneliness and happiness and relief that everything was all right again.

Eric waved to her diminishing figure on the ground. She waved back. His healing was complete now and he looked forward to the impending conflict with the Japanese. He felt confident and secure in his love of Nettie. He switched his radio on and selected the channel Nettie kept open for contact with the Nackeroos.

'Come in Tomahawk Plains,' he called.

He tried a few more times before Nettie's voice answered. 'Yeah receivin' Eric.'

'I love you.' He did not care that everyone on the channel could hear him.

'I love you too Eric. Look after yourself.' She knew John was probably listening but she did not care. It felt good that they could both express themselves publicly.

'See you when the war's over,' his voice came back.

CHAPTER 28

Nettie was missing Eric sorely after their brief intense reunion but gone was the lost feeling that had been with her ever since she had been advised that he was most likely dead.

She was tidying her room and found the small package John had given her for Christmas. At the time she had slipped it into her pocket so Eric would not see it and then later she had hidden it in her cupboard where it had lain forgotten.

She unwrapped the brown paper and found a lipstick. She smiled and thought what a nice gesture it was. The fact that it was a luxury he would most likely have only been able to get on the black-market suggested his feeling for her and caused a moment of guilt. She had never owned or used lipstick before and was curious to experiment. She was unfamiliar with the application technique but with careful slow strokes she achieved a reasonable result. She stood looking at herself in the mirror and thought how sophisticated she looked.

She went on with her chores until she heard a vehicle approaching from the west and went out on the verandah to see who it was. John pulled up at the gate and she walked out to meet him.

'G'day John.'

'Hello Nettie. Eric's gone I see.'

She laughed. 'Yeah you can come in this time without worryin'. I'll put the billy on.'

They sat on the verandah drinking their tea and Nettie thanked him for the lipstick.

'I see you're wearing it. You really are a good-looking woman Nettie.'

'It's the lipstick.' She laughed self-consciously.

'No, it's not the lipstick Nettie. It's the woman who is wearing it.'

She blushed and again experienced a twinge of guilt.

'I heard Eric call you on the radio the other day and I reckoned he'd gone then.'

'Yeah it finally dried up enough for 'im to get away.'

'When I last saw you, you looked really tense and I was concerned about you. Were you okay?'

'Not then I weren't. Eric was that bloody jealous of you an' I don't blame 'im really. It was terrible till we got it sorted out. For a bit there I reckoned we mightn't get through it.'

'I'm sorry. He could probably see how I feel about you and I don't blame him at all. I'd be the same if the boot was on the other foot. I know from experience how difficult it can be to maintain objectivity in love at times.'

'No it weren't you. It was me an' he just knew how I felt about you. Eric ain't stupid an' I ain't much good at hidin' me feelin's neither.'

'What do you mean, how you felt about me?'

'If Eric never turned up when he did I reckon it coulda been too late John. I'd started to fall for you an' he knew it without bein' told anythin'.'

'Well it's just as well he did turn up then and it's just as well I've done what I have now too.'

'What have you done?'

'I've applied for a transfer Nettie. I can't keep seeing you regularly and relying on you, knowing you'll never be mine. You're another man's wife and it's not right to feel the way I do about you.'

'You don't need to do that John. We ain't kids. We can keep it under control.'

'Yes Nettie, I do have to because I do love you. If I stay here it will either wreck me or make an enemy of you or Eric, or both of you.'

'Well if it's any consolation, I nearly loved you too.'

'I've really enjoyed working with you Nettie. You kept me sane when everything was daunting and new and hopeless. To tell the truth, I doubt very much whether my unit could have been as effective without your help. You're just so knowledgeable and capable and straightforward. You're not tricky like some women are.'

'Where will you go?'

'Active service I hope. I need to lose myself in something that will keep me too busy to feel sorry for myself for a while.'

'No chance you'll get back together with your wife?'

'I'm not sure that I want to anymore Nettie. I don't know if I could trust her again.'

'You're a good man John an' I hope you find someone nice to love in the long run.'

'Well just now I'm not looking. Maybe later on I'll think differently. Where's Eric being posted?'

'He didn't know when he left here an' I ain't heard from 'im since.'

'Well Nettie I'd better keep going. I just called in to say goodbye.'

'You're goin' for good now, not comin' back?'

'Yes this is it Nettie. Thanks for everything and I'll miss you.'

'I'll miss you too John.'

They walked out to the Jeep and he got in. Nettie leant over and kissed him on the cheek and then laughed.

'What's funny?'

'Have a look in the mirror.'

He looked in the rear-vision mirror and saw the lipstick on his cheek. He laughed too. 'I won't bath for a week Nettie.'

'Good luck John. I hope things pick up for you. You deserve it.'

'You too Nettie.' He squeezed her hand gently.

He drove off and Nettie realised a chapter of her life had come to an end but she knew it had to because she loved Eric more than anything else.

CHAPTER 29

Eric was assigned to a Spitfire squadron based at Port Moresby.

There had been grave fears Port Moresby would fall to the Japanese at the time when the Australian troops had been forced to withdraw from Kokoda. Greatly outnumbered, they had fought a rearguard action in pitiful conditions as they were forced back over the Owen Stanley Range. That woeful, blood-soaked track through the jungle-clad mountains had come to be called the Kokoda Trail.

They had finally blocked the enemy advance at the Battle of Ioribaiwa and gradually regained lost ground; slowly but relentlessly pushing the Japanese force back as the enemy supply line became overextended. However, the Japanese had got within sight of Port Moresby which had been a close call. In November the Diggers had recaptured Kokoda but the outcome was as yet by no means certain and it was tenuously held.

Eric's squadron had given support to a transport squadron that flew reinforcements into Wau under heavy Japanese fire. He had been blooded in the new theatre of war in that battle, scoring a Japanese Zero fighter. It had been a desperate battle and their squadron leader had been killed, along with five other pilots.

Eric was told to report to Wing Commander Sidney Dunstan's office. He went to Reception where he was told to wait. He noticed the clerks worked in full uniform in the humid office where sluggish fans moved the turgid air around uselessly. They looked uncomfortable clad as they were and it seemed incongruous to him. At least outside in his world they wore the bare minimum and mostly went shirtless.

'He'll see you now,' a female sergeant told him. She showed him to Dunstan's office and he knocked.

'Come.' The voice had an imperious tone, to which Eric instinctively reacted.

He entered as a florid-faced man with bushy eyebrows turned from the window. Eric saluted. 'Flyin' Officer McDonald sir.'

'Sit down McDonald.'

'You wanted to see me?'

'Sir!' the man snapped.

'Ay?'

'You will address me as sir, McDonald. Just because we're in this God-forsaken part of the world doesn't mean we let our standards slip.'

'No sir.'

Dunstan walked to his desk and opened a folder. 'I see you're new to your squadron.'

'Yes sir, three weeks ay?'

'I don't like familiarity either McDonald.'

'Sir.'

'I also notice you held the rank of squadron leader in England and have decorations for service and bravery.'

'Sir.'

'I also see you have twenty kills to your name.'

'Twenty-two sir.'

'It says twenty here.'

'I shot one down after that when I done some undercover Intelligence work an' one at Wau a couple of days ago.'

Dunstan frowned. 'I could be mistaken but your record gives the impression you could be regarded as a bounty-hunter.'

'Ain't that what we're all supposed to be sir?' Eric asked incredulously. It was common practice in the RAF and RAAF to paint a tally of enemy kills on their aircraft. The Luftwaffe was no different in that regard. Yet here was this pompous little desk jockey pouring scorn on a strongly held tradition.

'I run my command by the book McDonald and I do not tolerate personal glory-hunters.'

'Sir.'

'Your squadron is leaderless since the death of Squadron Leader Royce and you're the only man experienced enough to fill the position. I'm not sure I have much choice but to promote you to that role.'

'Sir.'

'I want discipline and respect for officers in my outfit McDonald. Do I make myself clear?'

'Sir.'

'And another thing McDonald, smarten up your salute. It's no example to set your men.'

'Sir.'

Eric was glad to get out of the office and return to his squadron, where the pilots lounged under the wings of their planes which were armed and fueled, ready to go at a moment's notice. Curly Jackson, a pilot who had transferred from North Africa, called out, 'What did the old man want Eric?'

'Made me squadron leader, as well as rippin' a fart outta me for not salutin' properly.'

'Well you're the right man for the job. What's our orders?'

'Apart from showin' proper respect for shiny-arse officers it's the same as before, we wait for a call an' then we go to work.'

Curly had little regard for authority. He was always scruffy and mostly unshaven. He had no front teeth and a scarred countenance. He had a reputation as a brawler but Eric liked the man. He had already shown himself to be a superb pilot, prepared to shoulder more than his share of the danger. Eric suspected he thrived on excitement and the rest was a bore to him.

Eric called the men together and told them he was now in charge. 'An' for Christ's sake if you see old Dunny comin' get your shirts on an' salute properly.'

'What about the rest of the time?' someone asked.

'Do what you always done. Salutin' don't matter two hoots to me.

Killin' Japs is what we're here for not parade-ground bullshit.'

★ ★ ★

They were supporting an infantry attack on a Japanese-held village. Eric organised his men to come in low to strafe the Japanese positions singly, leaving the others circling to guard against patrolling Zeros.

He flew low over a copra plantation, strafing briefly wherever he saw Japanese movement. A machine-gun nest disappeared in a hail of his cannon-fire, the men thrown aside like rag dolls by the big calibre projectiles. Another group ran for the cover of thick jungle and his machinegun fire cut them down like a scythe harvesting wheat.

He hated killing infantrymen because they had no chance against aircraft attack. Fighting an adversary in another plane was different, where it came down to skill and nerve and luck but massacring foot soldiers was a sickening business for him.

'Zeros three o'clock!' a call came on the radio.

'How many?' Eric asked.

'Squadron strength.'

'Engage!' he called as he pulled out of the strafing run gladly, making for where the dogfight had already started. He was in his element then and felt the adrenalin rush which turned him into an impassionate hunter rather than a reluctant killer.

The engagement was fierce. Eric quickly discovered that the Mitsubishi A6M Zero's reputation as a formidable dogfight machine was justified, even though they were slightly underpowered compared with Spitfires and not quite as fast. He was surprised because he had been led to believe by Allied propaganda they were an inferior craft. The suicidal nature of their pilots also made them formidable adversaries. If they ran out of ammunition or all else failed they were quite prepared to use their planes as weapons and commit suicide in the process.

Two Zeros were down and one Spitfire had sustained damage but was still flying. Eric relentlessly stalked one Zero in a frenzied chase until he got it in his sights and loosed a barrage at it. It veered hard to starboard and his fire missed. He swore and followed it.

'Look out Eric!' Curly called.

Eric glanced in the rear-vision mirror but there was nothing there. Then out of the corner of his eye he saw the other Zero close on collision course, coming straight at his starboard side. He dropped the nose but knew it would be a close call. The Jap must be out of ammunition and intending to ram him.

He watched the Zero coming as if in slow-motion, while to his speeding mind the Spitfire responded like an unwieldy cart. It was close enough so he could see the Japanese pilot clearly. Then the cockpit of the Zero exploded in a shower of torn metal and Perspex. Its nose lifted a fraction as the dying pilot involuntarily pulled the stick back when he was slammed by the hail of cannon fire. Eric's Spitfire started its dive as the Zero began to climb and they missed by inches. He heard Curly's maniacal laugh on the radio as the adrenaline rush hit his brain leaving him light-headed for a moment.

They drove the raiders off and headed for base, low on fuel and ammunition.

Eric was already realising that the dogfight strategy they had used in Europe may have to be modified to allow for the fanatical and suicidal mores of Japanese airmen. He had almost paid the ultimate price in his first skirmish due to inexperience where his new enemy was concerned.

They would have to take advantage of the Spitfire's power and speed to counter the new threat. Maybe it could be achieved by using higher altitude high speed attacks, rather than slugging it out with a devious opponent who seemed to be making the rules. The Japanese rules version was like an all-in anything goes brawl, compared to Marquis of Queensbury Rules boxing. Survival of his men was paramount and a new strategy was needed.

The weeks went by as they engaged in similar exercises and gradually developed Eric's strategy. The Japanese were ferocious fighters and had to be forced back every inch of the way, whether it was in the air or on land. It was a dirty war from Eric's point of view because it never seemed to matter how many men they cut down, they just kept coming as if there was an endless supply of mindless automatons. There were always others to take their place and to die in the blood-soaked jungle below. They were a fanatical enemy whose seemingly frenzied death-wish was in a way demoralising to saner men.

His war in Europe had not prepared him for the wanton carnage that was his New Guinea experience, where the endless close-up bloodshed blunted his sensibilities almost to the point of indifference. Benzedrine was now a way of coping with the horror of it all rather than for endurance.

The experience made him acutely aware that the Japanese must be stopped from setting foot on the ground in Australia and whatever means it took to do that was what he did willingly. If they were allowed a foothold on Australian soil everything that Australians held dear would be forfeited.

There would be no going back to the world they had all known pre-war. The innocence he had known all his life was gone.

CHAPTER 30

A gnarly big old scrub bull horned and trampled one of the Aboriginal stockmen who miss-timed trying to tail-throw it, after it had charged straight through the coacher mob and out the other side. It was too strong for him to pull down so he tried to jump on its hocks to bring it down and missed, ending up under the bull in reversed circumstances. Nettie flew him back to the homestead. She laid him on the verandah floor and called the Katherine Flying Doctor outpost on the radio.

'How bad is it?' asked the radio operator.

'He's got internal bleedin' be the look a 'im as well as a busted collarbone an' he's in a fair bit a pain.'

'Wait a minute. I'll get the doctor to come to speak to you.'

The doctor came on and Nettie repeated the information.

'We'll be five hours at least. Can he last that long?'

'Yeah I think so but he needs somethin' for the pain.'

'Give him morphine, one syringe intravenously. Can you do that?'

'I've inoculated plenty a cattle for pleuro in me time but always with a seton, never used a syringe.'

The doctor told her how to find the vein and to make sure there was no air in the syringe when she injected. 'That should hold the pain at bay until we can get there. Apart from that, just treat for shock. That's all you can do.'

Nettie thanked him and went to the army medical chest where everything was listed by number inside its steel lid. Then she got the patient onto a verandah bed and covered him with a blanket after giving him the injection. He was shivering uncontrollably, and she remembered how she had been after the injury she had sustained from the crocodile years before. At least the flying doctor would be on site in a few hours this time. She made a pot of tea and helped him drink some, heavily laced with sugar.

The mail truck arrived and she went out to get the mailbag while the driver unloaded the supplies.

There was a letter from Eric and she had one ready to send to him also which she slipped into the bag and gave it back to the mailman. He declined a cup of tea because he said he was running late.

She opened Eric's letter as she walked back inside.

Dearest Nettie,

I got made squadron leader again the other day, as well as getting a lecture for shooting down too many planes and not saluting properly. I don't reckon old Dunny likes me much and the feeling's mutual but we're stuck with each other for now.

We sometimes get to fight Jap Zeros but mostly it's covering troop attacks and I don't like killing men on the ground. It seems like cold-blooded slaughter. I know we've got to do it and they'd do the same to us but that's how I feel. If I've got to kill men on the ground I'd rather be on the ground too.

This place is stinking hot, must be really bad around the end of year but I suppose I'm not properly acclimatized yet. Two years or more in England wasn't good preparation for New Guinea weather. It rains every afternoon but it doesn't seem to cool things down much. Even sweating doesn't cool you. It just seems to turn to steam.

Thanks for your letter. It must have been hard for you saying goodbye to John. I know how well you worked together. I'm sorry about how I was towards him. Maybe he'll be happier somewhere else in the long run.

We don't have time for much else other than constant patrols. We get to see a lot of country though. Some of it is pretty mountainous and it must be rough going for the footsloggers, with the mountains the jungle and the rain, not to mention the bloody Japs.

Time to go on patrol again. Look after yourself.

I love you.

Eric. XXXX

The flying doctor's plane arrived. Nettie had hung a sheet out on the clothesline as a windsock so he would know the wind direction. She always did that for herself and knew it made landing safer.

Tommy and Lily helped her carry the man to the plane where the doctor gave him another injection and checked his pulse, respiration and temperature.

'I think the bleeding may have stopped and if it has he'll have a fair chance. They're pretty tough these Top End boys.'

She thanked him and he left after being on the ground only five minutes. He would refuel at Timber Creek or Victoria River Downs. He had to call at both places.

Nettie got the plane ready for the next days' flying. The muster was in full swing and she still had her duties with the Nackeroos as well.

The new CO at Ord River base had been briefed by John and seemed friendly. She had been nervous that her association with them could come to an end with John's departure but nothing had changed so far and she was grateful for that. It was good to be needed and to be able to contribute to the war effort. It made Eric's absence more bearable.

CHAPTER 31

As the months went by, Eric increasingly clashed with Dunstan and considered asking for a transfer to another unit. He was beginning not to like his job and knew it was time to move on if he could before they had an irreversible run-in.

He was on single-plane-surveillance and the mission brief was to watch over and give cover to a small boat which was undertaking an undercover operation to the north of the mainland. More than one plane would draw unwanted attention so he had organised his pilots to fly a shuttle service, relieving each other as fuel got low. That strategy also left most of the squadron available for other emergencies that might present themselves.

He flew low over the small boat and black faces looked up and their owners waved. He supposed the members of the operation would be white commandoes disguised as natives but maybe some of them were natives. He flew on ahead of the boat looking for enemy air or shipping activity but both sky and sea were barren that day. He knew just how quickly that could change though so was careful not to let it lull his diligence.

He went up to 15,000 feet for a more comprehensive overview but there was nothing in sight so he decided to turn back. It would soon be time for his relief to take over from him. He noticed that clouds were building quickly as he swung in a wide arc to cover an expanse of sea as he returned.

It started to rain, a sudden heavy downpour which was common and visibility fell to less than half a mile. He dropped to a lower altitude to check the boat again before he left and could just make it out in the pouring rain. With a shock he realised that it was listing badly and burning fiercely. Then he spotted the Japanese submarine that sat on the surface near it.

He went down to twenty feet above the sea as he began his approach. The sub came in range and he hit the gun-buttons. He saw a deck machine-gun crew cut down in a pink fog of blood and body parts and then it was behind him. He climbed and banked to come back for another run but as he turned he was just in time to see the sub disappear under the water. He backed off the throttle as he searched for survivors. Already he could see sharks feeding on bodies in the water and the boat was going down.

He came around again and could see one wounded man clinging to some wreckage only 100 yards from shore. Other than that there was no sign of life. He knew the man's chances were slim because one sleeve of his shirt was blood-soaked and it would only be a matter of time before the sharks found him. Eric's view from the air disclosed a whole school of the killers prowling and feeding.

The beach looked firm so he put the plane down lightly, ready to power up and abort the landing if necessary but found the sand as hard as concrete. He cut the motor after swinging around ready for a hurried take-off if it became necessary. He climbed down quickly and paused to undress before running to the water's edge and jumping in.

He expected sharks to attack him at any minute as he swam towards the head he could see bobbing in the waves. He was a strong swimmer and closed the gap easily.

'Here put your arm around me neck,' he told the wounded man and struck out for the beach. He knew the man was bleeding which made shark-attack even more likely so he put all his energy into dragging the victim as quickly as he could towards where the waves broke on the sand.

It seemed like a mile but eventually he helped the wounded man to his feet and dragged him towards the plane, where he climbed up and got a field dressing.

The man was staring at him as he got back down. 'Are you Eric McDonald?' he asked.

Eric recognised him then. It was John Holley.

'John what the hell you doin' here?'

'Getting myself into trouble it seems. You saved my life. You could have left me for the sharks.'

Eric bound John's shoulder tightly to quell the bleeding and then dressed quickly.

'Come on, I'll help you up but you're gonna have to sit on me lap. There's only one seat,' he told John.

They were only just airborne when he spotted Curly coming to relieve him.

'Mission aborted Curly,' he called.

There was no evidence remaining to show there had ever been a boat or men on the surface of the sea. The sharks had done their grisly work and even the oil-slick had been dissipated by the current.

They headed back to base.

★ ★ ★

The following morning Eric handed in his report for the previous day and then drove to the hospital in a Jeep. He asked to see John Holley and was shown to a ward, where John was sitting up in bed with his shoulder swathed in bandages.

'How's it goin' John?' Eric asked.

'Good thanks Eric. They took a bullet out of me last night and reckon I'll be back in action in six weeks or so.'

'That's good then. I was your scout yesterday. Some bloody help I turned out to be.'

'We never gave subs a thought either Eric. Enemy planes and shipping were our main worry. There was nothing you could have done unless you'd been right there when it surfaced and maybe not even then. We didn't even have time to retaliate it happened so fast. They'd obviously been watching us but we didn't spot a periscope.'

'No me neither. I was lookin' for planes an' ships too.'

'Eric you must have been wishing you'd left me there when you found out who I was.'

'No John, I don't hold no grudge against you. I know that with Nettie it was just somethin' that happened because of your situation. I've got nothin' against you over it or her neither.'

'I'm afraid I wouldn't have the same attitude towards the bloke my wife ran off with.'

'Yeah, except you never ran off with my missus John. If that was what you done I'd probably want to kill you too.'

'You're a lucky man Eric. Nettie's a very honourable woman and I know she loves you.'

'Yeah.'

'How do you like New Guinea? It must be a lot different from England and fighting the Germans.'

'I don't mind New Guinea but I don't like the jobs we get an' I don't get on with me CO. How about you?'

'I joined up to fight Japs and I jumped at the chance to volunteer for the Nackeroos. It seemed at that time it would only be months before they invaded and I believed we'd actually be defending our shore.'

'But it never happened.'

'No and I'm glad it didn't. I know the work we did was useful but if it hadn't been for Nettie's cheerful help I don't think I would have lasted as long as I did. Now I've got into the proper war I'm happy that I'm at last helping to defend Australia.'

'You in some kinda special force John?'

'Yes loosely I suppose you'd call us commandoes, although we don't have that official designation.'

'Was it a hard unit to get into?'

'No not really. The Nackeroos roughly fit into the same category.'

'Look I better get back John. I just wanted to see how you got on. Nettie'll want to know when I write to her.'

'Eric thanks, I owe you my life.'

'You can shout me a beer when they let you outta here. How's that?'

'I won't forget.'

He parked the Jeep at the motor pool and returned to the strip where they were on standby.

'Dunny's lookin' for you Eric,' Curly told him.

'What's he want?'

'Never said, didn't look real happy but.'

'You ever seen him look happy?'

Curly laughed. 'He said to tell you he wants to see you an' I told 'im to get stuffed.'

'You didn't?'

'Nah, like to but. He's got a broomstick up 'is bum an' he gives me the shits.'

Eric felt much the same but thought he had better report to Dunstan. He walked towards the Admin building but just then an air-raid siren wailed and he ran to his plane instead. Whatever Dunstan wanted would have to wait.

A Japanese bomber squadron was mounting an attack and the airfield would be their prime target.

The Spitfires swarmed into action, soon to be joined by another RAAF squadron of Curtiss P-40D Kittyhawks which in the USAC went by the name Warhawks. The Nakajima B5N torpedo bombers were escorted by a squadron of Zeros. The fight was brief but bloody and although the Japanese losses were high they were reluctant to admit defeat.

Eric and Curly simultaneously attacked a bomber and shot it down. They went after another one but were forced to break off the attack by a bevy of Zeros that swarmed at them like angry wasps. They each got one and then Eric's plane took a hit which damaged the rudder.

'I gotta head for home. This bloody thing's fallin' apart. You're in charge Curly.'

He battled with the stricken plane and eventually managed to get it down safely without any more damage. He taxied to the workshop hangar and told the mechanics, 'I want it back tomorrow.'

'What do you think this is Rolls Royce or somethin'?'

'No, Quick-As-Shit Airlines. Get it done for us mate ay?'

He waited for his squadron to come back. Curly reported they had lost one plane and another had landed on a beach. They had finally driven the

Japanese off for a loss of four Zeros and two bombers.

'Well at least they never got the airfield. How about Robbo? Did he get out?'

'No, went down with it, poor bugger.'

'Could easy have been worse I s'pose but he was a good bloke. Thanks Curly.'

A sergeant from Admin office approached. 'Squadron Leader McDonald sir?'

'Yeah?'

'Wing Commander Dunstan wants to see you urgently sir.'

'Tell him I'll be there directly or soon as I'm ready whichever comes first.'

The man looked dubious but left them.

'You better go Eric.'

Eric rolled a smoke. 'No bugger him, let him wait a bit. This is the real world.'

'You'll be in the shit.'

'I'm just about sick of this job anyhow Curly. I might just apply for a transfer.'

'Where to?'

'Anywhere but here.'

'Let me know an' I'll come too. He's a dead-set galah, a real poobah.'

Eric knocked on Dunstan's door.

'Come in McDonald!'

Eric saluted briskly. 'You wanted to see me sir?'

'I've waited three hours for you to grace me with your presence McDonald!'

'Yes sir. There was an air-raid sir.'

'Damn you man! I know there was an air-raid but when I leave you a message it takes priority.'

'Even over an air-raid?'

'Don't get impertinent with me!'

'I'm sorry sir. What was it you wanted me for?'

'You disobeyed orders yesterday!'

'What?'

'You landed your plane and left it unconcealed on a beach in enemy territory while you played hero.'

Eric stared at the man, thinking he surely could not be serious.

'My job was to protect that boat an' I had to assist after it was sunk sir.'

'How was it that you allowed it to be sunk? It was as you admit your job to protect it from such attack.'

'Nobody expected a sub sir.'

'I've a good mind to put you on a charge McDonald.'

Eric had had enough. He could put up with this idiot no longer. 'An' what in the name of Christ would that be?' He paused as he observed the shocked look on the man's face and then he added, 'sir,' in a sarcastic tone.

'That's enough McDonald! I'm charging you with dereliction of duty, failure to obey orders and insolence to your commanding officer. You are also relieved of your command immediately and confined to quarters pending court martial.'

'I want a transfer sir. I can't work with you.'

'You'll do time unless I'm very much mistaken and on your release I'll recommend you do not return to this unit.'

'Suits me down to the ground. Can I go now?'

'Yes, and remember confined to quarters means exactly that. You'll be shot if you attempt to leave your compound.'

'No wonder we're in so much trouble with the bloody Japs,' Eric commented.

'What's that?'

'Nothin' sir, see you in court.'

★ ★ ★

Three weeks later Eric was still confined to quarters waiting for a date to be set for his hearing. He had freedom of movement in the camp as long as he did not try to pass the gate, although he had not tested the guards' resolve on that score. He chaffed at the injustice of his situation but more than that he wanted to be back in action.

Curly had taken his place as squadron leader but he still regarded Eric as boss, reporting to him after each mission. That way at least Eric knew what was going on. Curly suggested they should kidnap Dunstan and dump his body in the sea.

'That's mutiny Curly. Don't be bloody stupid.'

'Yeah I know that but that's what the bastard deserves. I'll give evidence for you when the time comes Eric. Surely he can't get away with crap like this.'

'You ain't a witness. You wasn't there an' you never seen what happened. All the evidence you can give is to verify what our orders was that day.'

'I'll give you a character reference as well. You're the best squadron leader I ever had. That's gotta count for somethin'.'

'Yeah thanks Curly but I don't know that it will do much good. He's got it in for me. Wonder what he done before the war?'

'Headmaster of a bloody girls' school!'

'You're bloody jokin'?'

'No, fair-dinkum, he was.'

'Well he should of stopped there.'

An officer approached and Eric noticed he held the rank of major from the adornment on his epaulettes.

'This could be me lawyer,' he told Curly.

'I'll leave you then.'

The man who came over to him was tall and athletic looking, with swarthy complexion and a large moustache. He looked somehow familiar.

'Eric I heard you were in strife.'

The voice and face were familiar but Eric couldn't identify him for a moment. Then he suddenly realised it was his cousin whom he had not seen for years.

'Ben Abdul Henry! Bloody hell! What are you doin' here?'

'I was in North Africa but I wanted to get away from there for personal reasons.'

'An' now you're here. Fightin'?'

'Yes in a way you could say I'm fighting. It must be almost twenty years since I spent that time at Tomahawk Plains.'

'Yeah close. I never recognised you for a bit at first it's been that long.

You was pretty young back then.'

'I called in at Tomahawk Plains a few days ago for the first time since then and saw Nettie. We were all young when I was there and she's grown into a very capable woman.'

'Did you? How's she goin'? I ain't seen her for quite a while.'

'She's well Eric. What a woman she must be. I was reviewing the Nackeroo operations and discovered that unofficially she's one of them.'

'Yeah she's been doin' it for a fair while now. She's got the plane an' they need it. They ain't had all that much backup from the army from what I gather.'

'She had a narrow squeak with a Jap plane the other day.'

'Is she alright?'

'Quite alright. I think it would take more than that to daunt her.'

'An' what are you doin' here then Ben Abdul?'

'I'm setting up an operation, Special Air Services commando type of thing. We need men who can fly any kind of plane in any conditions, who are reliable under pressure and capable of surviving on the ground in an op; in other words individuals with multiple skills and nous.'

Eric laughed. 'I'd join up if I wasn't under arrest but right now I'm told I'll be shot if I try an' leave the camp.'

'I might be able to organise that Eric. Are you serious that you'd join up?'

'Yeah I been wantin' to get outta this place for quite a while, actually pretty much since I first got here. I can't get along with me CO.'

'I'll see what I can do but no promises. Oh yes, I almost forgot to tell you. I'm not sure if you've heard that Grandfather died.'

'Buster?'

'Yes Father found out recently and told me.'

'I knew Toby died but I hadn't heard that. He would of been pretty old.'

'Yes but I can't remember how old Father said he was.'

'When did it happen?'

'Not long ago.'

'How is Henry goin'?'

'He wants to retire when the war's over. He's been doing that job for a long time now.'

'He never wanted to get married again?'

'No. When my mother was murdered he swore he'd never put another woman in that position of danger again. He said to give you his regards if I saw you.'

'He's an amazin' man. He's got his finger in every pie.'

'Yes that's why he'll find it hard to retire. You have to die to get out of a job like his and I'm not even sure retirement is allowed then.' He gave a cynical laugh.

'You reckon you can get me outta here?'

'I'll try. I've just organised one operation that I hope will be successful and I want to get more similar ones going.'

'Are you in British Intelligence too?'

Ben Abdul gave him a look. 'You ask too many questions Eric.'

'You met me CO, Dunstan?'

'Yes. He's like many British officers even though he's Australian and not a career man, definitely not my type.'

'He won't be easy to swing an' I doubt if he'll drop the charges against me.'

'He'd be no trouble to handle if we were among my people.'

'Your people?'

'Yes I'm half Arab remember. My mother was Egyptian.'

'An' what would your people do?'

'Probably cut his tongue out and leave him in the desert.'

'Pity they ain't here.'

★   ★   ★

Dunstan refused to drop the charges as Eric had predicted and the case was scheduled for a weeks' time.

Ben Abdul had his degree at law from Cambridge and had practiced law in London briefly before the war so he offered to represent Eric.

'I'd rather defend meself Ben Abdul, no offence to you. You can advise me but, if you don't mind doin' that?'

'I'm happy to help in whatever capacity I can Eric. Let's go through the charges so you can get your case prepared. You'll need to organise witnesses too.'

Eric described every relevant situation since he had first met Dunstan.

'You'll have to plead guilty on the insolence charge. I know the man's just a petty bureaucrat but he'll have witnesses who'll bear him out,' Ben Abdul replied.

'Yeah I was insolent, never in public though.'

'All your mates know your attitude towards him and they'll be called so you can't ask them to lie for you.'

'Yeah I know that an' I'll need 'em as witnesses anyhow. Righto I'll plead guilty on that one but not on the others.'

'Yes that's what I advise. The other two are the serious charges, especially dereliction of duty, which thankfully will be very hard to prove. Provided you hold your tongue in check and don't antagonise the court I think you've got a good chance.'

Eric knew that United States Supreme Commander, General Douglas MacArthur, put a lot of pressure on his Australian subordinates and a number of capable officers had been relieved of command over their inability to hold Kokoda and the track over the Owen Stanleys. The top men usually covered their own backs and apportioned blame to lesser minions. His case was no different. Dunstan disliked him for his successful record and his ability to instill loyalty in his men, both attributes he did not possess himself.

The bench comprised three senior officers and Eric had the feeling they thought the case a waste of time in view of the war situation. Such trivia should be reserved for peacetime in Ben Abdul's opinion.

Eric was read the charges one-by-one and asked for a plea on each. He pleaded as they had agreed. The presiding officer announced that the court would first deal with the dereliction of duty charge.

'Sir, could both the charges I've pleaded not guilty to be heard together please?' Eric asked.

'On what grounds does the accused make the request?'

'On the grounds that both charges relate to the same incident an' are therefore just variations of the same charge sir.'

'Point taken. It should expedite matters. Are there any objections?'

There was no objection from the prosecution.

'The prosecution will present its case.'

The lawyer representing Dunstan called the CO as his first witness. He read from his diary his version of the instructions Eric and his squadron had been given relative to the event. He then read Eric's subsequent report on the incident.

Eric was called next. 'Would you agree as to the nature of your orders on the day in question and the contents of your report that you have just heard read?'

'Not entirely sir.'

'In what respect do you query the contents?'

'The orders were of a very general nature but specifically charged us with the duty to protect the commando operation. To my mind, that also included the individual members of that operation whether plural or singular.'

'Your opinion was not requested. In light of the sinking of the commando vessel by an unidentified Japanese submarine, would you admit that you failed in your duty to carry out your orders?'

'I scouted the area all around the boat before leaving it on a broader search from higher altitude. No sir, I do not feel I failed in my duty. I was patrolling as instructed.'

'Yet you admit that the boat you were supposed to be protecting was in fact sunk by a submarine on your watch after you left it on that broader search?'

'That's correct sir.'

'And as you were ordered to protect it, would you not then say you failed that duty?'

'I don't believe I did sir. I did fail to stop the boat being sunk but I didn't fail in my duty towards that operation or its members.'

'Is it not true that you are in the habit of interpreting your orders to suit your own modus operandi?'

'No sir not that I'm aware of, except in cases where our orders are discretionary, under which circumstances interpretation is required.'

'How did you interpret your orders on the day in question?'

'I didn't interpret them sir. They specifically charged us with the duty of protecting the operation but there were no specific instruction as to how that brief was to be achieved.'

'So you admit you did interpret your orders?'

'As regards carrying out orders yes sir but no more than on any other flight or mission.'

'So you admit that you regularly take matters into your own hands during an operation?'

'As squadron leader that is my responsibility sir.'

'I had planned to call other witnesses but in light of Flying Officer McDonald's virtual admission of guilt that will not be necessary. I have no further questions of this witness at this time.'

Eric called each member of his squadron and they all supported his understanding of their orders that day. He then called John Holley who took the oath.

'Captain Holley, what was your understanding of the duty of our squadron regarding your mission?'

'That you were to protect us and would respond to any request for help from myself as commander of the operation.'

'Did you make any such request?'

'No our radio went out in the first few seconds of the attack by the submarine.'

'Would you have requested help if your radio had been working?'

'Yes I would have. That was why you were there.'

'No further questions of this witness sir.'

The prosecution lawyer asked Holley, 'When your boat was sunk and to the best of your knowledge your men were all dead, would you have expected to be rescued by Flying Officer McDonald?'

'I believe he was at that time squadron leader not flying officer.'

'Well squadron leader then.'

'It didn't occur to me that he would.'

'So you are saying he took matters into his own hands?'

'No I would say he was interpreting his orders in the execution of his duty.'

'He left his plane unconcealed on a beach in enemy territory while he swam out to rescue you. By doing that, would you agree that he risked his plane as well as his life?'

'My view of proceedings was from water level, whereas his was from flying height. He made at least three passes over the area before landing so I can only assume he was satisfied it was safe to do so. As regards risking his life to save me yes I believe he did, especially as sharks were feeding on the bodies in the water. I have recommended him for a bravery award on that count.'

'Do you personally know the defendant?'

'I had previously met him once briefly.'

'So your rescue was not motivated out of friendship?'

'Not at all, on the contrary I believe.'

'Why is that Captain?'

'Because he had no way of knowing I was even in New Guinea. Also I was disguised as a native at the time so there was no way he could have recognised me. The very fact he rescued a man he thought likely to be a native tells me he was carrying out his duty to the letter.'

'Would you not agree that his action was over-zealous, that he exceeded his orders, and that you in fact would not have requested him to do what he did under the hazardous circumstances?'

'No I do not agree that he was over-zealous or that he exceeded his orders. As for requesting him to help me I was in no position to make that request, either from a practical point of view or from the overview aspect. He was the only one qualified to make the decision that he did.'

Both sides rested their cases and the officers of the tribunal conferred briefly before the senior officer stood up. 'The court will rise.' He waited for his instruction to be carried out.

'Flying Officer McDonald you have admitted guilt on the charge of insolence. How long have you been in detention?'

'A month sir.'

'You are sentenced to one month confined to quarters and your demotion from squadron leader to flying officer is noted. As far as this court is concerned you have served your sentence. With regard to the other charges, we find you not guilty on both counts. In the view of this court you discharged your duty in every way.

'I note you have requested transfer to another squadron or unit and I recommend your transfer be approved forthwith. There is clearly a clash of personalities between yourself and your commanding officer and no practical purpose can be served by prolonging the untenable relationship.'

★ ★ ★

Ben Abdul requested that Eric be transferred to his command. Eric was more than happy with that outcome and suspected Dunstan was also glad to see the back of him.

'Curly wants to volunteer too,' he told Ben Abdul.

Within a week they were both assigned to the new squad. Its headquarters was established in a disused igloo building constructed from corrugated iron and painted in camouflage colour. As well as being their operational headquarters the building also served as storage for their equipment and quarters for themselves.

It was a motley group who gradually gathered in the building. They had been transferred from units all over the place, all chosen for their skills and records of initiative.

Ben Abdul had set up his office in one corner of the huge building. It was basic to an extreme degree, consisting of a desk and filing cabinet, a table with a radio transmitter and some cane chairs. Regardless of the sparseness of their lodgings it was adequate for the needs of an irregular unit.

Training was done among themselves with each man training the others in his own particular skill. There were sappers, engineers, radio technicians, cipher experts and battle-hardened commandoes, including a Ghurka sergeant who instructed them to kill silently with the knife. Eric taught the rudiments of tracking, living off the land and parachuting.

There were twenty-six men in total once they had all arrived and begun training. Ben Abdul demanded absolute fitness of his men and trained them hard in two-hour sessions morning and evening. The rest of their day was spent learning the other basic skills they would need on the job and as Ben Abdul explained their job description was pretty-much open-ended.

Two weeks after Eric and Curly had arrived in the crew Ben Abdul called his men together as a group and addressed them. 'I want to introduce my new subordinate officer. Come up here John.'

Eric turned to see who the newcomer was and got a shock when he recognised John Holley.

'This is Captain John Holley. The rest of you will retain whatever rank you already held although that is pretty-much irrelevant because rank will not necessarily denote command on any particular operation. This is an irregular unit and there is one other such unit under my command but at this moment that is all you need to know about it. Everything I say to you is to be regarded as classified information because all of our work is top-secret.'

'I believe in self-discipline, and you have all been chosen with that attribute in mind because I hope no other kind will be needed. If it is necessary, I have failed.'

'You'll live your work from now on and there will be no leave. Your lives will depend on each other so get to know and trust each other to the same extent as mates.'

'Orders will only be given as necessary and will be obeyed. I'll shoot any man who disobeys an order in the field. In this unit you will not have the luxury of a court martial. Anyone who's not happy with that arrangement can leave now.'

'The role of section leader will change from operation to operation. The man with most relevant expertise will be in charge on each sortie or mission. On an operation all ranks are subordinate to the section leader and that includes me if I'm not the one in charge on a particular job.'

'Personal disagreements in camp will be settled in the boxing ring and that will be the end of the matter.'

'You'll be trained hard and fed and accommodated for endurance. By the time you go into action you'll look like racing greyhounds but you will be tough. I intend to be proud of you all and my standards are high.'

'As you can probably see from my complexion I have Arab blood. If you call me a Wop there won't be any charges laid but you'll find yourself in the ring with me and I warn you I can fight. The only racial intolerance I will accommodate is towards the enemy and then I expect total intolerance. No respect is permissible in that quarter.'

'Any questions? No? Good. As you were.'

Eric joined Ben Abdul and John Holley. Ben Abdul spoke. 'Eric, John has told me of your relationship. Can you work with him? If not you can go.'

'Yeah I can work with John. I got nothin' against him.'

John offered his hand and they shook.

'How's the wound?' Eric asked.

'It's healed well Eric but I'll need to get back in training before I'll really know if I'm up to it. Maybe I'll have to be the one who pulls out because I don't meet the criteria.'

Ben Abdul was as good as his word. He trained them hard and subjected himself to whatever he expected of his men. Eric soon came to respect his cousin who had grown up fast and hard in his father's company in the savage land of post-war Egypt. He was adept in almost every skill himself. As well as being multi-lingual and highly educated he was a highly trained fighter pilot and Special Air Service commando.

A canteen was set up in the building with a limit of three beers per man. In the canteen at night they learnt to speak Pidgin, the universal language of New Guinea, as well as rudimentary Japanese.

Ben Abdul encouraged boxing matches for sport and participation was compulsory. One-by-one they all got to fight him as well as each other and learnt respect in the process. In an unequal bout the superior boxer had to fight one-handed to even the chances.

For training they joined a battalion in action for two weeks after humping their packs for sixty miles over the Owen Stanley Range.

They also parachuted into the jungle in pairs and had to get back to base while evading the enemy and living off the land as they went.

They all had to give up smoking, not only in the interest of fitness but also to enhance their sense of smell Ben Abdul told them. Their lives could depend on being able to smell the enemy first.

They had the name Special Air Irregular Unit or SAIU but they called themselves The Flying Circus.

Ben Abdul called for six volunteers for a mission once he considered they were ready for action and the whole unit volunteered.

Ben Abdul picked the squad which included Eric, John Holley, the Ghurka, a wireless technician and a former commando. Curly was selected to fly the plane for the mission.

Ben Abdul briefed them. 'The Japs have pulled out of Guadalcanal but they still hold New Britain. Our two separate targets are at Rabaul, a fuel depot and an ammunition dump. You'll operate as two separate groups of three. You'll be dropped at night and Curly will fly the drop-off plane. You'll have plastic explosive and the charges will be set to go off at the same time so there's less chance of the enemy being alerted and finding one set of charges before they detonate.'

'You will then rendezvous at a predetermined point and establish radio contact once both sections have reached that rendezvous. The contact must be brief because the enemy will be targeting you by then. You will be picked up the following night by boat.'

'I thought you reckoned two teams of three but you only got five in total,' Eric pointed out.

'I'm going too Eric. I make up the six.'

CHAPTER 32

They waited in the cargo hold of the transport plane, watching the open door as they flew through the early night. They all wore their packs and parachutes. It was too noisy for casual talk with the air rushing past outside and the roar of the engines but each man was busy with his own thoughts anyway.

Each section would be dropped separately as an extra precaution to ensure at least one group would be successful in their mission.

'One minute deadline for A Section,' Curly called loudly over the intercom.

John Holley, the Ghurka and the wireless man hooked their ripcords to the wire over the door.

'A Section ten second countdown. B Section twenty seconds to deadline.'

The three men disappeared out the door in the dark and the others clipped their ripcords to the wire. The parachutes had to open immediately because they were only flying at 500 feet. Curly had eased back on the throttles.

'B Section ten second countdown.'

The darkness loomed up as Eric jumped. The straps snapped tight against his body as he tried to make out what lay below but it was too dark to see anything. He hoped Curly had navigated accurately.

The ground collided with his feet and he stumbled briefly before grabbing the cords to begin hauling in the parachute. He could hear surf breaking softly and knew he was on the beach, right on target. He quickly got the harness off and scooped a hole in the sand to bury the chute. Then he gave the curlew call and got two answers. They were no more than 100 yards apart.

They joined each other and Ben Abdul asked, 'All okay?'

'Okay,' they both answered. Ben Abdul led and set the pace, walking on the water's edge so that the rising tide would hide their tracks.

The moon rose and they left the beach striking out for the fuel dump which was their target. Their faces were blackened for camouflage and their only weapons were commando knives and pistols fitted with silencers. The commando who was sapper-trained carried the detonators, fuse and timer, Ben Abdul carried the plastic explosive and Eric the wireless. Each group had their own wireless in case they could not rendezvous for some reason.

They reached the barbwire perimeter of the fuel dump and began cutting through the fence. It took half an hour before they were inside but they were still on schedule.

They heard a guard coming and went to ground in the long grass just inside the wire.

Eric heard the footsteps come close to where he lay. They stopped and he waited as the seconds ticked by. Suddenly the sentry switched on a torch and it shone on the grass, not six feet from where he lay. It swept backwards and forwards and Eric knew he would be seen on the next sweep. He had his knife out ready.

The sentry grunted and pitched forward almost landing on top of him before Eric had time to act. The torch went out and in the moonlight he could see the knife protruding from between the man's shoulder-blades. Heart blood welled copiously around its hilt.

Ben Abdul retrieved his knife and Eric hid the body among some crates stacked nearby. They moved on.

Twice more they hid as sentries passed them and then they were among the big steel fuel tanks. There were stacks of forty-four-gallon drums as well but the tanks were the primary target.

Ben Abdul attached the explosive while Eric ran the fuse wire and the sapper prepared the detonation circuit. The sapper cursed under his breath.

'What's up?' Ben Abdul asked quietly.

'Detonators got wet. I came down in the surf and only just realised the pack was wet too.'

He checked each of the detonators in the box and picked six. Then he wired them doubly into the circuit and connected the timer, which Eric set for 0500 hours.

Then they closed the opening in the barbed wire behind them and made for cover, pausing in a clump of trees.

'It's not going to work. All the detonators are wet. I used the driest ones and wired two in each circuit but I don't reckon it'll go off,' the sapper said apologetically.

'Is there any other way we can set it off?' Ben Abdul asked.

'A hand grenade might do the trick but a pistol bullet wouldn't for sure.'

'How about aircraft machineguns or cannons?' Eric asked.

'Yes cannon fire would set it off no trouble.'

'What are you thinking Eric?' Ben Abdul asked.

'I could borrow a Zero an' set it off if it don't go off by itself when it's supposed to.'

'But by then the ammo dump will have gone up and there'll be alarms blaring all over the base. They'll be looking for us. It's too risky Eric.'

'I could get into their airfield beforehand an' wait. If both lots of explosives go off, all good an' I'll just get out. If our charges don't detonate there'll be a panic anyhow an' I can grab a plane. Probably won't even get noticed in the scramble.'

Ben Abdul knew how highly his father regarded Eric and he was beginning to understand why. He knew Eric had pulled off the most daring undercover operation of the war in Europe.

'Is it feasible Eric? Do you really think you can steal one of their planes right from under their noses? You're not just gambling everything? My unit in Africa stole German planes regularly but the circumstances are completely different here. There we had a whole Bedouin outfit backing us.'

'Yeah I reckon there's a good chance I can do it. It'll mean killin' the pilot though I imagine but what's wrong with one less Nip? Once the first explosives go off the place will be bedlam an' it should be easy to pinch a plane, easier than it would be right now for instance.'

'Okay. We'll come with you to give you cover if it goes wrong.'

'Righto, let's go then.'

'You're section leader now Eric. This is your baby.'

Eric nodded and they loped off heading for the airfield where they cut the wire hurriedly and Eric went in. He found concealment near a parked Zero fighter that stood in a row of similar planes. The others waited outside the fence.

The waiting time was always the worst part of an operation and the minutes ticked by slowly as he waited to see whether the two lots of charges would go off or not. His watch showed 0455 hours.

He heard vehicles start up down by a hangar and then trucks with their lights dimmed came towards where he was hiding. They stopped regularly to drop off pilots and he realised the squadron was off on a mission. He tossed up whether to wait for the explosion or steal the plane while he had the chance but decided there was no point in taking the risk if it was not necessary.

Plane engines fired to life further down the line as the trucks came nearer. One truck stopped near where he lay and a pilot jumped down and went to the plane Eric had chosen. He climbed up and started the motor and then got back down while the motor idled. His watch showed 0459 hours and there was a glow in the east. It would be daylight soon.

Eric heard the thud of an explosion combined with an enormous whoomph as the charges at the ammunition dump exploded, followed by ongoing spectacular fireworks as individual munitions exploded in a fiery display. He watched in the direction of the fuel dump, knowing he might not hear the charges go off with all the plane engines running but that the explosions would be clearly visible.

The Japanese pilot stood still and stared in the direction of the exploding ammunition dump which looked like Guy Fawkes night, as explosion after explosion rocked the early morning and tracer bullets arced skywards like fiery rain. He turned urgently towards his plane as he flicked his cigarette away. The fuel dump charges still had not gone off and Eric knew he had to seize the moment or lose the opportunity.

'Ay Tojo!' Eric called sharply. The man spun towards him in panic and the silenced pistol cracked. The pilot had a stunned look on his face as he slumped almost at Eric's feet, the inertia of his sudden turn carrying him toward rather than away from Eric.

He unbuckled the man's parachute and fitted it himself, then ran to the idling plane. He waited for the other planes to take off, planning to be last of the pack so he had less chance of being noticed when he slipped away from the formation.

Finally his Zero bellowed down the strip and was airborne a quarter of a mile shy of the last plane in front of him, heading towards where the ammunition dump fireworks entertained the gods.

He throttled back and swung towards the fuel dump, knowing that once he made his attack he would have plenty of unwanted company almost immediately.

He came in low, throttled right back to give himself more time to acquaint himself with the use of the guns as he lined up the stacks of drums. He pressed the buttons and watched as the drums burst into flames one after the other. He was on line for the middle tank and kept firing at the spot where he knew the plastic explosive was attached. He kept firing until he had to hit the throttle and the stick together to avoid colliding with the tank but it still had not exploded. The drum stacks erupted behind him and he knew he had holed the tank. It would most likely catch fire but he wanted to be sure of the result.

As he swung for his next approach he could see a swarm of planes coming at him. It was already daylight in the air and they were clearly as visible as he also was to them.

He lined up the patch of grey explosive and started firing as soon as he got it in the cross-hairs, keeping the throttle back as before for a slow approach and more time to set it off. The other Zeros were narrowing the gap fast. Sweat trickled down into his eyes.

The tank loomed up. He hit the throttle and pulled back on the stick simultaneously. The motor coughed momentarily and then took the fuel. He was not going to clear it by much margin.

Suddenly he was engulfed by fire. The explosion rocked the plane, sending it wildly off-course as it came out of the fireball but the motor was still bellowing which was a relief. He fought for control of the craft as he swung away in a turn.

One pursuing Zero which must have been right on his tail had been caught right in the middle of the fireball and thrown skywards. He saw its tank explode as two others turned to follow him.

'Time to go Tojo,' he called on the radio as he climbed towards high cloud at full throttle.

He could hear the frantic radio calls between the pursuing pilots and knew his only chance of survival was to evade them if possible. He was heavily outnumbered and had lost any advantage of surprise. He was also inexperienced at flying the Zero. To try to shoot his way out would be suicide.

There was light cloud at 10,000 feet and he decided to use the same tactic he had used before in Germany. Two pursuing planes were not far behind as he entered the cloud and bailed out, hoping they would not spot him or collide with him.

He dropped out of the cloud, plummeting toward the ground, not spreading his arms and legs to slow his fall. He had lost sight of his immediate pursuers but could see more Zeros flocking towards him. His only comfort was that he would be all but invisible to them until his parachute opened.

He pulled the chute just in time to slow his fall before he hit the canopy of the jungle. There was a brief sensation of being slammed by branches and then he could not remember any more.

CHAPTER 33

Ben Abdul watched Eric take off in the Zero before he rose from cover and led the way again. Eric was on his own. There was no point in waiting. He would have to make his own strategy up as he went but it was imperative they head straight for the rendezvous point and get away from the scene of their raid as quickly as possible.

There were troops on the move everywhere heading for the exploding ammunition dump. They had to wait in hiding beside a busy road that swarmed with speeding vehicles but the pall of dust would aid their safe crossing.

Finally there was a lull in the traffic and they sprinted across the road. They had just crossed it when a huge fireball shot high in the air from the fuel dump. They watched a Zero carried up by the blast, before it too exploded. Ben Abdul shook his head in disbelief. Eric had unintentionally blown himself up in the process of setting off the charge! He had pushed his luck just one time too many, played Russian roulette for the last time.

'Let's go,' he said soberly. There was no sense in waiting any longer. Eric had done his job and paid the supreme sacrifice. Ben Abdul was no stranger to violent death but he was shaken as they headed for their rendezvous, with planes searching for them as they made their way through the jungle.

It was late afternoon when they reached the cave close to the secluded beach where they would rendezvous with their pickup. The three other men were waiting there and he told them what had happened to Eric.

'You're related to him, aren't you?' John Holley asked.

'We're cousins, yes.'

'He was a brave man.'

'He'd already proved that 1,000 times. He was a fighter ace in England as well as one of their most successful undercover agents. He never shirked danger, just ran the gauntlet one time too many I'm afraid. Anyway we'd better send the message. We'll climb the hill so there's a better chance of getting through.'

There was no talk among them as they walked up the hill. Ben Abdul particularly was stunned by the finality of Eric's death. He could have forbidden his plan but was not sure Eric would have obeyed. Further conjecture was counterproductive though, as was over-emotion. What was done was done. Soul searching would change nothing.

CHAPTER 34

Nettie pushed the plane out of the hangar and loaded the mail and supplies for the Nackeroos. She thought of Eric and wondered what he was doing.

She had received his letter telling her of the court martial and the outcome of proceedings. He also said Ben Abdul was organising some secret operation and had recruited him. He told her he would not be able to write for a while because it was all top-secret.

That was three months prior. The news broadcasts on Radio Australia said the Japanese army was being pushed back little-by-little but the fighting was fierce. The cruiser Hobart had been torpedoed in the Solomon Islands only a few days earlier. It was badly damaged but had not sunk.

She suddenly realised she could hear the sound of a rapidly approaching aircraft so she hurriedly pushed her plane back into the hangar and shut the doors.

It must be Eric! She ran past the cattle yards and headed for where the plane had taxied up to the house.

She arrived breathless to see it was Ben Abdul. She immediately thought he may have news of Eric but she was disappointed that it was not Eric himself.

'Are you alright Nettie?' he asked as she panted for breath from her run.

'Yeah I thought it was Eric.'

'You'd better come inside.'

'What is it? Has somethin' happened to 'im?'

'I'm afraid so. Come inside and I'll tell you what happened.'

He told her the whole story and she listened in silence, white-faced toward the end.

'Are you sure it was Eric you seen get blown up?'

'No I'm not totally sure but he was trying to set the explosives off and it's ninety-nine percent likely that it was him Nettie, I'm sorry. He died bravely if that's any consolation to you.'

'He was always brave Ben Abdul, ever since he come here as a kid to run the place, too bloody brave for his own good sometimes. He could ride any horse an' throw any bull an' he could fight. I never seen 'im afraid of nothin'. I idolised 'im as a kid an' I still do. But why did it have to be 'im? I need 'im. Tomahawk Plains needs 'im. Our bloody kids need 'im.'

'I've recommended him for a decoration and also for his rank of Squadron Leader to be reinstated.'

'He already had two medals. What use are medals to a dead man or to a dead man's wife?'

'I know that but he deserves at least one more. He was one man in 1,000 and I've known some brave and capable men in my life.'

'Well thanks for comin' in person to tell me. It's what I was always scared would happen. Did you come specially from New Guinea or was you in the area?'

'No. I'm sorry Nettie I had to fit it in with work. I'm heading for Exmouth Gulf on secret war business but I did want to be the one to tell you. It was on my mission and I'm responsible for all my men. Apart from that Eric was a friend as well as my cousin.'

'Can you stop here for a bit?'

'No, sorry I can't. I'll write and tell you all the things he's done if you'd like that?'

'Yeah I would thanks.'

'Did you know he saved John Holley's life? You know John don't you?'

'No, he never told me that.'

'That was what his court martial was over.'

'I knew he got into trouble for savin' a man's life. He told me that an' it's bloody ridiculous but I never knew it was John that he saved. Yeah John an' me was friends when he was here with the Nackeroos, pretty good mates actually.'

'Yes I thought you were. Will you keep helping them now Nettie?'

'Yeah I'll need to now more'n ever Ben Abdul, otherwise I dunno if I can keep goin' anymore. I'll need a purpose for quite a while I reckon, a reason to get outta bed in the mornin'.'

CHAPTER 35

Eric gradually became aware of voices speaking a Pidgin variant, as if waking from a dream. The owners of the voices were trying to decide whether he was a Japanese airman or not. He looked about him but all he could see were treetops. Then he realised he was hanging by his parachute, high in the branches of a tall tree. He looked down and could see two natives looking up at him from the forest floor.

'Yutupela helpim dispela?' he called for assistance in his basic Pidgin and saw them smile when they realised he was not an enemy pilot.

He hung suspended at least thirty feet from the ground. His head hurt and he could taste blood. He had no idea how long he had been hanging there so he checked his watch. It was 1500 hours, which meant he had been unconscious for quite a while. But at least he was thankful that Japanese patrols had not found him.

One of the natives scaled the tree nearest to where he hung. He shot up its trunk and paused level with Eric. He grinned broadly and then went higher until he reached where the parachute was tangled in branches.

Eric feared he was about to be dropped. 'Nogat pundaun dispela!' he called urgently but the man just laughed and began swinging the parachute. Eric realised what he was trying to do and helped the momentum until it swung like a pendulum. Eventually he managed to hook a branch with his foot. He kicked off it and increased the swing until he was able to grab a limb and climb aboard.

When he felt that his balance was secure he unbuckled the chute harness and looked up to the man to get him to bring the parachute down and pack it away. 'Orait, bungim karamap kwiktaim.'

The man grinned and began unhooking the chute where it was caught up in the foliage. Eric buckled the harness to his limb and when the man dropped the chute he climbed down the ropes and dropped to the ground. Then he watched the man slide down to where he had been to unhook the strap and drop the harness. Then he came down the trunk as agilely as he had ascended.

They bundled the chute up and he knew they would use every part. Then they set off, with him following for miles through the trackless jungle. They finally reached a small village high on the crest of a mountain ridge. He knew they hated the Japanese invaders and that he would be safe with them. It was almost dark but without the radio which he had given to Ben Abdul he had no way of letting his unit know he was still alive. They would most likely think he was dead when he did not rendezvous with them for the pickup.

★ ★ ★

The natives who had rescued him had their own bush telegraph and always knew when there were Japanese patrols in the area long before they arrived. They melted into the scrub and he went with them and hid until the enemy left, before returning to their village.

Food was plentiful enough. They cultivated papaya, sweet potatoes and corn, as well as raising domestic pigs which doubled as a source of milk and meat.

He thought of trying to get back to Rabaul to steal another plane for a getaway but realised his chances, of first outrunning pursuit and then getting through the Australian defences on the mainland without being shot down, were exceedingly slim. That was if he managed to steal one in the first place.

He took the two men who had found him and went to the coast where he found the cave that had been their rendezvous point. The tracks told him the others had all arrived there safely and had been extracted. He doubted that they would expect him to have survived and would be unlikely to return to look for him. He scratched his name and the date on the wall of the cave anyway, in the vain hope it may be found by someone.

On the way back to the village he shot a wild boar with his pistol. The men gutted it with their sharp knives and carried the carcass suspended between them on a pole slung over their shoulders.

On the perimeter of the village a tall tree of great girth stood proud of the forest. Footholds were cut in the trunk and wooden pegs had been driven in for hand grips. He followed one of the men up above the canopy 200 feet above the ground. The view was spectacular. He could see Rabaul about thirty miles away and well out to sea in most directions. He could see Japanese ships clearly enough to identify them and realised that if he had a radio he could pass on shipping and aircraft movements but then if he had a radio he could also get out of there.

Although the men carried steel axes and sharp knives the tribal group lived in fairly primitive fashion. A few of the men understood some words of Pidgin but they conversed in their own tongue which bore no relationship to the Aboriginal dialect he knew. As the weeks went by he gradually picked up words of their language, at first mostly words for food items; papaya, sweet potato, corn and pig. He already knew the Pidgin words, popo, kau kau or kumu, kon and pik which helped until he learnt their words.

Each day he climbed the lookout tree and kept track of the planes and ships he saw by making marks in the bark of the tree. He also kept tally of the days in the same way.

Sometimes he climbed the tree at night and could see distant flashes of artillery or ships' guns. He knew there was a push to get the Japanese off the island of New Britain and that it would only be a matter of time before the Allies invaded. In the meantime he felt safe where he was, even if he fretted about Nettie and about getting back to his unit.

His main concern was that Nettie would again be told he was dead but there was nothing he could do about that.

Every week he made the trip back to the cave but there was never any sign anyone else had been there again. He was there on one of his visits when he recognised the sound of a Spitfire engine. He ran down to the beach and saw it fly over. He continued waving until it was out of sight and then sat down despondently on a drift log on the edge of the beach.

Then it came to him that many planes had been shot down in the past couple of years and that it may be possible to find one that still had a salvageable functioning radio. He knew batteries would go flat and radios would succumb to the humidity quickly but it would at least give him something positive to do.

By word and sign he asked his hosts if they knew of any such planes. They grinned broadly and indicated he should follow them.

They walked for three days before coming on a crashed P-39 Airacobra with US insignia. He was aware that many inexperienced US pilots had come to grief in the P-39s when they ran low on fuel, which could affect their centre of gravity to the point of going into a spin. It had lain on a ridge for some time with the dead pilot still in his seat in an advanced state of decay. The radio was corroded and unserviceable. He buried the man with a cairn of stones to mark the grave and then hung his dog-tags on the uppermost stone.

Then they found the first USAF P-61 Black Widow night fighter Eric had ever seen. He had heard they were being produced but this was the first evidence he had seen of one in the Pacific Theatre. It was a twin engine, twin hull and tail machine with four 20 mm cannons and four .50 calibre Brownings. He studied it with interest but the radio was unserviceable.

The next day they came on a burnt-out USAF B-17 Flying Fortress and he gave up, discouraged for the time being.

A week later, he saw a sea-plane land near the beach from his vantage point in the tree. He climbed down quickly and set off to walk to the coast in the hope it would still be there but, when he arrived half a day later, it was gone.

He scrupulously maintained his pistol, drying it when it got wet and greasing it and the ammunition with pig fat.

He celebrated Christmas by shooting a wild pig which they roasted whole. He told them it was a celebration but knew Christmas meant nothing to these people.

Nevertheless he felt particularly homesick for Nettie, for his children and for Tomahawk Plains, even though he had never been particularly traditional in his attitude toward Christmas. His optimism was at its lowest ebb for quite a while.

CHAPTER 36

The months went by while Nettie again struggled to come to terms with Eric's apparent death. Like the previous time she knew there was the slimmest possibility he was still alive and that it was also possible she would not know for sure until the war was over. It was also possible she may also never know for sure. In a way it would be easier to cope if she knew he was dead. Her nature was straightforward and vague hope was more difficult for her to deal with than even the harshest reality.

She hoped John would not contact her while she was in emotional limbo because that was a complication she did not need on top of her grief at this time. A card came from him at Christmas, handmade from a piece of brightly coloured cardboard.

Merry Christmas Nettie. I think of you often and hope you're coping with your loss. I hope to see you again one day if this war ever finishes. Best wishes, John.

She cried when she read it. At least she was not likely to see him soon, which was a relief. She was not ready for that yet. Every day had to be got through without giving up hope and losing her will to keep going.

She spent more and more time with her Nackeroo duties and realised the plane was long overdue for a major service but all she could do was change the oil and plugs and check the machine daily. She was able to repair tears in the fabric of the plane but her main fear was that the propeller would eventually de-laminate and crack from stress. Aeroplane parts were one thing the Nackeroos could not get for her either legally or illegally and it was quite likely that parts were difficult to obtain even for those who legitimately ran aircraft. Shortages of all kinds were a fact of life in wartime. They had always been a reality in the more remote areas, which was why bush people were resourceful.

She flew to her outposts just after New Year and was on her way home when she spotted a Japanese fighter plane on the ground. It seemed intact but she did not dare land to check. Instead she flew to the Ord base to report the find.

The CO Ian McKenzie said he would go back with her if she would take him in the plane.

They landed near the enemy craft and approached with their Tommy-guns at the ready but there was nobody there. The plane appeared to be undamaged. She cut for tracks and found where the pilot had set out on foot. After an hour spent tracking she realised she would have to give it away if they were to get back to base before dark.

They returned at daylight and resumed tracking until they found the pilot, who had obviously perished from thirst only a few days prior. They buried him after taking the contents of his pockets. It seemed most likely that the plane had run out of fuel because the tank was dry. There was no visible damage and the prop turned freely, which proved that the engine had not seized.

'We could keep this plane,' Nettie suggested.

'Are you serious? I'll have to report it.'

'You could say it crashed or not even mention it. Nobody else knows about it.'

He looked dubious. 'Where would we keep it and what use would it be to us anyway? I'd rather not have it at our base.'

'At Tomahawk Plains. My plane'll break down at some stage an' then I'll be stuck without it. I could use this one instead if that happened.'

'Could you fly it though?'

'I suppose I could. I flew a Spitfire once.' She knew this was only a half-truth but was keen to try to keep this unexpected prize. It seemed too good an opportunity to let pass.

'We'd have to paint RAAF roundels on it or else you could get shot down by one of our own planes.'

'Yeah we could do that easy enough. Will you help me to keep it?'

'Fly me back to camp now and tomorrow we'll come out in a Blitz and bring fuel. Then we'll clear you a good enough strip so you can take off and we'll give it a go. What you're suggesting makes sense if you're game to fly a strange machine.'

'Thanks Ian. You know how valuable any plane is to us don't you?'

'We'd have a tough time without you and your plane Nettie. I think it's a good idea but I just hope we don't get found out.'

'I won't be tellin' no-one. I ain't even got a pilot's licence an' I ain't meant to have the Tiger Moth now neither so from my point of view I got nothin' more to lose.'

Thinking about it that night she realised this plane was probably fast like a Spitfire. Could she manage to take off and even more importantly could she land? She felt that she had committed herself and could not back out. She knew Eric would fly it if he was home and she would give it her best shot, although she was somewhat nervous.

They took six men the next day and got a strip cleared by mid-afternoon. It was open timbered country which meant there was not a lot of clearing and grubbing involved. The ground was even enough for take-off. The enemy pilot had managed to land with no cleared strip and the plane was undamaged so with a cleared strip she was reasonably confident she should be able to manage the exercise.

They filled the tanks from the drums they had brought but Nettie decided it was too late in the day to attempt the flight so they camped the night there where they were. She hoped the men did not think she was procrastinating out of self-doubt or fear.

The next morning she again checked the plane all over and then climbed into the cockpit. The controls were different to those of the Tiger Moth but similar enough and she worked them until she felt confident of not making a mistake.

She pulled the throttle out a little and richened the mixture, then switched the ignition on and pressed the starter button. It cranked over and coughed. She tried again and it fired and then stalled. On the third try it started and ran raggedly. She leaned the mixture adjustment until it smoothed to an idle.

Then she climbed down and arranged with Ian that he would send someone to collect her at home to take her back to the Nackeroo camp for her own plane.

'Are you sure you still want to do this? You can change your mind you know. I won't think you're a coward.'

'I'll be alright Ian. I know I'm just bein' nervous over nothin'. I got hundreds of hours up in my plane now. It oughta just be a matter of gettin' used to the speed.'

'It's a hell of a way to learn. You'll only get one go at it.'

'Wish me luck.' She grinned and hoped she looked more confident than she felt.

She climbed into the cockpit and took a few slow deep breaths to settle her racing pulse. She eased the throttle out a little and held it with the brakes, forcing herself to stay calm as she opened the throttle full bore and released the brake. It surged forward. At half strip she knew she was committed. There would not be another chance. It was racing towards the trees at the end of the makeshift strip at a rapidly increasing rate.

By the time her groundspeed seemed more than fast enough the strip was running out. She eased the stick back and the wheels lifted off the ground. She was flying!

The sense of relief left her feeling slightly light-headed but extremely elated. It was a great boost to her confidence, which she knew she would need if she were to make a successful landing back at the homestead.

Guide me Eric. I know I could do it if you were here with me.

CHAPTER 37

Eric carved another notch on the lookout tree and hoped he had not lost track of the days, not that it mattered much he supposed. The year 1944 had come without event. Nothing much had changed except that by then he had learnt most of the language of his host tribe and had become familiar with the terrain over a wide area. He knew where the Japanese troops were likely to be and avoided them at all times.

He seldom went to the rendezvous cave anymore but he had visited just before Christmas and scratched the date on the wall on the off-chance that somebody found it and may come looking for him.

As the months had passed he had realised that there was no winter in that country. The only noticeable thing was that the nights were cooler in the middle of the year than in summer.

He scratched the notch on the tree and counted the marks. If he had not lost track, that day was the twins' 14th birthday, 15th September 1944. They had been nine when he had last seen them. Nat would be twelve in October. He felt lonely for them and Nettie and wondered if he would ever get home to lead a normal life again. It seemed a lifetime ago that he had enlisted to go to England.

By the time of Nat's birthday it seemed that the war was coming closer to him. His sightings of allied planes and shipping were more regular occurrences. He hoped an invasion would come soon and give him the chance to be reunited with his unit or at least an Australian force.

Allied planes were attacking Rabaul and he watched dogfights in the sky along the coast from his lookout. He could see a convoy of ships nearing the island and realised the Allied invasion was coming at last. There was a heavy bombardment of shelling during the night, as well as bombing of Rabaul and other Japanese bases. By morning it was apparent that Allied troops had landed on the island during the night. The sound of distant battle came on the breeze. It was time to go to try to link up with an Australian unit.

He said farewell to the tribe who had been his hosts for the past sixteen months and was sad in a way to be leaving these simple cheerful people. He had been happy with them, apart from fretting about his family and his responsibilities. He realised how complicated Western peoples' lives were by comparison and he was not sure they were much better off as a result.

The two men who had rescued him that first day came with him and they set out for where the fighting was in progress. By then the only part left of his original clothing was his webbing belt with the pistol and commando knife. He wore a lap-lap like the natives and was burnt brown by the sun. His hair and beard were long and his bare feet were as tough as those of his companions.

CHAPTER 38

Nettie checked the calendar and realised it was the twins' birthday. She wished she could call them but knew the radio blackout which had been in force for the past eighteen months prevented that. She felt isolated from the world and missed her children and Eric.

She also realised the twins were almost young adults now and they had still been children when she had last seen them. She had sent them a letter for their birthday and enclosed a cheque so they could buy themselves presents. She thought how fortunate it was that Eric had arranged for her to be able to sign cheques before he had enlisted, because she did not know how she would have managed to run the business without that legal detail. She had never had a personal bank account in her life.

The proceeds of each mob of sale cattle which were sent under Bluey's management to the Cape River Meatworks, or Pentland Meat Store as it was initially called, was deposited in their account. Since the war had started they had previously been going to Brownson's Slaughter Yards at Charters Towers which had struggled to keep up with the demanded kill-rate. The new facility at Pentland was built by the Army to service the extra supplies for the huge number of troops stationed at Macrossan Army Base on the Burdekin River and at Townsville. Pentland was closer than Charters Towers and was also on the same rail line, which saved considerable droving distance.

Recently the Army had built another new abattoir on Manbulloo Station near the Katherine River which was killing 700 head per day to feed the Northern Territory troops. However, it seemed impractical to bring fats back west from their Barkly fattening depots so she decided to stick with what had proven successful and leave the new market for others who could supply slippery cattle from the surrounding region.

It was apparent from the balances on the bank statements that there was much more money in the account than came from the sales, although cattle prices had risen somewhat. She wondered if Henry still paid money into their account, even without any diamonds being sold anymore. She had not notified the bank that Eric was probably dead because she feared they would freeze the account if she did. If that occurred there would be no way of continuing. Apart from buying and cartage of stores at wartime rates there were odd wages, land rent and a war levy to be paid if Tomahawk Plains were to survive as a cattle station.

She fought back the feeling that threatened to engulf her. She had to keep busy. There were colts to be broken in so she mustered them and drafted two off to begin handling. By midday she had caught them both and begun the breaking process. She decided to give them a spell for a couple of hours in the hottest part of the day to have lunch and wait till it got cooler.

She heard a plane approaching and waited apprehensively as she always did when she was not expecting anyone.

It hove into view approaching fast and she realised with a start that it was a Japanese Zero the same as hers. It dropped altitude as it neared and suddenly its guns started firing as it swooped low over the house.

Anger flared in her as it banked and came back for another attack. The machineguns hammered again and then it passed over her. Then they fired again as it shot up the Aborigines' camp on its way.

She lost her temper. Strafing her house was bad enough but shooting up the Aborigines' camp enraged her. She ran to where her Zero fighter sat parked under a tarpaulin and camouflage net that the Nackeroos had supplied especially. She dragged the cover off it hurriedly and climbed into the cockpit.

She had been starting the engine regularly to keep the battery charged and had taken it up a few times so she felt capable of flying it adequately.

She had even fired a short burst from its guns so she knew that they worked and also so she was sure how to fire them. It was full of fuel and ready to fly.

The Japanese plane had headed in the direction of the Nackeroo headquarters on the Ord River. She started the motor and held her foot on the brakes while she idled the engine fast.

Once she was airborne she set a course for Nackeroo headquarters. She thought it would probably also shoot them up and hoped to catch it there before it did too much damage. Her blood was up and she felt no fear, only the dry-mouthed sensation of her adrenalin rush.

As the Nackeroo headquarters came in view she could see the enemy plane passing low over the camp strafing everything. Vickers and Lewis machineguns fired at it from the ground but she knew they were no match for its guns. She was glad her plane was now painted Army drab green, with the red, white and blue roundels on it. Otherwise the Nackeroos could mistake her for a second Japanese raider.

She had the throttle wide open coming up behind the enemy and closing the gap fast. The pilot did not seem to have spotted her. He was most likely overconfident that he had the sky to himself and was not expecting an attack from that quarter.

As the gap narrowed she pressed the gun-buttons and the plane shook from the recoil of all four guns, the two 7.7 mm machineguns and the two 20 mm cannon. The machineguns were mounted in the engine cowling and the cannon in the wings.

She saw metal torn from her target's fuselage and then it wheeled hard and climbed sharply. She knew she had to stay close on its tail so that it could not turn the tables on her. She was also acutely aware that she would be no match for an experienced fighter-pilot where aerobatics were concerned.

She got it in her sights again as it banked to come back at her. She fired a burst and saw the sun glint on aluminium shards torn from its wing like a shower of shiny confetti.

She swung her Zero hard to follow but it was quickly apparent she was no match as a pilot for her adversary. Try as she might she could not prevent her enemy gradually getting into position for a counterattack.

Her teeth were clenched and she knew she could die at any minute but she still felt no fear. None of it seemed real. It was like a dream sequence.

It was coming at her and she saw the muzzle-flashes as its guns fired. She pulled hard on the stick with the throttle wide open and saw shiny metal torn from her wingtip before the other plane flashed past.

She banked hard. If her life was not so urgently on the line she knew she would love the full-out flying. She had never flown like that before and it thrilled her, just as it had when Eric had done his aerobatic manoeuvres.

She levelled out and saw her enemy had completed his turn. They now faced each other at a distance of a quarter of a mile and the gap was narrowing rapidly. She saw the flashes of its guns and pressed her own gun-buttons.

She realised its guns had stopped firing but kept her thumb on the buttons and saw a shower of Perspex explode from its cockpit. Then she banked to come back, thinking it must have run out of ammunition.

She brought the plane around to pursue her quarry and her pulse raced. She knew she had him at her mercy.

As she came up behind it she realised he was not taking any evasive action. Had she hit the pilot when she saw the glass fly?

She got it in her sights and fired again. There was a flash of fire as its fuel tank exploded. It felt good as she throttled back and watched it spiral into a dive. She looked back as it crashed into the ground and then turned her plane for home.

She was almost back to Tomahawk Plains before the adrenaline rush settled.

CHAPTER 39

Ben Abdul flew on his way to Exmouth Gulf. His other irregular unit which was based there had successfully emulated the MV Krait's Operation Jaywick and got into Singapore harbour in a disguised fishing boat and blown-up Japanese shipping over a year earlier. Since then they had engaged in further raids on the Japanese-held island of Java.

The planned assault on New Britain was imminent and he only had time for a brief visit to the unit before he was needed back at Port Moresby.

He planned to call at Nackeroo headquarters at Ord River on his way through and wished he could also visit Nettie but knew he could not spare the time.

He circled the Nackeroo camp before coming in to land on the short bush strip and spotted the burnt wreckage of a plane nearby. It looked like a Zero.

As he taxied towards the camp a Jeep came out to meet him and he recognised Lieutenant Ian McKenzie at the wheel. He had one arm in a sling.

'What happened to you Ian?' he asked, as he got into the jeep.

'Did you see the wrecked plane as you came in?'

'Yes?'

'It shot up our camp and I got a flesh wound but luckily only a bullet and not a twenty mm. Also, luckily for us Nettie McDonald arrived and shot it down.' He stopped, realising he had let the cat out of the bag about the plane. Ben Abdul noticed the pause.

'How did she shoot it down?'

McKenzie told him the whole story. 'I thought no harm would be done by not reporting we had the plane.'

Ben Abdul laughed. 'She surely is some woman. I'm glad she's got it and I'm sure you are too.'

'Yes I just wish we could recognise her officially. In a way she's the backbone of this company, regardless of the value of our work.'

Ben Abdul resolved to see what he could do in that regard. He knew the efforts of many people went unrecognised by official channels. It was more often the case than not in intelligence work. He knew that if she was a male member of the Nackeroos it was likely she would be decorated for her bravery and service.

It was a pity he could not spare the time to call on her but at least he knew she was coping with Eric's death. She was strong that one. He recognised her as an equal, giving her the code name, 'Joan of Arc'.

CHAPTER 40

Ben Abdul led his party ashore at the same little bay from whence they had been evacuated all those months prior. He wanted to check the cave which had been their rendezvous on that mission in the faint hope that Eric had been there afterwards. He knew it was an unlikely possibility and that even if Eric had arrived later his chances of still surviving were remote. Nevertheless, he wanted to set it beyond doubt in his mind.

They were the advance party for an assault that would be mounted in the next few days. Their mission was to set up an observation post and establish a radio base to assist in the invasion of the island.

They unloaded the small fishing boat and he instructed his men to sink it in the shallow water where they may be able to salvage it later if it was needed.

They carried their equipment to the cave. It was slow going in the dark but eventually they had everything stowed away.

He switched on his torch and shielded the beam in case there were Japanese troops in the area. At first glance the cave was as they had left it. Then he spotted scratch marks on the wall. He looked carefully and made out the name Eric and a date. Then he saw more dates. Eric had come there only a day or two after they had been evacuated. The last date was 23/12/1943, eleven months previously. He had still been alive then but had he died since or just given up returning?

He showed the others and they discussed the likelihood of finding Eric alive after all the time that had elapsed since the raid and even since

Christmas 1943.

The next morning they would move out in search of a suitable site for their observation post. There was no time to consider looking for Eric but at least there was tangible evidence he had survived his attack on the fuel dump and a distinct possibility he was still alive. Ben Abdul fervently hoped he was because he had been responsible for the mission during which Eric had gone missing in action.

One thing in Ben Abdul's favour regarding Eric's whereabouts was that if he was still alive and in the vicinity he would be sure to try to make contact with Australian troops once the invasion started. Whereas, mounting any search for him would be like looking for the proverbial needle in a haystack. If he had survived on the island with all the Japanese troops he would obviously have studiously avoided them.

CHAPTER 41

Eric propped suddenly. His now heightened olfactory senses had identified a foreign aroma that did not belong among the other musty jungle smells of decaying vegetation and exotic fungi. Sound was muted in the dense rainforest and the carpet of rotting leaves underfoot made their passage almost totally silent.

His companions went to ground at his example but they like him had smelt it too. He crept forward, every sense alert to danger, calling on instincts that had become keenly developed during the time of his involuntary exile. He had grown up in his own Top End bush environment trained by his Aboriginal tutors and his past months with the natives in this place had sharpened those instincts even further.

He crawled to the edge of the ridge, peered over down the slope and listened. There were no bird sounds! The smell was stronger there. His eyes roamed the slope as his head turned imperceptibly following his vision.

There was movement below him. He focused on the spot and made out the figures of three well camouflaged Japanese soldiers.

In the distance he could hear sporadic fire as the engagement proceeded. He pulled back from the rim and moved further along, pausing to observe regularly as he went. After a thorough assessment of the area he realised that the Japanese force dug in on the slope below him was at least company strength.

He had planned to head for where the fighting was in an effort to make contact with Allied troops but now realised that to be able to do so he would have to get through enemy lines. He had no illusion as to the ability of the Japanese soldiers where jungle warfare was concerned and decided his undertaking to make contact with an Australian force would not be as easy as he had hoped.

He sent his companions back because he did not want to endanger them unnecessarily and was also aware that he would be less visible alone. He would skirt the enemy positions and hope to find a weak spot where he could get through their lines.

His evasion took him wider and wider as he kept locating more and more Japanese troops. He found himself heading in the direction of the cave he had visited so often, which meant that he was in an area where he knew the terrain quite well.

Darkness fell early in the jungle and he slept on a bed of leaves between the buttressed roots of a huge tree. To continue in the dark was to risk stumbling onto a Japanese outpost. He moved again at first light. His belly felt empty but he ignored its plea for food. His perception was akin to that of a small animal dwarfed by the forest as his instincts guided him through the dense tall scrub, smelling the enemy out before he saw them.

He paused in a ravine and studied the slope that faced him. He knew he would be disadvantaged and vulnerable from above as he climbed. Half an hour passed while he waited and studied the terrain before he felt ready to continue.

As he neared the crest of the ridge he picked up man-scent again. It seemed subtly different somehow but he took no chances and moved forward warily. He reached the crest and cautiously looked over. Nothing seemed amiss as he watched and waited. Still there was nothing. Even though he knew that somebody was close he had not yet managed to locate that somebody, whose ambush he could walk into at any moment. He would have to backtrack and go around again rather than risk walking into a trap. He realised in frustration that he was working his way around in a circle, neither gaining nor losing ground and was now only a couple of miles from the sea. It was beginning to look as if he was not going to find a chink in the enemy lines between where he was and there.

He warily climbed a tree on the spine of the ridge, going all the way up to the canopy where he could look out over the surrounding scrub. From that vantage point he could see the smoke of battle away to his left and hear artillery fire. His eyes roamed the forest in every direction until something caught his eye momentarily, but he could not be sure what it was because he could not locate it again. He swept the area time and time again but could see nothing odd. He was just about to concede that he had imagined whatever it was that had caught his subconscious notice when he had a sensation of deja vu. He stared and worked the focus of his gaze range-wise rather than laterally. His eyes blurred from the effort.

There it was! There was something not quite right about a tree around 100 yards along the crest from him. As he studied it he realised that what had caught his attention in the first instance was something slim and straight and there were no straight lines in nature, not animal, bird or plant. What he finally identified was a well camouflaged radio aerial in the canopy of the tree. The straight line had caught his highly tuned mind's eye as being different and alien somehow.

His hackles rose at the knowledge he had got so close to a possible enemy. He slowly descended from his perch with all of his senses on high alert but he was not challenged as he did. He reached the ground and wormed his way towards the tree with the radio aerial. Nothing moved or seemed amiss at ground level but he continually scanned the canopy overhead as he went, feeling extremely concerned that he would be a sitting duck from above.

Then he came upon a single boot track. It was similar to an Australian Army boot, not the split-toed camel-like track of a Japanese one. There were more tracks but they were unclear in the leafy mulch that absorbed tracks the same way a carpet does.

There was an intermittent low-pitched alien sound in the vicinity. He listened and heard it again, a low vocal hum. It was a voice speaking quietly, not the high pitched chatter of a Japanese voice or the nasal twang of an American one. He looked all about him but could not locate the source.

The smell was different from that of the Japanese, the tracks were similar to Australian ones and the voice was low-pitched. However, even if it were Australians he was stalking he was still in danger of being shot by them. He knew they would be taking no chances in this jungle with its heavily entrenched Japanese troops and he was also acutely aware that he no longer even resembled a white man in his present suntanned near-naked condition.

He heard the unmistakable snick of an automatic weapon being cocked and his skin crawled. They had him under surveillance and he hardly dared breathe.

Then came the mournful wail of a curlew's call and his heart skipped a beat, knowing that there were no curlews in that environment. It had to be someone who used the call like he did. He answered it with his own call and the minutes ticked by agonisingly slowly. Sweat trickled into his eyes and dripped off his face. The call came again and he replied in kind.

'Stand up and raise your hands!' a quiet command came from very close nearby.

He obeyed, having little choice but not totally confident he would not be shot as he complied with the direction.

'I'm Australian. Don't shoot,' he said anxiously as he stood and raised his hands cautiously without making any sudden moves.

A man stepped out from behind a tree not twenty yards distant and he recognised him as a member of his own Flying Circus unit. 'Nugget, it's me Eric McDonald. Thank Christ for that!'

Men appeared on all sides. They had been watching him but obviously still did not quite trust he was who he said he was because they kept their weapons trained on him as they approached warily.

'Eric!' The voice was Ben Abdul's.

Eric turned, keeping his hands raised. 'Ben Abdul, thank God it's you lot an' not a mob of trigger-happy Yanks.'

'You'd have spotted us and probably heard us, if we'd been Yanks Eric. Put your hands down.' He holstered his weapon and embraced Eric.

'I knew you were here but for the life of me I couldn't spot you,' Eric told him.

'We never spotted you either until you came down out of the tree but we couldn't take the chance that you weren't a native spying for the Japs. You certainly don't look like a white man garbed up like that.'

Eric smiled. 'Garbed down like that might be more like it ay? I reckoned I'd never see you all again. You got no bloody idea how good it feels Ben Abdul.'

'How long since you've eaten? You look a bit on the lean side Eric.'

'Yeah I'm hungry enough to eat a bloody sandshoe without tomato sauce. I ain't had a feed since early yesterday but it ain't like I'm gonna whinge about it now that you coves are here.'

'Well you'd better go down to our camp and get a feed and then report back here. We've got a war to fight.' Ben Abdul pointed the way towards the campsite. 'You can't miss it with your instincts Eric, about 200 yards.'

CHAPTER 42

The Flying Circus returned to Port Moresby in early 1945 soon after New Year. The fighting continued while pockets of Japanese opposition were mopped up. However their job was, to most intents and purposes, done. New Britain and Rabaul were once again in Allied hands.

Eric was not allowed to write to Nettie but Ben Abdul told him he would get a message to her through the Nackeroos so that she would know he had been found.

They had two weeks of relative ease before preparing for their next mission, which was similar to the role they had played in New Britain but on the mainland in preparation for an assault on Wewak. They would be further ahead of the attacking force this time and their job would be to set up a long-distance radio post as before, as well as gathering critical intelligence on enemy strength and position.

During the invasion of New Britain Eric had enlisted the help of his two native rescuers and had done extensive reconnaissance behind Japanese lines, so that whenever possible an artillery barrage could be brought down on enemy units before ground troops went in. Ben Abdul realised that many Australian lives had been saved by having that detailed intelligence. They would attempt to set up a similar network of native spies at Wewak.

Ben Abdul was proud of his unit. They had undertaken many dangerous missions and had always acquitted themselves well. Since their formation he had only lost seven of the original twenty-six men.

It had been a great relief to him when Eric had turned up alive. They had been friends as youths even though Eric was quite a bit older than he. He knew they had both inherited the tenacity that ran back through their bloodlines to the now legendry Eliza Henry their paternal great-grandmother, who had survived a life of danger and notoriety in the early days of outback settlement, to die not far short of her century a wealthy and respected woman.

CHAPTER 43

Nettie heard of the recapture of Rabaul on the short-wave radio. About that same time, Australian forces took over from the Americans at Bougainville.

Gradually the Japanese invaders were being driven back. Although she knew everyone wanted the war over she also knew that once it was over and the Nackeroos pulled out she would be left with a hole in her life that she would find difficult to fill. She desperately looked forward to having her children back and hoped they would be enough to satisfy that need and fill the void left by Eric's death.

She heard vehicles approaching and cantered the colt she was riding back to the house, where she saw a Jeep arriving followed by a Blitz. She hobbled the horse and greeted the men, Ian McKenzie and two Nackeroo privates.

'G'day boys, I'll put the kettle on. Come on in.'

Ian followed her inside. 'I've got a message for you from Major Henry, Nettie.'

'Yeah?'

'It said, 'Tell Joan of Arc that Eric is alive'.'

'Eric alive? Who the hell's Joan of Arc?'

'That's all I know Nettie. It was in code and I have no idea who Eric is but I do know that Joan of Arc is Major Henry's code name for you.'

She sat down at the kitchen table stunned by the news. A sense of unreality gripped her. What the hell am I supposed to believe? First Eric's dead and then he turned up. Then he's dead again and now he's not dead after all.

I know I ought to be excited but I just can't trust what I'm hearing anymore. It's not that I don't trust Ben Abdul just the same but he's been wrong before.

She had undergone so much disappointment and grief since Eric had gone away that her emotions had almost reached the point of immunity, where they refused to respond anymore. She hoped she would know the truth about him before too long.

'You alright Nettie?' Ian asked anxiously.

'Yeah I'm fine Ian. We'll see eventually won't we? I'm sorry I don't sound too excited about this but I really bloody well don't know what to believe anymore.'

'I can understand that. Life is all a bit unreal these days, isn't it? Not wanting to spoil the news for you but I've managed to get hold of some Jap ammo of both calibres for your Zero, Nettie. The boys will re-arm it after smoko for you.'

'Yeah that's great Ian. Thanks.'

She went with the men down to the plane because she wanted to know how to load the guns in case she had to do it herself. After it was done, there were ten boxes of 7.7 mm and ten of twenty mm left over for her to keep. She wondered how they had been obtained but did not ask.

'Alright Nettie we'd better get going now. We'll drop you off at the house.'

'I'll walk thanks Ian. Thanks for the message an' thanks for the ammo.'

'Who's Eric? I'm totally in the dark.'

'He's me husband.'

'You must be really relieved then.'

'Yeah I'll be relieved if it's true. I'll see you next time Ian.'

She watched them drive off and did not really feel relieved. She felt depressed and knew she could not keep going like this, having her heart broken each time she learnt of Eric's death. It had recovered after they had sorted out their differences when he had come home from England but now she did not know what she felt anymore.

She had also gone through the conflict of her feelings towards John at that time and now she felt drained of all emotion, unable to respond. Or was she just being stoic?

She walked slowly up to the house where she unsaddled the colt and turned it loose. She did not feel like doing anything. She looked disinterestedly at the bullet holes in the roof and went inside.

There was a bottle of rum in the kitchen cupboard. She took it out and poured a drink. Maybe when she was drunk she could take the Zero up and put it through its paces.

CHAPTER 44

As the time for their departure neared Ben Abdul worried about Eric's state of mind.

He had seemed fine when they had been reunited in New Britain and he had thrown himself back into the work enthusiastically but now since they had been back in Port Moresby, he seemed withdrawn and uncommunicative.

He wondered if Eric's period of involuntary exile had seriously affected him emotionally. It had not appeared to have done so at first but he knew Eric had been through a lot in the years leading up to that. Maybe the pressure had been building in him. The only leave period that showed on his record since he first enlisted was the months he had spent recovering from his injuries after his undercover operation in Germany.

Ben Abdul wondered how he had avoided being ordered to take leave at some time during his service. Many men had broken down under the pressure of war, especially in the high stress fighter and bomber squadrons.

Eric had not said anything when he had been told that he could not write to Nettie but Ben Abdul had seen near-rebellion in his eyes.

Maybe it was all catching up with him and Ben Abdul wondered if it was wise to include him in the next mission. It only took one man to break down and not only would their lives be at risk but the success of the mission would be in jeopardy as well.

He would have to talk to Eric soon because a decision would have to be made. On one hand he did not want Eric to feel he was no longer wanted but on the other he was inclined to recommend he be released from service. He had already done much more than his share, more than was expected of most men.

Eric was also thirty-nine years old, older than most in the services, although Ben Abdul knew of plenty of older men still serving.

He walked over to the bar where Eric sat talking to Curly and noticed Eric pop pills into his mouth before quaffing them down with beer. Maybe he suffered from headaches.

'Can I see you for a few minutes Eric?'

'Yeah pull up a stump an' have a beer.'

'Privately if you don't mind.' Ben Abdul jerked his head.

Eric followed him over to the office section of the shed, where a man sat at the radio wearing headphones.

'He can't hear us Eric,' Ben Abdul said.

'What's up Ben Abdul?' Eric's eyes looked wary and the tone of his voice was slightly antagonistic.

'A couple of things actually. First there's this.' He went to his desk drawer and took out a slim wooden case which he handed to Eric.

He opened it. Inside was a bar to go with his Flying Cross and the commendation that went with it.

'What's this for?'

'I recommended it for your attack on the fuel-dump at Rabaul. That was straight out bravery Eric, some would say lunacy. Your rank of Squadron Leader has also been reinstated. Your action at Rabaul was aerial so you also deserve that.'

'Thanks but I never done nothin' special. I was just doin' me job like everybody else on the operation.'

'I've had it for a while and I should have sent it to Nettie. I thought you were dead but just hoped somehow you weren't.'

He saw a flicker of emotion in Eric's eyes at the mention of Nettie's name.

'Do you get headaches Eric?'

'No. Why?'

'I saw you popping pills at the bar.'

'Just Bennies.'

'Benzedrine?'

'Yeah.'

'Where did you get them?'

'Off one of the blokes in the Spitfire squadron, why?'

'Do you need them? You know I don't like drugs.'

'They're Air Force issue, for Christ's sake Ben Abdul. What's your bloody problem? You suddenly got a social conscience or somethin'?'

'Yes I know they're RAAF issue but do you really need them?'

'I been feelin' a bit unmotivated since I got back to work, too long of a holiday I suppose. They help me get me head in the right place.'

'You're annoyed with me for not letting you write to Nettie.' It was a statement.

'I'll get over it. You're just doin' what you gotta do.'

'If it wasn't war you'd bail up over it, wouldn't you?'

'Yeah. Probably.'

'Do you want to go home to her now Eric, call this quits?'

'Yeah we all wanna go home. I just wanted to write an' tell her things, that's all. You get plenty of time to think when you're in a situation like I was, you know? But call it quits? No never, not while I still got two arms an' two legs.'

'I wouldn't blame you if you do want to go home Eric.'

'What are you comin' at Ben Abdul? Come on, out with it. You reckon I can't handle it no more? You reckon it's got to me? That I'm a security risk?'

'Can you handle it Eric?'

Eric gave him a hard look. 'You met old Eliza, didn't you?'

'Yes I was there at your twenty-first birthday remember?'

'What'd you think of her?'

'Amazing, still as tough as nails and she was eighty-six at the time, as I recall.'

'We all got her blood Ben Abdul an' we can all handle it, whatever that is. Just harder to manage sometimes, that's all. You of all people oughta know that.'

'Are you sure?'

'Yeah I won't let you down. I'd tell you if I couldn't do it. I ain't that self-involved that I don't care about me mates.'

'I just had to know Eric. I had no intention of annoying you or insinuating anything.'

'Yeah I understand an' I'd be toey too if one of me men weren't happy.'

'And you aren't happy, are you?'

'No but like I said, I'll get over it.'

Ben Abdul made a snap decision then. 'I don't want you to get me wrong over what I'm about to say. Okay?'

'Yeah? Go on.' Eric had a sceptical look on his face.

'I've been trying to get away again to go to Exmouth Gulf. I've got an operation organised there and should go and make sure it's all properly finalised, all the loose ends tied up you know?'

'You want me to take over this operation so you can get away? Fine by me, I can handle that alright without buggering up.'

'No I want you to go instead of me. You're capable of doing what has to be done there and I'd rather not have to leave here right now.'

'Why Ben Abdul? You're tryin' to let me out gentle ain't you? Make me feel a bit half-useful without givin' me a real job.'

'No you're wrong Eric. I can't let you write to Nettie for security reasons but I also can't stop you spending a night at Tomahawk Plains with her each way, if that's what you decided to do.'

Eric looked at him. 'You're bloody serious ain't you?'

'Deadly serious Eric. Someone should go there because I'm concerned things aren't quite right. But I want you back with your mind fully on the job because the next few months are critical. I think you do really need to see Nettie before you will be ready for whatever is coming up and I'm sure she's in the same boat. She's been through hell too. What do you say? Will you do that for me?'

'You sure you want me back on this job when I get back?'

'Yes of course I do. There's a second unit to go in after we've set up the radio base anyway. I want you to lead the group that recruits the fuzzy-wuzzies because you know them better than anyone else. You've had most experience with them.'

'An' you sure you wouldn't mind if I seen Nettie?'

'You've got to see her if you're going to be able to do this next job properly. That's perfectly clear to me.'

'I appreciate that Ben Abdul. I reckon she'll need to see me too, after thinkin' I been killed again. It's probably done her head in too. I'll do it but you're gonna have to brief me on this operation that I'm goin' to check on.'

Ben Abdul handed Eric the file. 'I'll talk to you about it in the morning.'

'Thanks Ben Abdul ay.'

'You might not think it Eric but I do know what it's like to be in love with a woman.'

'You wanna talk about it?'

'No not really Eric. I think she's dead. She's missing believed dead on a mission in North Africa so that's well and truly out of my control but it is within my control to let you and Nettie have your moment together.'

'What was her name?'

Ben Abdul paused before he answered, 'Mad Dog.'

'Mad Dog?'

'Her nickname. That's all I'm going to say about her.'

'Fair enough and thanks mate ay.'

CHAPTER 45

Nettie heard a call on the radio and ran to listen. It came again. 'Curlew to Joan of Arc, come in Joan.'

She realised with a start it was for her and it sounded like Eric's voice. Her heart skipped a beat.

'Yeah receivin' Curlew.'

'Got time to put the kettle on love?' It was Eric!

'How long have I got Curlew?' Her voice sounded funny even to her, in a slightly breathless way.

'About five minutes ay.'

'I'll be ready.' She laughed with pure joy and realised she was trembling with excitement.

She had been castigating herself over her binge on the rum a week earlier. Since then she had recovered from the hangover and also the melancholy that led to it and had started to dare hope that Eric really was alive. But she had also been praying that she would never again get the news that he was dead.

Now he was coming, almost there. She whistled as she put the kettle on and cut bread to make toast. How had he managed to get away to come and see her?

She heard the plane coming and ran out to watch him land. She realised that her scrap with the Jap plane had left her with a yearning for that sort of flying.

The plane came to a stop and she climbed up on the wing as he opened the cockpit and got out. They embraced and her heart sang.

'Jesus it's good to see you Nettie.'

'At least you knew I was alive this time Eric.'

'Yeah sorry, nobody except me knew I was but. Weren't nothin' I could do about it just the same.'

'What happened?'

'How's that pot of tea comin' along?'

'Oh hell! I bet the toast's burnt.'

They laughed as they walked arm-in-arm to the house.

'What happened to the roof,' he asked.

'After you've told me your story Eric.'

She made fresh toast as they talked and Eric told her about his time in New Britain.

'Weren't you scared the Japs would find you?'

'No I was with the blackfellers but there was no way to get outta the place. An' except that I was worried they'd tell you I was dead again I weren't too worried about meself. I knew it was only a matter of time before our mob come back to shift the Japs.'

'I think I nearly went batty. You was dead, then you turned up an' then you was dead again. Then I really didn't believe it the other day when I got the message from Ben Abdul that you was alive.'

'You believe it now?'

She laughed. 'I ain't sure. You better kiss me again.'

He kissed her. 'Happy now?'

'Yeah but I'll be happier when you're home for good an' this bloody war's over.'

'What happened to the roof?'

'Did you hear about the Jap plane I shot down?'

'No. How'd you shoot a plane down? With your Tommy-gun I s'pose?'

'I'll tell you all about it, even if it sounds a bit far-fetched.'

She told him what had happened; how she had got her own Zero and what had happened that day. 'I just seen red Eric. Lucky as it turned out nobody got killed in the blackfeller's camp but I never knew that then. I jumped in the Zero an' went after the bastard. I just wanted to kill 'im an' I did too.'

'You was takin' a big risk goin' after an experienced fighter pilot in a plane you hardly knew how to fly.'

'Yeah, I got the shakes after it was all over but at the time I just wanted to kill 'im for shootin' up the blacks' camp an' I was just lucky he ran outta ammo before he shot too many holes in my Zero.'

'You're crazy girl, you know that?'

'I'd join up an' fly fighter planes if they'd let me Eric. I enjoyed that fight. Do you understand that?'

'Yeah I know the feelin' an' you must be a natural but I'm glad you can't go an' do that.'

'I wanna keep that Zero for my own when the war's over Eric.'

'If the army don't know about it there's no reason you can't. They're pretty good planes, not junk like the propaganda reckons.'

'How long can you stop here with me?'

'I gotta go to Exmouth Gulf early in the mornin'. I'll be there for a day or two, I ain't sure how long yet. Then I'll spend a night here on me way back again.'

'Well we better not waste time yakkin' then.' She laughed.

By the time he flew out the next morning their tensions of the past two years had been assuaged. Eric also knew that John Holley was no longer any threat to their marriage. Nettie was her old self again.

CHAPTER 46

Eric and Curly waited in the shade of a coconut palm for the charges they had laid to detonate.

Eric had returned from his trip to Exmouth Gulf and seeing Nettie. He had then taken his team of men into the area near Wewak. They had established contact with Ben Abdul's radio unit and then Eric had begun recruiting a group of native spies to report on enemy movements and installations. Once that was done he had put each of his men in charge of three of the native agents. Information was assessed and passed on to Ben Abdul's unit where it was coded and sent out.

Now that the offensive was underway each of his groups was engaged in sabotage.

He and Curly had planted explosives at a Japanese radio base and waited on a ridge to see the results. When it detonated they would go in and mop up any survivors. The other groups each had a target for the day. By that stage they had been reinforced by the rest of the Flying Circus unit.

This strategy was vital to the offensive, which they all knew was the culmination of the past two months of intelligence gathering and hiding from the enemy while so doing. For their operation to be successful it had been imperative that the enemy did not even suspect they were in the area. To maintain cover over that period had required tight security at all times and a certain amount of luck.

They spotted two men coming their way. John Holley and the Ghurka were moving cautiously through tall Kunai grass, alert for danger with their Owen guns at the ready.

A shot cracked unexpectedly right above Eric and Curly. The Ghurka went down. John swung his gun to retaliate, as Eric and Curly also reacted. The shot had come from the foliage of the tree under which they sheltered, totally unaware of the sniper right above their heads.

The rifle cracked again and John went down just as he raised his weapon to return fire. Eric and Curly poured a hail of bullets into the fronds above and the body of the sniper plummeted down almost on top of them.

'Cover me Curly.' Eric ran to where the two men lay.

The Ghurka was obviously dead and John was coughing pink frothy blood. His lungs gurgled as he struggled for breath. Eric carried him to cover and inspected his wound.

'Go get a medic Curly,' he instructed and Curly left at a run.

John pawed at his sleeve as Eric wiped the blood from his mouth, knowing he would not last long.

'Eric,' he wheezed. Then he coughed up more blood. 'Eric I'm finished.'

'You'll be alright mate. Curly's gone for a medic. Just save your energy an' don't talk.'

'Not worth it Eric. Waste of time. I won't last that long.'

'Yeah you will.'

'Eric, get my wallet out for me,' he croaked.

Eric dug the wallet from his pocket and handed it to him. John opened it and handed him a piece of paper.

'What is it John?'

'My will. I had it ready. I always knew somehow that I wouldn't make it through to the end.' His voice was a gurgling wheeze and he struggled for breath.

'You'll make it mate. Just take it easy.'

John coughed up more blood and Eric wiped his mouth with his sleeve again.

'Here, Eric.' He handed Eric a well worn photograph of Nettie posing with her Tommy-gun in front of the Tiger Moth.

The next coughing fit was his last. Eric laid him down and closed his eyes. Then he returned the will and photo to the wallet, before stowing it in his own pocket without any further thought. John had given him Nettie's photograph because of who he was but obviously he had been given the wallet because there had been nobody else. He would attend to it once the heat of battle was over.

Wewak was secured in the next week of heavy fighting. During that time Eric had no time to think of John or even Nettie for that matter.

On the last day of the battle he sustained a wound to the calf of his leg, inflicted by shrapnel from a Japanese hand-grenade. It was not serious but kept him from the last few hours of the action.

Then he and scores of other wounded were evacuated to Port Moresby.

Being the only member of The Flying Circus at their base in Port Moresby Eric manned the radio. He had been treated as an outpatient at the hospital because his wound was only superficial. Every morning he went to have his dressing changed. There was little to do and even the radio traffic was mostly no longer of any urgent nature. He had the distinct feeling that the war was almost over. The mood felt slightly anti-climactic after the tension and danger of the past few years.

He sipped a beer as he listened, waiting for a call that would give him something worthwhile to occupy his attention.

Realising he still carried John's wallet and had not even looked at the contents he took out the photograph of Nettie and set it up on the table in front of him. He accepted that John had also loved her. Otherwise he would not have carried her photo. A brief pang of jealousy came unbidden and he pushed it aside. It was all in the past. John was dead and Nettie loved him. That was all that mattered. He realised that if he had been the one killed John would most likely have courted Nettie after the war. That was the luck of the draw in war and he held no animosity for the man who had been a comrade and a good officer.

He read the will which was dated in April 1943, about the time the Flying Circus had been formed and after John had been wounded when Eric had rescued him. It seemed that apart from his personal effects his estate consisted solely of his bank account which he bequeathed to Nettie.

John was a victim of the circumstances of war. His wife had left him for another man and Eric wondered if that man still survived. Then he had fallen in love with another man's wife who believed her husband was dead. It somehow seemed tragic that he had died leaving just a bank account as the only legacy of his life, nothing for which he would be remembered. War was a sad thing. It tore people's lives apart, not just their bodies. Maybe John had wanted to die. Nobody would ever know if that was so. A wooden cross in a graveyard at Wewak was his only record of having lived and it was unlikely anyone would ever care or visit.

Eric was sick of the war and knew it would sour him if it went on much longer. It had begun as an adventure, where you pitted your skill against an enemy who had no face and you revelled in the thrill of proving your superiority as a warrior. You proudly painted the stripes on your plane, each one representing a contest you had won rather than an unknown man's life taken. You were reckless and cocky in the company of others like yourself. Life was a game, a game that got deadlier as time went on until it eventually became ugly and awful.

He guessed you either died or you tired of the senseless killing. He thought of Nettie and desperately wanted to be home with her and his kids living a normal life. But would life ever be normal again? Could he forget what he had experienced? Could she? He knew they loved each other but also knew they could not go back to the carefree life they had known when they were young and first in love.

He opened another bottle of beer and composed a letter to Nettie in his head.

He took out the letter from her which had been waiting for him when he had come back to Moresby from Wewak. He had read it every day and now he read it again. It was dated March, 1945.

Dearest Eric,

Thanks for coming when you did. I needed that to convince myself you were real, that either of us actually was. Two nights together helped to get my head sorted out.

A good part of our lives since you first went away hasn't seemed real and of course I worry about you as always but now I sort of trust that you'll come home to me in the end. I do hope this damn war finishes soon.

I got a letter from the kids the other day. They're well and at least they're going to school there. I couldn't have taught them much here even if I did have the time but that's the only good thing about being apart from them.

The only excitement that I've had lately was when I crashed the Tiger Moth. It's a write-off I'm afraid. I've done a lot of hours flying in it and the propeller eventually cracked and de-laminated. I couldn't get a new one so I just patched the split up with a Cobb-and-Co twitch to hold it together and tried to keep it going as long as I could but the weight of the wire put it out of balance and it vibrated a bit. I was flying out to one of the Nackeroo camps when it let go and broke in a big way. It ripped the top wing off and the motor stalled. I think something broke inside the engine from the big vibration when it let go. I tried to land but it got out of control and hit a tree. I only got a cut on my forehead and a bruised leg but I had a forty mile walk to get home. That took two days with the sore leg but I got here all right.

I'm sorry about the plane Eric but I've still got the requisition order for it from the Army. We might be able to get them to pay for a new one. They don't know I still had it.

The Zero needs more room to land. It's not anywhere near as good for my work but at least I've got it and I'm getting used to flying it.

I hope you're still safe.

I love you more than you'll probably ever know.

Nettie. XXXX

P.S. Then just after I finished writing this, out of the blue Ian McKenzie turned up here with the news that the Nackeroos are being disbanded because the threat of invasion is past, or so he was told. It was a hell of a shock for me that I will no longer be needed. I'll have to adjust to that though.

There is more that I better not put in the letter. I'll have to tell you when I see you.

Love, Nettie.

He hoped the censors had not read the letter because she had mentioned the plane but usually it was only outgoing mail that was censored and security had also become more relaxed of late anyway. He also wondered what it was she had not told him about the Nackeroos and realised she would find the adjustment difficult after all that time helping them.

He fretted whether Nettie would be safe flying the Zero but she would not need to use it with any luck now that the Nackeroo work was finished. As she had said, the Tiger Moth had been perfect for what she had been doing and it was a shame to lose it but it had served her well and she seemed relatively unhurt by the crash. That was all that really mattered. They could get a new plane.

News came that troops had landed on the mainland of Brunei and Labuan Island. The enemy was being pushed hard. The Flying Circus was still occupied in the area around Wewak. Eric applied to go back to join them but was told they would be finished there soon and to stay where he was.

Australian troops landed at Sarawak and then Borneo. He hoped the Circus would not be needed anymore. It now seemed that the result was inevitable but he knew that it could still drag on and mean months more fighting. Even though they were being hammered in battle the Japanese forces stubbornly refused to capitulate. He also realised that once Ben Abdul and the unit returned to Port Moresby they would probably all be sent to Borneo.

After considerable thought, he wrote a brief letter to Nettie telling her of John's death so she could grieve for him in private, rather than waiting to relate it to her in person. He hoped that on top of her disappointment regarding the Nackeroo work the shock would not just add to her burden.

He planned that when he did finally get home they would go to Kalgoorlie to collect the children. It was also years since he had last seen his parents after Ben's accident. His father now walked with the aid of a frame and had never given up hope that he would walk unaided again. He had never stopped work and still went to the mine office every day. Eric realised that his parents were getting old. He would be forty that year, which meant that they must be in their sixties.

He and Nettie should also get married. They had never got around to it and the twins would be fifteen that year. Maybe they could get married while they were in Kalgoorlie. That would save any inconvenience of travelling for his aging parents.

He found some white paint and painted the wall of the office area as far up as he could reach. While he was at it he painted THE FLYING CIRCUS on one of the doors, which he kept open all the time to let a breeze through the hot building.

He killed time waiting for something to happen. A stray blue cattle dog turned up and stayed. He supposed he and it had something in common. It killed the rats, which meant it was welcome to stay. He called it Blue and that seemed to be alright by the dog because he answered to the name. Blue brought fleas with him so Eric went to the quartermaster's store and got some DDT powder which he sprinkled around. It got rid of the fleas but made him sneeze if it got up his nose.

He unpacked all the crates of weapons and cleaned and oiled them because they rusted fast in the humid environment. It gave him something to do.

After a while there seemed to be fewer rats for Blue to kill and he thought the DDT must also be killing them. He wondered if Blue would be next to succumb to the poison.

Ben Abdul and the unit returned, now only nine of them left, ten including Eric. Ben Abdul said they had acquitted themselves well but were feeling the effects of their months of privation and danger.

Balikpapan in Borneo had fallen to the Australian forces a few days earlier. It was July.

'Will we be sent to Borneo?' Eric asked.

'I hope not. The men need a break. We all do, except you by the look of you. You're looking well,' Ben Abdul answered.

Eric felt guilty. He had been idling the time away while his mates fought and died.

'I tried to get back to rejoin the unit but they wouldn't let me.'

'There was no point Eric. It was just mongrel dirty work and you of all people deserve a break anyway. Nobody's had as hard a time as you have.'

'I'm bored Ben Abdul an' I never been bored before in me whole life.'

'This war's almost finished now and I suspect we'll all be bored for a while when it is over. Everyday life will be too tame for a time I reckon.'

'Yeah I know. It's a bit like a mob of drovin' cattle that been on the road a long time an' can't settle once they get where they're goin'. They just keep walkin' like they're used to. It's like that already for me an' it ain't over yet.'

'You'd better get back in physical condition. You look as if you've been drinking too much beer. The rest of us are going to have a rest for a few weeks. Then we'll need to recruit some more men to get our unit strength up to the original level. When that's done, we'll see about Borneo.'

'Yeah I know I got fat. I couldn't leave the radio.'

'Well you can now.'

Eric put himself back into training and as he lost his soft fat the boredom also went. Blue ran with him and followed him everywhere.

Nevertheless, he could not help feeling that he was just marking time, going through the motions like those droving cattle.

CHAPTER 47

Nettie heard the news that an atom bomb had been dropped on the city of Hiroshima in Japan and then another three days later at Nagasaki.

She did not know where Eric was at that time. The war had moved north since she last saw him but she had received his letter telling her John had been killed.

She felt sad about John and hoped his death had been quick but there was no real grief. They had been friends and had possibly almost been lovers but that seemed long in the past. The war had inured everybody to grief and she was not sure that was a good thing. She was glad Eric had told her that way because she had been free to remember without feeling guilty and had been able to close the chapter without tension.

Japan surrendered. The war was over. Eric would be coming home soon and she wondered how long before that would happen. She did not suppose it would be immediate.

The Nackeroos had gone about five months earlier and for quite a while since then she had felt that her life was in limbo.

As they were pulling out, Ian McKenzie had sent three blitzes over with equipment he had been ordered to destroy. He had said he would much rather she had it and assumed some of it could be useful to the running of the property. There were a couple of radios, generators, telephones and unmarked crates of other supplies but she doubted he had been ordered to destroy the cases of .303 ammunition or the two Bren-guns. There was also a crate of Tommy-guns and cases of .45 calibre ammunition to match. He had however mentioned that Owen guns had replaced the Tommy-guns and they were now surplus to requirement.

They had made three trips in total, also delivering three broken-down Jeeps and crates of spare parts to get them going again, as well as a few Army tents which would be useful for the Aborigines' camp. He had also left a stock of forty-four-gallon drums of petrol, saying that she would find it useful while rationing continued.

He had said that he hoped it would compensate her to some extent for all the unpaid assistance she had given them during his time and previously.

At least the radio blackout had been lifted and she was able to talk to her children for the first time in two years. They sounded so different and grown up.

Eric called her on the radio from Port Moresby. He had been flying troops into Borneo when the war ended. He sounded cheerful but did not know how long before he would be coming home. They could not talk for long but at least she knew where he was and that he was safe.

She realised just how much new technology and the war had changed everyone's lives and she looked forward to the future when she would be reunited with her family and they could make up for lost years.

CHAPTER 48

Eric knew he should feel elated now that the fighting was finished and he would be going home soon but he had a nagging feeling it was not as simple as that.

Nettie had been running Tomahawk Plains ever since he had left to go to war and he knew she had done a good job. She had handled it without help, as well as managing her considerable involvement with the Nackeroos. She had made all the decisions that had been needed in that time with nobody to call on for assistance.

Could he now go back into her life and take it over from her? Would she let him? He thought she probably would let him but at what price to her self-esteem and to their relationship? He avoided making any definite plans in his mind while these thoughts plagued him.

He loved her dearly and wanted everything to be as if the war had never happened but he knew that impossible. He felt anxious that once again their relationship would be tested, ironically this time by their propinquity rather than their separation. For that reason he had reservations about the future.

He knew he had money from the bank robbery in Germany. He did not know how much but knew it was enough to buy the rest of the string of cattle stations he had dreamt of in his youth when he had aspired to emulate Sid Kidman. He was not sure his dream was still the same as it had been then and realised he would not know the answer to that until he got back into his old life and readjusted. He knew that he could involve himself in that dream without threatening Nettie's world if it came down to that.

He would have to wait until he got home and they worked together again before he would know.

He sat alone with his thoughts, as he gazed out over the sea of Torres Strait from a high point. It was a peaceful and balmy vista, in sharp contrast with how it had recently been.

He saw Ben Abdul approaching.

'What are you doing here Eric?' Ben Abdul asked, as he sat down beside him.

'Just thinkin' about goin' home.'

'Yes. I sometimes wish I had one.'

'You live in England but.'

'Yes but where is my home? My roots are in Australia. I was born in Egypt. I live in England. I have no wife and no family to go home to. I have no desire to go and live in my father's house again. I have money, a university degree, a profession. I can get almost any job I want with the connections I have but where is home?'

Eric thought about it but had no answer.

'Eric do you have any money?'

'Yeah some, why?'

'Do you want to invest it? Now is a time of opportunity for investment.'

'Do you reckon?'

'I'm sure of it. In fact there are so many opportunities one could easily do oneself a disservice by taking a lesser one than possible.'

'What sort of investments you thinkin' about?'

'Mining, steel, land development, who knows? The whole world will boom in the next twenty years. I do know that Japan would be a good place to invest.'

'We just been killin' the bastards an' now you wanna give 'em your money? That's crazy Ben Abdul.'

'They'll be rehabilitated, just as Germany will. There'll be huge profits to be made in both of those countries, as well as America and even

Australia. It will be a period of prosperity for the whole world.'

Eric was thoughtful and knew that Ben Abdul was likely right.

'Father made a lot of money after the First World War; legally too most of it. He took the opportunities that presented themselves.'

Yeah, Henry's a wealthy man. He's got power as well but he's got no wife to share his life. He's got a job they'll never let him retire from. Is that a happy life?

'Why ain't you ever got married yet Ben Abdul?'

Ben Abdul gazed at the sea for a long time.

'I was almost four years old when my mother was murdered and I was there when Father opened the first package that contained one of her fingers. I've never forgotten that Eric. I have been tempted though, not long before I came here when I was in North Africa. She was younger than me but …' he paused and Eric saw a wistful look on his face, 'I never got the chance to find out if it could have worked out for us.'

'You wanna talk about it?' Eric asked and then immediately remembered asking him the same question previously.

'No.'

'Get outta this intelligence game Ben Abdul before it's too bloody late for you, while you can still have a life of your own. Don't be like your old man.'

'It may already be too late.'

'Old Eliza changed her life an' her past never caught up with her.'

Ben Abdul laughed. 'It always comes back to Eliza, doesn't it? She's dead and gone but she still guides all of us who have her blood legacy and influences our lives in one way or another.'

'Yeah I suppose she does.'

'Eric I'm flying to England in the next few days. Father wants to see me. Why don't you come with me? It will be about business and he'll have investment ideas for sure. He's already hinted at it.'

'I dunno Ben Abdul. I'd rather go home if I could.'

'We could both cheat the system and jump the queue and go home but we won't. I'll be coming back here, not staying there. Come with me. You'll still get home to Nettie just as quickly. It will give you something to do while we're waiting, something to be thinking about.'

'I'll think about it an' let you know.'

'Don't take long to think about it Eric. It won't make any difference for us. We're not going to get home from here until all the troops have been brought home from the islands north of here, the prisoners of war from Malaya and Burma and Japan, all the wounded. We'll be among the last you can bet, but that's how it should be. We're the fortunate ones, if anyone's ever fortunate in war.'

CHAPTER 49

They saddled horses at Henry's stables and Eric was intrigued by the Light Horse saddles and equipment in the tack room.

'Father would like to see these saddles so well looked after,' he commented.

'Yes it goes back to the first war I suppose. I got so used to them that I prefer them now. They're so light and almost never gall a horse's back,' Henry said, 'but I don't suppose poor old Ben will ever ride again.'

'He still reckons he'll ride again one day Henry.'

Eric noticed that there were no servants in attendance and remembered that Henry liked to conduct important meetings outdoors away from prying eyes and ears. He knew they were not just going for a social ride to take in the sights. Henry would have his own agenda which he would reveal when he was ready.

Henry showed them his broodmares and foals as they rode. The stallion was stabled and they had already inspected him. They moved on through a gate into some heavily wooded country leading towards a high hill.

'If we keep quiet we'll probably see some deer,' Henry told them.

'Father's very proud of his deer herd,' Ben Abdul explained.

The breeze favoured them and they came on a flock of the timid creatures grazing in an open glade. They reined in covered by the thick forest and watched. A large stag raised his head exhibiting perfect antlers.

'Want a shot?' Henry asked quietly.

Eric shook his head, having no desire to kill anything unnecessarily.

'Ben Abdul?'

'No Father. Killing isn't fun for me, never has been.'

'Good. I don't like to see them shot either. The English shoot everything that moves and they think it sport to run down mangy foxes with packs of overfed dogs. It's a wonder there are any deer left in this country, or foxes for that matter.'

The stag spotted them then and he and his hinds quickly disappeared into thick forest. They moved on up the slope and Henry reined in at the top of the rise in an open area that overlooked the country for miles. They followed Henry's example and hobbled the horses. He led them to the edge of a steep craggy slope, leaving the horses to graze.

'There are no ears to hear now,' Henry said as he selected a rock and sat down. They waited for him to come to the point, having flown halfway across the world for this meeting. Eric realised that he never wanted to end up like Henry, whose life and work had made him security-conscious almost to the point of paranoia but he was curious to hear what the older man had to say nevertheless.

'Firstly I want to give you some background to the cause of Hitler's invasion of Poland which in effect began the war. Not many know that Stalin made a pact with Hitler to divide Europe up between them but then Stalin reneged and came into the war on our side instead. I also want to tell you both a secret I've been sworn not to reveal but it's eaten at me long enough. Reasonably early in the war the British got hold of the German Enigma code which enabled them to decipher Nazi messages. To cover up the fact, they only used the information sparingly so the Germans wouldn't suspect.

'Then after the Americans came into the war a similar Japanese code machine was stolen. That gave England and America access to coded radio traffic of both enemies. Now that was a good thing of course and an intelligence bonanza but the thing that worries me most is that neither of those allies shared that intelligence with the Australian Government, even when invasion was imminent. In spite of being their major ally and often at the cost of men and shipping, the Australian government and military was not entrusted with that valuable knowledge. I can only assume that was because Prime Minister Curtin was either unable or unwilling to stand up to the trade unions who had put him in power and who constantly sabotaged the war effort.

'As an Australian that fact worried me considerably. Now that I've told you, you must swear to me that you won't reveal this fact but I think it's something you both should know. The truth is that in war you can't always even totally trust your own government or your allies. Will you both give me that undertaking?'

Eric and Ben Abdul both agreed.

'Who was responsible for that Father?' Ben Abdul asked.

'Who do you think?'

'Churchill?'

Henry didn't acknowledge Ben Abdul's observation except to add, 'However to Churchill's credit, he did instruct General Percival not to surrender Singapore to a smaller Japanese contingent but he ignored the instruction, which caused much suffering to a great many Australian troops. I just reckoned it might be of use to you in the future if you keep these facts in the back of your minds. It helps in our game to have a bit of an edge sometimes.'

Eric noted the inference and wondered whether Ben Abdul's future had not already been laid out. He was shocked by the revelation but had no questions.

Henry went on, 'Now we can move on to the reason I invited you here. As you probably know I made some successful financial moves in the period following the last war. If I'd been more experienced I could have done better but that's in the past now. Over the years I've built on those investments, until now money is just something to play with. I have learnt that there is no satisfaction in just having money. What use is it in the bank? The thrill is in the cut and thrust of the business deal and being able to see the chance for profit in the first place. It's no different than a dogfight in a Spitfire Eric. You live or die on your wits, so to speak.

'Money is little use to me for my own sake and I'll soon be old and need it even less. This will all be yours when I'm gone Ben Abdul and it's a pity you have no son to pass it on to. You should address that issue before you're much older.

'But now regardless of that, there's another period of opportunity at our feet. Our world is much bigger than this.' He paused to survey the view.

'Eric you did very well with the bank job. I know much of the spoil was lost but that is no different than betting on the last card in a poker game. The truth is that I seriously underestimated how much there would be in the haul. It's been difficult to transfer large amounts of money during the war but I've been trickling a little into your account, enough to keep Tomahawk Plains going.

'Ben Abdul, Eric, this is your world now and we have money to spare. I propose we form a company and invest that spare money. I'd hold a one pound share and be chairman of the board but you two would own the company and be directors. What do you think?'

'You mean that all I'd be puttin' in would be some of the money from the robbery?' Eric asked.

'Most of the money from the robbery Eric. But when you look at it, it's just monopoly money really.'

'But you said you been payin' money into my account. Some of that's probably already been spent.'

Henry waved his hand dismissively. 'Pocket money Eric, a negligible amount.'

'I'm in favour Father, as I've been telling Eric,' Ben Abdul said.

'Eric?'

'Why not? It ain't gonna cost anythin'.'

'I think it cost you quite a bit at the time, in one way or another.'

Eric remembered the look on Odette's face in the instant she knew she was going to die. He remembered the guilt he had felt towards Nettie over his infidelity with the spy. He remembered the anxiety it had caused Nettie. He remembered the months he had spent recovering from his injuries but it already seemed a long time ago.

'I'm in Henry. Deal the cards.'

'Good man Eric. Ben Abdul can draw up the contract.'

'What will we call the company Father?' Ben Abdul asked.

'I thought Curlew Investments would be appropriate?'

Eric and Ben Abdul both smiled. Eliza still guided their lives from the grave.

'Good, it's settled then. I've already taken the liberty of entering into negotiations with the Australian and American governments, regarding salvage of excess war equipment at Port Moresby but I don't want to put all our eggs in one basket. That's why I chose just Port Moresby because it's close to the Australian mainland. Australia will boom now the war is over and the demand for equipment will be high in the next few years.'

'What sort of equipment you talkin' about?'

'Trucks, Jeeps, bulldozers, Tournapulls, graders, cranes, generators, welders, barges, aeroplanes, you name it, basically whatever the Allies leave behind when they pull out.'

'And scrap steel,' Ben Abdul added.

'Yes there'll be demand for that too and plenty of it is available in and around Port Moresby. Japan will be rebuilding and they have steel mills and foundries.'

Henry held out his hand. 'Gentlemen, let's shake to Curlew Investments.'

They all joined hands. Eric thought, Joined by money and the blood of Eliza Henry.

CHAPTER 50

Nettie was nervous. Eric would be home in the next hour or so. He had called her on the radio to tell her he was en route from Darwin.

She wanted to look nice for him and had chosen the green dress of the two she owned rather than the blue one she had worn last time. Should she wear the diamond necklace? No, she would feel silly wearing it.

Her olive skin glowed from scrubbing and her hair shone. She had thinned it but left it at collar length. She agonised whether to wear the lipstick. Because it had been a present from John she decided it would not be appropriate.

The table on the verandah was set. She had made fresh biscuits and also had a pikelet mixture ready to pop on the stovetop at the last minute. The heavy cast-iron kettle was simmering ready to make the brew of tea in the big enamel pot.

She had got bunches of the exotic opium-poppy flowers from old Tommy's garden and they sat on the table in blue castor oil bottles.

When the plane came she went out to watch as Eric circled. She was glad she had remembered to hang a sheet on the line because there was a stiff breeze blowing and he would be landing with a tail wind. The small plane touched down on the racecourse and taxied towards her enveloped in a cloud of dust. She could see it was bigger than the Tiger Moth, a twin engine bi-plane with a closed in cabin, either a four or six seater she guessed.

Eric opened the door and she kissed him before he could get out. He cut the motor and grinned at her. 'You look nice.'

'Are you really home this time Eric?'

'Yeah home for good if that suits you.'

'Oh yeah, it does!'

He unpacked his gear and then reached back inside and retrieved a bunch of flowers wrapped in wet newspaper. They were white frangipani and the perfume was exotic.

She kissed him again. 'Thanks Eric, they're lovely.'

'I got 'em in Darwin.'

'Who owns the flash plane?'

'We do. I reckoned we'd need a six seater but this was what was available. It's an eight seater ex-RAAF de Haviland Dominie, which is really a DH89a Dragon Rapide. Each engine is 200 horsepower an' she'll cruise at 130 mile-an-hour all day, 157 mile-an-hour flat-out.'

She remembered the trip to Kalgoorlie with the children in the Tiger Moth.

'It's just what we need Eric. Won't be as good for musterin' as the old Tiger Moth but.'

'I'm plannin' to get another Moth to use on the place. This can be our goin' to town crate.'

She helped him carry his things and they walked to the house. She thought he looked brown and healthy.

'How was your trip?'

'I stopped overnight in Darwin after I picked the plane up. It's in pretty good nick an' flies well, only been used for flyin' army brass around.'

They talked as she cooked the pikelets and then sat on the verandah and talked some more. He told her of his trip to England and the Curlew Investments deal they had made.

'Will that mean you'll be goin' off all the time on business?' she asked apprehensively.

'Not necessarily. Why?'

She looked disappointed. 'I been lookin' forward to havin' you home.'

'I won't get in your way if I'm here all the time?'

'No, course not. Why do you even ask that?'

'Well it's pretty much been your show for the past six year. I reckoned … I dunno what I reckoned.'

'Oh Eric, I waited that long for this moment an' I never want us to be apart again. I only been lookin' after the place while you been gone an' it needs you too. Things have slipped a bit I'm afraid. Fences need fixin', yards need patchin' up.'

She saw relief in his eyes and realised he had been unsure of his place in her world. She knew that in a lot of ways they would have to get to know each other again. Six years was a long time apart and their experiences had been so different during that time. Hers had been unusual enough and she could only guess what his had been like.

'Eric I only done what had to be done to keep the show runnin'. Tomahawk Plains is yours, it's a part of you an' yeah it's become part of me too. We both need you, it an' me both.'

'Thanks Nettie. I weren't sure what you'd reckon about it all.'

'Well I am. You're the boss, you always been the boss. Remember when you first got here on the mail truck?'

He laughed. 'You had buck teeth then.'

'Yeah, it's a long time ago now Eric.'

She kissed his ear and just doing that gave her goose bumps. 'Do you feel like what I feel like?'

For answer his lips found hers and his hands wandered.

Later she made sandwiches. It was getting late but the normal routine of the day had stepped aside for their more urgent need.

'What you got planned now you're home?' Nettie asked.

'Pick the kids up an' get married. How's that for a start?'

'Sounds perfect to me. We really should be married. We could do it in Kalgoorlie.'

'That's what I reckoned too.'

'Let's do it then Eric?'

'You'll need a weddin' dress.'

She laughed. 'I can get that in Kalgoorlie. Lily an' Sarah will know more about that sorta thing than what I do.'

'Henry reckoned he'd be goin' there soon too. He ain't been to see the mines since before the war.'

'It might fit in good then. I'd like to let the kids finish their school year before we move 'em though if you don't mind?'

'It's the middle of October now. By the time we have a honeymoon they'll be finished an' we can all come home then.'

'A honeymoon? Just bein' with you is a honeymoon.'

'Don't you want one?'

'You know what I'd really like for a honeymoon?'

'No?'

'Dad never knew 'is father an' 'is mother died when he weren't much older'n a baby. He was born in a drovin' camp an' grew up in one like I done. I know Mum's father was Afghan an' her mother was half-caste but I never really knew me mum neither. She cleared out when I was too little to remember her much.'

'Yeah? So what are you gettin' at?'

'You've got family goin' all the way back to old Eliza Henry the bushranger.'

'An'?'

'I'd like to meet all a your family. I'd like to take the kids to meet their family so that they'll know 'em too.'

'You mean take the kids on our honeymoon an' visit all me relations?'

'Yeah it'd be good for all of us I reckon.'

He laughed. 'Bit of a different sorta honeymoon than what most people have but yeah I like the idea.'

'The muster's finished an' the bullocks an' spayed cows is on the road so there ain't much to stop us doin' it. Could we take Dad with us? Me an''im had never even been past Darwin till I went to Kalgoorlie with the kids when I took 'em down.'

'Take him on our honeymoon too?'

'No just to our weddin'. He could fly back after that on a charter.'

'You reckon he'll do that?'

'I hope so. 'is only daughter never got married before this.'

They started planning the trip but their propinquity distracted them often. Neither of them minded that.

CHAPTER 51

Eric could not get over how much his children had grown up in the last six years when they met at the Queen Victoria Mine airstrip on arrival in Kalgoorlie.

Lenny at fifteen was tall and already filled out, dark like both his parents and tall like Eric but blocky like Nettie. Lily reminded him of his mother with her graceful figure and fair hair. Nat was the image of Nettie.

His father had aged noticeably. His hair was grey but in spite of his disability he stood straight as he hung onto his walking frame. His mother was still a beautiful woman, her hair a silver-blonde in late middle age.

There were hugs, kisses and handshakes all round as they greeted each other and Nettie introduced her father. Len opined that it was good to 'get outta that bloody contraption'.

Lenny drove them to the house in a big Buick sedan and Eric noticed he drove confidently.

'You two look like you been on a holiday, not a war,' Ben commented.

Nettie laughed. 'Yeah. we been catchin' up a bit the last couple a weeks.'

'And not before time either,' Sarah said approvingly to counter Ben's insinuation.

'Mum can I help you pick your wedding dress?' Lily asked.

'Yeah I was hopin' you would. I got no idea about dresses. I only own a couple.'

'I like the plane Dad. Where did you get it?' Lenny asked.

'I got it in Darwin on me way home an' you all gotta learn to fly it yet.'

'I already can. I fly Granddad's plane when he goes to Perth.'

'An' how about you Nat? Can you fly too?'

'No they won't let me. They reckon I'm too young.'

'I can,' Lily said and Eric looked at her. Yeah, I bet you can do whatever you want. She already had that confidence that beautiful women seemed to take for granted. Lenny punched her on the shoulder. She was riding beside him in the front seat.

'What's that for big-head?'

'You can't fly. Just because you've taken the controls in the air doesn't mean you can fly.'

'Well I nearly can then and I can bash you.' She poked her tongue out at him.

'That's because you don't fight fair.'

'Well you'll all get a chance to fly before we get home,' Eric told them.

'How come?' Nat asked.

'We're goin' to New South Wales an' Queensland to see all your other relations before we go home.'

'That'll be some honeymoon for you!' Lily snorted.

'That's what I want,' Nettie answered, 'It was my idea.'

'When I get married, I won't take anyone else on my honeymoon.'

'You're fifteen an' I'm just about forty.'

Lily gave her mother a sly look. 'I bet you haven't got much work done since Dad got home.'

'That's enough familiarity out of you young lady!' Sarah intervened.

Eric thought Lily was just like Nettie had been at fifteen but obviously much more worldly-wise. He supposed they all were. Times had changed dramatically since they were young and they all had yet to get used to each other.

Later when they had a chance to talk Ben asked, 'What was it like mate?'

Eric knew he meant the war. 'Pretty bloody long an' narrow Father but it probably weren't anywhere near as bad as Gallipoli was. I'd had enough by the end of it but. An' I see you proved the doctors wrong.'

'Yeah I knew I'd walk again. I'll chuck this mongrel thing away yet too. Them doctors dunno too much but they kept me alive just the same so they ain't too bad.'

'How's the mine goin'?'

'Gold's been good durin' the war but prices have already dropped again now it's over, like they did last time. We got the most up-to-date plant on the goldfield so we'll be alright in the long run.'

'I seen Henry the other day. I say the other day but I meant about two months ago an' he reckoned he was comin' out to have a look at the mine.'

'Yeah he said he seen you an' he reckoned you gone into partnership with 'im too.'

'How much did he tell you about that?'

'About that much.'

'He organised it an' I done it. We robbed a bank in Germany while I was over there in England. Now we're startin' a company with the money. It's called Curlew Investments an' that about tells the story. It's an investment company.'

'You won't regret goin' into business with 'im. I never did.'

'No I trust him. You know when he's comin' out here?'

'Next week.'

'That's good. He'll be here for the weddin' then.'

'I heard you tellin' the kids you was takin' 'em to meet the rest of the family for a honeymoon.'

'Yeah?'

'We got a little cottage on the beach a bit south of Perth. Why don't you go there by yourselves for a bit first? You'll want at least some time to yourselves I reckon.'

'That sounds good. I'll have a yarn to Nettie about it.'

That night all Eric's siblings came with their families. It was a rowdy and happy reunion but then there were rowdy reunions taking place all over the country, with men coming home from the war. Eric, Gordy and

Tom got raging drunk and sang while Sarah played the piano. Everyone sang but the drunks dominated for volume if not for tune.

Nettie had met them all when she brought the children down. Len Chambers and Ben sat together drinking rum and reminiscing about common Territory acquaintances.

Everyone enjoyed the night. Eric had not seen any of them since his twenty-first birthday celebration, except Ben and Sarah at the Tomahawk Plains races and the others briefly at the time of Ben's accident.

Lily took over from Sarah at the piano and it was the first time Eric and Nettie had heard her play. 'Eric, we missed out on so much of their growin' up because of that bloody war.'

'Yeah I know what you mean. I reckon Lily's just like you was at that age.'

'No she's much better lookin' than I ever was Eric an' I bet the boys are all after her already. Nobody was ever after me except to run the horses up or tack a set a shoes on, 'ere do this, do that, all them sorta things.'

'I was after you too but it just took a while before it happened.'

CHAPTER 52

Sarah organised the wedding reception which was to be held in the ballroom at her Palace Hotel in Hannan Street, the leading hotel in Kalgoorlie.

Herbert Hoover, who was later American President, had been a regular visitor to the Palace in the boom days when he was a mining engineer on the goldfield and he had reputedly fallen in love with a barmaid there. When Hoover left Kalgoorlie he had presented the hotel with the ornately carved mirror which still graced the foyer.

Sarah now employed a French chef and she had told him to use his imagination with the catering and to spare no expense.

'French champagne Madame?'

'Of course, you have to have French champagne at a wedding.'

Nettie and Lily went shopping for a wedding dress and all the dresses looked exotic to Nettie. She was more than a little overwhelmed.

'We'll pick yours first,' she told Lily.

'No, we can't do that Mum. We've got to know what you're wearing before I can pick mine. It has to go with yours if I'm to be bridesmaid. Come on, I'll help you.'

Lily took charge and had the saleswoman running. Finally it came down to a choice between two dresses, both floor length, one in coral pink silk the other in emerald green silk. Right from the beginning Nettie had refused to wear white, saying, 'How can I wear white like a bloody virgin when me daughter's old enough to be me bridesmaid? Even I know that would be a bloody joke.'

'You'll wear your diamonds of course Mum?'

'Yeah I gotta wear 'em Lily, I never worn 'em yet an' they're just so bloody nice that nothin' else would be right for the job. Anyhow your father give 'em to me when you was born an' I know he'd like to see me wear 'em now.'

'Well, that's not much help anyway because they'll go with either of the dresses.'

'I like the green one. It sorta goes with me eyes an' I like it anyhow even if it don't. What do you reckon?'

'Well that's decided then. If that's the one you like, I agree.'

'Now you. What do you like?'

Lily chose a floor length floral chiffon dress with a sweetheart neckline. Nettie bought the dresses and shoes to match. It cost a lot of money but she supposed it was only once in a lifetime one got married.

Eric and the boys had less trouble buying their grey suits, white shirts and black shoes.

'Do you want bow ties to go with the suits sir?' asked the assistant.

'Bugger that fancy townie stuff! Just ordinary black ties is what we want ay.'

'Silk?'

'Yeah why not? You only do this job once.'

Sarah organised a photographer to take photos at the church and a band to play at the reception.

The day arrived, the church was arranged, the hall was decorated and the men had gone off to Gordy's place to dress. Sarah ironed their dresses and poured them all a glass of champagne. She had long ago got over her phobia regarding champagne.

'Can Lily have one Nettie?'

'Just one for now an' maybe another one at the reception.'

Lily scrubbed Nettie's back as she luxuriated in the scented bath and then shampooed her hair.

'I never washed me hair with anythin' but laundry soap in me life before. I feel like a bloody queen already an' I ain't even got dressed yet,'

Nettie joked. She dried herself and went to the bedroom, leaving Lily to bath.

She clipped the diamond necklace around her neck. Then she looked at herself in the mirror and then looked again. Her nipples had darkened and they felt tender. Her period was overdue and she had been praying it would not turn up to spoil her wedding night. She realised with a shock that she could quite likely be pregnant. She smiled and hoped she was but decided she would not say anything yet just in case.

'You've got lovely boobs Mum.' Nettie had not heard Lily come in. 'I wish mine were big like yours.'

'Give 'em time Lily. Nothin' the matter with yours anyhow. Sometimes I wish mine was smaller, like when I'm tryin' to pull a bull down or somethin'. They get in the road at times like that an' get sore as hell if I run too much or when a horse bucks.'

Nettie pulled on a silk slip and Lily helped her do her hair and makeup before they carefully fitted the dress. She had refused to buy or wear a corset.

Finally they were all ready and Sarah drove them to the church where Len was waiting for Nettie. The plan was that he would proudly walk her up the aisle and give her away to her husband.

Eric grinned at her and winked as she joined him at the altar and she relaxed.

'You're beautiful,' he whispered and she blushed.

The wedding went off smoothly and the reception at the Palace got past the speech stage.

'I'm glad that's over,' Eric said.

'You spoke pretty good an' you're the handsomest man here.'

'You shouldn't be lookin'.'

She giggled and he looked at her and saw she was drunk.

'I drunk too much champagne Eric. You don't mind do you?'

'You're funny when you're drunk, long as you don't start fightin' like one time I remember.'

'I promise I won't get in a fight. I won't need to anyhow.' She went into a fit of giggles and Eric roughed her hair and laughed.

'I'm glad I married you Eric.'

The band played and they danced the bridal waltz as well as they knew how.

'Where's Lenny?' Nettie asked as they circled the dancefloor trying not to tread on each other's feet.

'I dunno. He's here somewhere.'

Even with just the family and a few close friends who had been invited there was still quite a crowd because Eric's siblings all had children of their own.

Eric noticed Stanley Gibbs, who had worked at the Queen Victoria Mine since before Ben's time, hurry over to Ben and then they headed for the door. Something was happening outside.

'Hang on love I better have a look what's goin' on out there.'

'Where?'

'I'll be back in a minute.'

He hurried out the door and went down to the street in front of the hotel, where a fight was in progress and a crowd had gathered. It was between Lenny and a man about thirty. The other man's face was cut and Lenny danced around him hammering blows to his head. Eric recognised some of his young nephews in the crowd and spotted Ben and Stanley among them. He went over to join them.

'What started this?' he asked.

'I dunno what started it but it's pretty plain who's gonna finish it. Don't stop 'em Eric,' Ben said.

'I won't, looks like he's doin' alright.'

The other man was tough but was no match for Lenny.

'Where'd he learn to fight like that?'

'I got 'im taught. Don't hurt to be able to look after yourself.'

Eric remembered the night he and Nettie had got drunk at the Tomahawk Plains races.

'I seen you do the same anyhow,' Ben said.

The other man finally went down just as the police arrived. They grabbed Lenny. Ben let out a shrill whistle and everyone turned to look. 'We got this under control if you don't mind there Sergeant.'

The two police officers turned and then recognised Ben.

'Sorry Mister McDonald, we didn't know he was one of yours,' the sergeant apologised and it was plain to Eric just how much weight his father pulled in Kalgoorlie.

'I'll take care of it. You can go.'

Eric patted Lenny on the shoulder. 'You alright mate?'

'Yeah he's just a mug. He called us a mob of pansies because we're wearing suits.'

'Better come back inside now.'

They went back inside and Eric looked for Nettie. She was talking to Lily and as he approached Lily marched off in a huff. 'What's goin' on?' he asked.

'I just chipped her for dancin' too close to a boy.'

Eric laughed. 'Nothin' wrong with our family. Lenny's just got into trouble with the cops for fightin' an' Lily's just got into trouble with you for doin' exactly what you was doin' with me five minutes ago yourself.'

Nettie laughed. 'C'mon, let's have another drink.'

It was almost daylight when they left the reception and went to the bridal suite which Sarah had prepared for them. The suite was full of exotic flowers and the scent was heady.

Eric helped her undress because she was too drunk to manage the dozens of tiny buttons down the back unaided and he wanted to anyway. It was done slowly, with much kissing and laughter.

'You gotta get undressed too,' she told him, trying to look sober but not quite managing.

She fell back on the big double bed spread-eagled, wearing nothing but the diamond necklace and confetti in her hair. She wriggled her toes and giggled. 'I like me diamonds Eric. Now I wanna watch you strip off.'

He undressed. She was stroking her belly and mumbling to herself.

'Who you talkin' to?' he asked.

'I reckon I'm up the duff Eric. I got a bun in the oven be the look of things.' She burst into a fit of giggles.

'Well you will play around.'

She rolled over on one side and shut one eye. 'That's better.'

'What's better?'

'I can see you properly if I shut one eye.' She giggled again. 'I really shouldn't drink champagne but you don't mind do you?'

'What about?'

'If I'm up the duff?'

'All the better if you are. Now, are you feelin' like horsin' around or just plain too drunk?'

'All three.' She giggled again. 'I better get on me back. That'll work the best cause I'll probably fall off if I'm on top. I can shut me eyes an' oughta be able to keep up with what's goin' on that way.'

Eric was laughing at her antics.

'C'mon we gonna do it or not?' She rolled onto her back, spread-eagled again. 'Reckon you can work it out by yourself? I'm as pissed as a parrot, probably not much help to you.'

'I reckon I'll work it out somehow.'

He switched the light out and they started making love.

'Hang on Eric.'

'What's wrong now?'

She wrapped her legs around his hips and locked her ankles behind his back.

'Alright I got a grip now. You can go for it.' She giggled again. Their lovemaking was a ribald romp with plenty of laughter.

CHAPTER 53

Sarah returned from her morning walk to the paper shop. It made no difference that she had only managed to snatch a few hours sleep. She was always up early regardless and the morning paper ritual had been part of her life since Ben had been away at the first war.

She handed Ben the paper. 'Have a look at the front page.'

He unfolded it. The headline was in bold print.

WAR HERO WEDS SWEETHEART AVIATRIX

There was a big photograph of Eric and Nettie kissing at the altar.

Fighter ace, Squadron Leader Eric McDonald, DSO, Flying Cross and bar, a war hero with 25 enemy planes to his credit, married his childhood sweetheart yesterday. Annette Chambers, his bride, is also a war heroine, having unofficially served in a top secret commando unit and shot down one Japanese fighter plane in a dogfight. She has been recommended for a commendation as a result of that sortie.

Squadron Leader McDonald is the eldest son of Kalgoorlie mining magnate, Ben McDonald, who also served with distinction in the Great War. After a flying honeymoon, the newlyweds will reside at the well known Northern Territory grazing property, Tomahawk Plains.

'Where did they get all this stuff from?' Ben asked.

'I know nothing about it Ben. Someone in the family must have told them.'

Henry was staying with them and he came into the kitchen.

'Morning you two early birds.' He looked over Ben's shoulder and chuckled.

'You know somethin' about this?' Ben asked him.

'Yes I told them and that's a mild write-up compared to what they both deserve. They're both heroes. I really enjoyed the wedding thanks Sarah.' Henry knew Sarah was responsible for most of the organising.

'I don't suppose we'll see the newlyweds for a while,' Sarah commented.

'That Nettie can put the champagne away,' Henry said.

'Well as long as they both had a good time I don't care how much champagne she drank. I drank a bit myself if the truth be known,' Sarah replied.

'That young Lenny can fight too.'

'You seen it?' Ben asked.

'Yes, he's got ability and plenty of courage too. I can see his father in him.'

'Yeah first time we met Nettie, Eric got in a fight over her. Well she got in the fight first. She can be a bit toey too.'

'You don't mind that I'm involved with Eric in this business venture Ben?'

'No, I'm pleased about it. He said you robbed a bank in Germany.'

'He robbed it. I just planned it up to a certain stage but he took over and did it. He pulled off one of the most brazen stunts of the war and got a lot of valuable documents for Britain in the process, not to mention a fair swag of Nazi cash and treasure for us.'

'You mean it was legal?'

'Yes it was an undercover operation and as a result we're bringing charges of war crimes against a number of Nazis. The deal I had with the Government was that we got the money and the War Office got the documents.'

'Much money Henry?'

'Enough so that Eric is already a very wealthy young man. By the time young Lenny is ready to take over it should be an empire if they run it well.'

'They?'

'Eric and Ben Abdul own Curlew Investments. I'm just the nominal chairman of the board.'

Gradually the household came to life.

Eric and Nettie arrived for lunch and Lily called her mother aside. 'Mum you're not still mad at me are you?'

'No I never was. Why would I be?'

'You roused on me last night.'

'No I ain't mad at you an' I hope I never spoilt your night by sayin' that. I had a good time.'

'You're supposed to have a good time at your own wedding. I had a good time too Mum. I'm glad you didn't get married before I was born.'

'Why's that?'

'I would have missed your wedding and I'm glad I could be your bridesmaid.'

'Lily I just reckoned you was gettin' a bit too close to that young feller last night. Don't be in a rush with boys. Some of 'em don't take too much encouragin' if you give 'em the wrong idea. Your time will come soon enough.'

'How old were you when you fell in love with Dad?'

'Thirteen but I never even got to even kiss 'im till I was over twenty-one.'

'And you've been together ever since?'

'Yeah pretty much but we never got engaged till a few months after that.'

'When are you leaving to go to the beach house?'

'In the mornin'.'

'I hope you have a nice time. It's lovely and peaceful there.'

'I reckon we will.'

'I'm glad we're all back together now. It's been good here but I want to go home.'

'You an' Lenny fight a bit do you?'

'No we're good mates. We get into a few fights at school but not with each other.'

'You get into fights too?'

'I've had a few.'

'With other girls?'

'No, mostly with boys. Some of them annoy me. Girls aren't worth two bob in a fight. They just bite and scratch and squeal.'

'An' what do you do when they annoy you?'

'I just bash them. I knocked one boy's tooth out and I got into trouble over that.'

Nettie laughed.

'What?' Lily asked.

'I got into a fight with a bloke once too but I was too drunk to fight. Your father fought 'im for me after he belted me in the mouth.'

'Were you drunk last night Mum?'

'Yeah I was very drunk last night. I drank champagne all night an' I never even tasted it before. An' talkin' of which, you oughta be careful drinkin' it because it makes you wanna do things you ain't supposed to be doin' at your age.'

'I thought you were pretty drunk but you seemed to be having a good time. Did it have that effect on you?'

'You're supposed to have a good time at your own weddin' like you said. An' what I done later is me own business.'

'Did you see the newspaper this morning?'

'Yeah, I wish they never made so much fuss over me though.'

'Uncle Henry says you're a hero too.'

'I just give 'em a bit of a hand.'

'You shot a Jap plane down though.'

'Yeah, I just lost me temper, a bit like you with the boys.'

'I'm proud of you Mum.'

'An' I'm proud of the way you all coped with us bein' apart all this time too.'

'Did Dad mean it when he said we'd be learning to fly the plane?'

'Your father always means what he says an' if I know 'im you'll all be flyin' by the time we get back home from our trip.'

'Nat too?'

'Yeah, Nat too. Your dad was runnin' Tomahawk Plains when he was

Nat's age an' I was workin' there with me dad then too.'

'That's how you met?'

'Yeah.'

'Come on you two old women, lunch is on the table,' Sarah interrupted them.

CHAPTER 54

Eric and Nettie spent three idyllic weeks at Ben and Sarah's beach house, swimming, lazing in the sun, walking on the beach and catching up on lost years. The war was already fading into the past for them. They bought a camera and Nettie became an avid snapper.

They returned to Kalgoorlie and spent another week there before the school year was finished. Then they set out on the second part of their honeymoon, flying to Adelaide and Melbourne staying at each place for a few days to have a look about.

Eric instructed the children as they flew and one by one they took control of the plane when he considered conditions were favourable enough.

Lily was at the controls with Eric sitting beside her as navigator and instructor when they flew over a sizeable town.

'That's Bendigo. It was a gold-rush town in the early days. Follow the railway line there Lily. Somewhere up along here old Eliza an' Buster an' Toby held up a train an' stole a gold shipment once.'

They were all fascinated to learn something of their family history and watched out the windows as they followed the line.

'That's where it would have been.' Nat pointed. 'That would be a good place to rob a train. See there's a patch of scrub where they would have hidden on top of that hill.'

Eric laughed. 'Yeah you could be right. I know Buster an' Toby unhooked the wagon an' it got left behind the train on an uphill grade.

Would of stopped about there.'

They flew to Bathurst and stayed the night. Eric told them that one of Eliza's first robberies had been carried out there. 'I think it was a stock an' station agency on a sale day. They raided the office an' took all the cash.'

That night Eric rang Elizavale near Armidale and spoke to his cousin Clare. She gave him directions to find the property and said they should be able to land the plane near the homestead. She was surprised to hear from the cousin she had never met.

The next morning Lenny flew the plane and Eric let him take off because he was quite capable.

Nettie dozed in the back where she had two seats to herself, with the swags and luggage stacked behind her. The ride became bumpy and she woke. As she looked out the window she noticed how overcast the weather was and she thought the mountainous country looked grey and forbidding.

They had passed Tamworth and then saw a small town. 'That'll be Uralla Lenny. We head due north now an' it ain't far from here.'

The ride became rougher and it was not long before they crossed a range of hills. A narrow valley of mostly open country lay before them.

'This'll be Elizavale an' the homestead oughta be at the head of this valley.'

'I can see it,' Lenny said.

'Want me to take over?' Eric asked.

'No, I should be alright.'

'Just watch the wind currents in this valley mate. She'll be a bit choppy an' unpredictable down there.'

Nettie had a nervous moment as they came in to land. There was a strong crosswind and Lenny held the nose into it but the plane did not want to touch down.

'It'll be a bit rough,' Lenny said and dropped it on the deck as he spoke. The plane bounced but he held it against the wind with the rudder and made a good landing.

As they taxied toward the house a woman and a boy came out to meet them. Nettie thought the woman looked slightly younger than herself.

The boy looked about Nat's age and they wore riding gear with heavy coats and felt hats.

As they got out of the plane a cold wind buffeted them and the sky was clouding over quickly.

'You must be Clare. I'm Nettie.' The two women kissed.

'This is my son Mark. Our name's Logan by the way.'

They all introduced themselves and Clare said, 'You must be freezing without coats. Welcome to our typical weather. Come inside where it's warm.'

Eric and Lenny drove in steel mooring pegs and tied the plane down securely. Then they all moved inside, where a fire burnt comfortingly in a stone fireplace. An old grey-haired woman sat in a wheelchair in front of the fire. Clare spoke to her. 'Mum this is Eric and his family. Do you remember meeting him when you went to Kalgoorlie for the family reunion?'

The woman was looking straight at them but there was no recognition or response in her eyes.

'She had a stroke last year poor dear. She doesn't speak anymore and I'm not sure how much she understands.'

Eric recognised Eliza Jane from when he had met her previously and explained to the family that she was his father's younger sister and that she had come to Kalgoorlie with Eliza at the time of his twenty-first birthday party.

'She looks much older than Ben does,' Nettie said.

'Yes she's aged dreadfully since the stroke,' Clare told them. 'Dad died of a heart attack only two years ago and she has never really been the same since that. They were very close.'

'Where is your husband?' Nettie asked.

'Hamish was killed at Tobruk.'

'I'm sorry. I didn't know.' Nettie remembered her own grief each time she had thought Eric was dead.

'We've got over it now Nettie. Life goes on, especially when you're busy like we are. Mark and I do most of the work here, except when the muster and shearing is on. We employ men then but it's mainly been old men and boys during the war.'

'Yeah I know what that's like Clare. I been runnin' our place with just blackfellers since Eric went away.'

Clare had lunch ready for them and they sat at the big old dining table in the warm room. After lunch she brought out her albums and showed them photos of the various family members taken over a long period. She knew all the family history intimately and gave a story or an anecdote to go with each lot of pictures, which they all found informative. Even Eric knew very little of past events other than some of the highlights.

'This one is of all of them at the big wedding when Eliza married Paddy, and Buster married Toby at Cave Creek. I think the minister must have taken it.'

'Who's that?'

'That's Buster, Mother's and Ben's father. I've never met Ben. He had gone off to the Territory and then would have been at Kalgoorlie before I was born. That's Ben. He beat Buster in a horse race that day and later on won the Melbourne Cup on that same Cave Creek mare that Buster rode that day. He was disqualified in the Cup but won the race just the same. In the saddling paddock after the race he accidentally killed the jockey who came second. The police tried to arrest him but he ran away and went to the Territory. Then he came back to Cave Creek a few years later and married Sarah.'

Nettie studied the photograph and could see the family likeness they all shared. Even Clare had it. Buster had his arm around Toby's shoulder. He was a dashing looking man and Toby was pretty. She wondered if her own mother looked something like her.

'It looks like Buster's got fingers missin'.'

'Yes he lost part of his hand in a gunfight in Taroom and he killed the other man. I think the man accused him of stealing cattle that he hadn't.'

What a family, thought Nettie, old Eliza a bank robber, Buster a gunfighter, Ben a fugitive from the law and now Eric a war hero. She felt a sense of pride, knowing she was part of this close-knit but scattered family and that her children would carry on that line.

She wondered what life had in store for the baby she now carried.

'This is the wedding photo of Edgar and Alice McDonald, Eliza's parents. They took this small homestead block up in the early days and Eliza was born here in 1840. Since then most of the valley has been bought up and added to this original holding.'

They talked all afternoon. None of them felt like braving the cold outside and Clare had a fascinating repertoire of anecdotes and stories of the family. She told how Edgar had been killed by Aborigines and Eliza kidnapped by them as a child. Then, years later some of the Aborigines had returned to the valley under the leadership of a young firebrand warrior, Jimulka, who was notorious for terrorizing white settlers and for the brutal murder of scores of them and police troopers over a period of years.

'Jimulka was Eliza's childhood sweetheart apparently. Eventually the police wiped out all the others of his band of renegades at a cottage a few miles further down the valley from here and captured him but Eliza and Buster broke him out of jail in Armidale. He came back here to die because his heart was broken by his failure. He and Eliza and Paddy are all buried on the hill behind the house, right where Jimulka died. Eliza died there too alongside the graves of the two men she loved, you know.'

'We never heard she died till later.'

'Yes Mum and Dad took over here when Eliza got too old to run it anymore and she went to live in town but she wasn't happy there and eventually came back. She often used to spend time up at the graves and that's where she died lying between the graves of her two lovers. That's where she always wanted to be buried and she is.'

'She must a' been an amazin' woman.'

'Oh yes she was and still as sharp as a tack till the day she died. We thought she'd never die, that she would still be here when we were all dead and gone.'

Clare showed them the sword that hung over the fireplace, a Claymore.

'That belonged to Edgar. He was Laird of his branch of the McDonald clan in Scotland but left it to come here. I think the family in Scotland was broke then, like many of the old Scottish families.'

'I'd like to see the graves,' Nettie said.

'I'll show them to you before you go. You'll have to stay a while if you can spare the time. I'll show you around the place and there's also lots of old letters and documents and newspaper cuttings to show you.'

'We're plannin' to go to Cave Creek for Christmas so there ain't much rush.'

'Well that's a couple of weeks away. You've got plenty of time.'

The night was cold and bleak. The wind howled outside and Nettie slept close to Eric. She woke in the morning feeling sick. She told Clare she was pregnant and had morning sickness.

'That's a shame. I was going to take you all for a drive today.'

'No. You all go but I might stop here if you don't mind. I can keep an eye on your mum.'

'Are you sure? We can wait until you're feeling better.'

'No, we been on the go pretty much lately an' a bit of a rest is what I need. You take Eric an' the kids though. They'll be interested to see the place.'

'Alright I'll do that if you're sure you don't mind. Mum doesn't need much looking after. Just make sure she stays warm but you don't have to stay with her all the time and if you want to have a look about I'll lend you a coat.'

Clare took them off in her big old Humber sedan and Nettie made a pot of tea and took it into the dining room. She spoon-fed a cup to Eliza Jane as she had seen Clare do the previous evening and then drank her own.

She soon felt better and decided to have a look about. She rearranged the shawl over Eliza Jane's knees, stoked the fire and put the brass screen in front of it to stop any sparks spattering into the room.

As she went out onto the verandah she thought it looked like rain. She had the big coat on she had borrowed from Clare but decided to wear an oilskin as well. She hoped it did not rain because the others might get bogged if it did. She pulled her hat on and went to look at the shearing shed and the stables.

She saw some gravestones on the rise between the house and the little creek and went to look. Edgar McDonald's grave was the oldest and there was also one belonging to John Denton. Between the two was the grave of Alice Denton and she realised Alice must have married again after Edgar's death. There was also the recent grave of Clare's father, James Gordon.

Then she decided to climb the hill and see the other graves there. As she went, she kept imagining she could hear footsteps following but every time she stopped to look and listen there was obviously nobody else within miles. She also had the distinct feeling she was being watched but was not afraid because she knew it was just her imagination.

Once she arrived at the graves the feeling was even stronger. Jimulka's grave had an inscription neatly chiseled on the bole of a large tree instead of a headstone. It had obviously been done a long time ago because re-growth bulged over the edges of the blazed area. A simple marble headstone marked Eliza's grave. It read, Elizabeth O'Reilly, born 1-8-1840 died 29-10-1939. She had died about the time Eric had enlisted for the war and had been ninety-nine years old. That was more than twice Nettie's age and already she felt as if her life had been long.

The other grave had a similar stone proclaiming, Patrick O'Reilly, born Dublin, Ireland, 1838, died 3-4-1915.

Nearby a brass plaque was riveted to a large boulder.

Nettie looked around quickly, sure she could hear a horse approaching but there was nothing. The clouds sat low on the ridge and the wind had dropped but the chill still seeped through her clothing as if into her very soul, causing her to feel very small and insignificant.

She could see right down the valley from there and could see it raining further to the west, blotting out the distant hills as it rolled quickly closer. She shivered and turned up the collar of the oilskin.

The plaque had been cast in a foundry and at the top was some scrollwork around a revolver. At the bottom was more scrollwork around a branding iron. She began to read and the light was fading fast as the storm approached.

She heard horses galloping and spun around expectantly. Rain converged like a thick white blanket and that was all there was. But she could still hear the increasing thunder of galloping horses that were almost on her now. She strained her eyes until she could make out the moving grey clump of horses and riders in the rain. There was a spark of light like a muzzle flash and the sound of the shot came to her. The storm hit her then, fine heavy rain that cut visibility to a few yards. It was suddenly as dark as if she was in a cave. The hoof-beats of the horses gradually faded and more faint shots came as they retreated into the distance.

She hurried down the slope to get out of the rain, somewhat rattled by her experience. It was darkening and the rocks were slippery for her leather-soled boots. She picked her way carefully in the gloom and could still hear horses faintly. She slipped and twisted her ankle, sitting down hard.

A hand took her arm then and she got up, grateful for the help. She went to thank her aide and gaped in shock.

There's nobody here! I'm alone!

She stared around her in fright. She could see no more than ten yards but nobody had been there to give her assistance, of that she was sure. She had imagined it and her scalp prickled in superstition.

Then, faintly over the whisper of the rain she heard a curlew call. She was suddenly very conscious of the tiny life in her womb. Was it an omen and if so was it a good or bad one?

She forced herself to stay calm as she limped back to the house, looking behind her often but no-one followed. She must have imagined it all but could not believe that she had. There was no sound but the rain, no thunder or lightning. No thunder or lightning! I couldn't have imagined the shots. They were real. She shivered involuntarily.

She took the oilskin and her wet boots off on the verandah and took the boots inside to dry them in front of the fire. Eliza Jane still sat staring at the glowing embers, exactly as she had left her. Nettie felt her hands and they were cold so she pushed the wheelchair closer to the fire and stoked it with another log. She put a blanket around the old woman's shoulders. It was an eerie feeling caring for a zombie, especially in her own present emotional state.

She talked to the old woman as she stood warming her back at the fire but knew she would not get an answer. Time passed and she felt Eliza

Jane's hands again. They were still cold. She picked one up to rub some warmth into it but it was stiff. She felt her forehead and it was cold too. Her eyes had a glazed look.

She's dead! Oh, bloody hell! This is too much. Nettie sucked in a breath at the realisation. The old woman had died sitting in the chair while Nettie had been out but now looked no different than she had before. She was suddenly sure it had occurred when she had been up at the graves. The horses, the shots, the curlew call were all part of her dying and her spirit joining those of her forebears. They came for her, old Eliza, Buster and all their old gang! Tears prickled her eyes at the thought. These McDonalds are no ordinary people.

Nettie shut Eliza Jane's eyes and sat down on a couch trembling, convinced it was her fault. She felt very alone and scared. The breeze had picked up considerably. The strange house was enveloped by the blowing rain and wailing wind in a dark ominous world of its own. The walls and surrounding trees were buffeted by savage gusts. There was the slightly unnerving sound of a loose sheet of iron rattling on the roof and an unidentified metallic scraping sound, possibly caused by a branch touching the roof. Maybe.

The hours passed and she kept the fire stoked against the psychological chill in her as much as that of the real cold. The others must be bogged somewhere, otherwise they would be back. She watched the hands on the grandfather clock. It was six o'clock but already night outside and still raining. She found a lamp and lit it. By then she had become used to sitting with the dead woman and had got her nervous superstition under control. In a bizarre way Clare's dead mother was even company. It seemed a cynical, irreverent thought.

She thought of taking horses and going to look for the others but it was dark and she had no idea which way to go anyway even if she could find the horses. It was an impractical idea in the circumstances. She instead lit a hurricane lantern and hung it on the verandah to guide them if they were walking in the dark.

She went to the kitchen and prepared a stew, thinking they would be cold and hungry when they did arrive home. The meal was cooked and sat warming in a pot on the hearth. The clock showed 10 pm and she hoped they were safe, knowing how cold it was outside. The rain was steady on the iron roof and the wind gusted. She dozed off.

The clump of boots on the verandah woke her at midnight and she hurried out to meet them. 'You must be bloody freezin'.'

'We got bogged,' Clare told her, as they all stripped wet oilskins and boots off.

'You better get in near the fire,' Nettie said and then realised she should warn Clare that Eliza Jane had died.

'I dunno how to tell you but your mother is dead Clare. She just died, sittin' in front of the fire.'

Clare put her arm around her. 'You must have got a fright Nettie. I've expected that would happen and even hoped it would but I'm sorry you had to be here by yourself when it finally did occur. I should have warned you that it could happen at any time.'

They went inside, where Eliza Jane sat in the wheelchair as if nothing had happened. Clare knelt in front of her and brushed the hair off her forehead and kissed her cheek.

'You'll be happy Mum,' she said. 'You can be with Dad now.'

The rain had stopped by morning and Clare rang their family doctor to tell him her mother had died. He said there was no need for him to see the body. He would issue the death certificate and arrange for the minister to come for the burial when the road dried.

Eric and the three boys dug the grave beside that of her husband. The sun was out and the wind had dropped.

Nettie helped Clare lay the body out and prepare it for burial while Lily watched gravely.

'Don't be sad Lily. It's a mercy she's died. If she'd been a horse I'd have shot her a year ago,' Clare told her in a matter-of-fact tone.

Nettie realised that all those of the McDonald clan were and probably always had been strong people. Life and death were just part of their world. To them death was just part of life. They were not sentimental in the maudlin way many others were. She liked Clare, who just seemed to take things in her stride.

Everything was done and the minister would bring the coffin when he came.

'He should get through tomorrow because the road dries out fairly fast but we won't get the car out of the bog for a few days because it's all black soil down that way,' Clare said.

Nettie told Clare she felt responsible.

'Nonsense Nettie, she'd have died just the same if we'd all been here and may even have been dead before you went for a walk. She often looked as if she was dead and I'd check her pulse. She was never very far from it, poor old thing.'

'Mark's takin' it well.'

'Yes he's alright. He was pretty upset when his father was killed though. He's grown up a lot since then.'

'How did you feel when he got killed?'

'When I got the news, I was relieved to tell the truth. He was reported missing in action almost a year before and he could have been a prisoner but I knew in my heart he was dead. I'd already done my grieving by then.'

'I was told twice durin' the war that Eric was dead. The first time he was in England an' it was almost a year before I knew he wasn't. The next time he was in New Guinea an' he was missin' for sixteen months that time.'

'It would have been terrible the second time. How did you cope?'

'I had to. I was there on me own. I had to run the place an' I was doin' work with the Nackeroos too, never had time to feel sorry for meself.'

'What are the Nackeroos?'

'A commando unit that was coast-watchin' in the north an' I helped 'em with the plane.'

A mutual respect was growing between the two women.

★　★　★

The minister read a simple burial service and they filled the grave, even the women taking turns on the shovel. There were only themselves and the minister present and Eric wondered about that.

Clare had prepared afternoon tea. A bottle of rum and a bottle of whisky sat on the verandah table with the tea and cakes.

'We'd better drink to Mum,' She said.

Eric poured them each a drink and asked her why there were no others at the funeral.

'Dying is private Eric. You share happy times with your friends but you die with your family.'

'You sound a bit like old Eliza.'

She laughed. 'If I was half the person she was I'd be happy.' She raised her glass in a toast to her mother. She drank straight whisky and swallowed it at a gulp. She held her glass out and Eric refilled it.

Later, after the minister had left and they had cleared the table Clare suggested she show them Eliza's grave. 'While we're on the subject of graves,' she added.

Nettie had told Eric of her visit to the graves and now she looked relieved that she had company. He took her hand as they climbed the hill.

Clare had organised the bronze plaque to be cast at a Newcastle foundry and it had raised letters.

ELIZABETH O'REILLY was born three hundred yards from this place where she lies evermore and she died where she is buried. She was born Elizabeth McDonald and during her life was known as Elijah Henry or Eliza Henry. She married Patrick O'Reilly, the policeman who had previously hunted her for her alleged crimes, including bank robbery, murder, train robbery, payroll robbery, cattle duffing and horse stealing.

She was as respected as she was notorious and leaves her family with a legacy of which to be proud. May we who follow her strive to live up to the example she set.

'Amen,' said Eric with a lump in his throat after he had read it aloud. He squeezed Nettie's hand and she looked at him proudly.

'There never was the like after her,' Clare said.

'An' probably never will be neither,' Eric added.

CHAPTER 55

Nat's first landing was on the strip at Tomahawk Plains.

Eric and the boys had come on ahead leaving Nettie and Lily to fly the second-hand Tiger Moth they had bought in Darwin. Including the Zero, they now had three planes.

They had spent Christmas and New Year at Cave Creek near Taroom in Queensland, with Eric's uncle James McDonald and his family. From there they had inspected their own three other properties as they flew across the Barkly Tableland, spending a night at each place. Then they had gone to Darwin to check whether the equipment Eric was expecting from New Guinea had arrived and also to buy the Tiger Moth.

The first shipment of freight had arrived but Eric was told that, as had happened all through the war, the stevedores union was refusing to unload the cargo because it was war material and it could be weeks before the dispute was settled. He learnt that much of the loss of shipping in Darwin Harbour in the first air-raid was said to be due to such union action. It enraged him that while men fought to protect their country the waterfront unions had played politics. He found that hard to stomach, as did many others.

Jack and Ethel Miller had both died since they had last seen them. Their daughter Enid had kept their block and they had stayed a week with her while they waited for a break in the weather so that they could fly home safely. While there they had made a landing strip so they could use it in the future because it was unlikely Nettie would ever get her pilot's licence and legally be able to land in Darwin.

The Tomahawk Plains country looked a picture in the middle of the wet season.

Flying conditions were good so Eric let Nat land the plane and it was a competent effort for a first attempt.

'Well there you are Nat, you're the first of you three to land on our strip. How's that feel?'

'Pretty good Dad. Thanks for letting me do it.'

'I want you all to be good pilots. Flyin' is part of our lives now, just like ridin' a horse is too. Taxi over to the house so we can unload our gear.'

Two hours later Lily put the Tiger Moth down, to Nettie's congratulations. She parked beside the other plane.

'What's happened to the roof?' Lily asked as Eric met them.

'Mum'll tell you.'

'The Jap plane I shot down did that,' Nettie told her.

When they went inside Eric handed Nettie a letter addressed to her, from the pile of mail on the kitchen table that the mailman had left in their absence. It had OHMS printed on it and was sealed with red wax. She opened it and read the contents.

'Eric I'm a Nackeroo!'

'What is it Mum?' Lily asked.

'They made me an honorary member of the Nackeroos an' I got a commendation for shootin' down that Jap plane.'

'Good on you girl.' Eric kissed her.

It rained that night so they were all housebound the next day as the monsoon deluge continued. Eric lay on their bed reading mail while Nettie unpacked their things.

'You still ain't unpacked one a' your bags since you got back from New Guinea,' she reminded him.

He tipped the contents of the bag out on the floor and sorted through it. Nettie spotted her photograph and picked it up.

'How did you get hold of this?' she asked.

'Oh yeah I forgot all about it, I'm sorry Nettie.'

He picked up John's wallet and handed it to her. 'I was with him when he died an' he give me this to give to you.'

She got quite a shock when she discovered John had left her as sole beneficiary of his will. 'Why would he do that Eric?'

'He loved you Nettie. An' he obviously had nobody else that he cared enough about.'

'I feel terrible. I can't take it.'

'Someone's gotta take it or the government will an' he wanted you to have it. I know he did because he told me.'

'I'll bank it for our baby when it's born then. I don't want it. You're the one I love.'

'Alright take it easy. I come to terms with the business with John long ago. Otherwise I couldn't of worked with him like I did.'

'Well, I'd feel happier if I did that anyway because I feel a bit ashamed of meself over it all Eric.'

'An' I shouldn't be ashamed about what I done?'

'I never think about that. It's now that matters, not the past.'

'Well I don't neither because I don't want to ever think about what I done again.'

CHAPTER 56

Nettie often revisited her experience at Eliza's grave the day she had gone there alone. She tried to explain it to herself in sensible terms, realising that perhaps her Aboriginal blood made her susceptible to superstition and sought a practical explanation to put that superstition to rest.

When she had thought she had heard the horses it could have been the sound of the approaching rain. The flash she had seen must have been lightning and the shots must have been thunder but she was sure there had not been any thunder and lightning in the storm. She definitely remembered realising that fact at the time.

She could have built the whole experience in her mind from nothing mysterious at all but it would not go away and she instinctively felt it had some significance. Had she imagined the curlew call too? And there was also the hand that had helped her up when she fell.

She spoke to Eric about it.

'I dunno love but I do know I wouldn't swim in the crocodile hole without the diamond. Call it superstition or whatever you like. Maybe it really was old Eliza givin' you a hand up when you fell. An' maybe it was all of 'em comin' with a spare horse to get old Eliza Jane's spirit. Who knows?'

She did not take part in the muster because Eric did not want her flying all the time or overdoing things while she was pregnant. He did most of the flying but also gave the kids practice.

They had built a shed for all the gear the Nackeroos had left. The boys had already got one of the Jeeps going, having both spent time in the Queen Victoria mine workshop while they were in Kalgoorlie. The little four-wheel-drive vehicle proved its worth during the last of the Wet, being light and nimble in the heavy black soil. Its skinny lugged tyres cut a track without picking up too much of the sticky clay.

Nettie thought she should learn to drive the Jeep after the baby was born, just as she had learnt to fly all those years earlier. The old world they had known had gone by the wayside along with the war and it would be silly not to keep pace.

The baby was due about the middle of July and while the muster was on Eric brought Lily home and stayed most nights so she knew she would not be alone when the time came. The boys stayed in the mustering camp with the men and Eric had left Johnny in the position of head-stockman. She was glad he had because Johnny had served her well through the war years and had proved his reliability. His pride had been obvious when Eric told him.

Lily was thrown by a horse and broke her arm. Nettie called the flying doctor who came and set the arm in plaster. The doctor noticed Nettie's advancing pregnancy.

'You'll call me when the baby's due, won't you?'

'I wasn't goin' to. The two Lilies can help me.'

'I want you to call me Nettie. That's my job. Will you do that for me please?'

'Yeah righto, as long as you can spare the time. I don't wanna be no trouble to nobody an' I ain't expectin' no difficulty anyhow. I already had three kids with no trouble.'

CHAPTER 57

Eric waited on the verandah feeling redundant and slightly anxious. The doctor had been with Nettie for quite a while and Lily was fetching for him. She came striding past him heading for the kitchen.

'How's it goin' Lily?'

'I've never seen a birth before Dad and I don't know. It seems to be taking a long time though.'

Eric fretted because he knew Nettie's earlier births had been quick and easy for her.

The doctor came out on the verandah and lit a cigarette. 'You want the good news or the bad Eric?'

Eric's heart sank. One of them was not going to make it.

'Gimme the bad news first Fred.'

'The bad news for you is that it's a girl.' He grinned broadly. 'And the good news is that they're both well. You can go in and see them now.'

'You just frightened the livin' daylights outta me then.'

'Sorry. I never meant to do that Eric. I was just joking.'

Nettie was sitting up in the bed, trying to get the squirming baby to latch onto a nipple. She looked tired and her hair was wet with sweat but she smiled proudly.

'Come an' look at her Eric. Ain't she just bloody beautiful?'

Lily sat on the side of the bed with a look of wonder on her face.

Eric kissed Nettie and touched the baby's nose gently with his finger. 'She looks pretty good to me. What do you reckon Lily? She pass muster you reckon?'

'She's my own little sister. Yes, she passes muster Dad and yes she's just beautiful. I can't wait till I have a baby of my own.'

'You got a while yet,' he growled.

The baby finally took the nipple and sucked greedily and instinctively.

'How does she know to suck Mum?' Lily asked.

'It's just like breathing. It's just nature. Calves and foals are the same.'

Eric sat on the bed and watched. Nettie looked so happy.

'What are you going to call her Mum?' Lily asked.

Nettie looked at Eric and he shrugged. 'I had Tom picked out but that obviously ain't much help.'

'I want to call her Elizabeth Eric. Do you like that?'

'Eliza. Yeah why not?'

'An' Sarah after your mother. I like Sarah as a person an' I like the name as well.'

'Elizabeth Sarah McDonald, I like that Mum,' Lily said.

'C'mon, Lily we better leave 'em be. They both look as tired as each other.'

He had noticed Nettie's eyes shutting involuntarily and the baby had already gone to sleep.

He kissed Nettie on the brow and they went out onto the verandah.

It was 20th July, 1946.

CHAPTER 58

Nettie was too exhausted to keep her eyes open any longer.

She felt Eric kiss her forehead and she smiled. They had got through the stresses and tensions of the war years and she now had her baby, born out of their love that had endured all the obstacles it had experienced.

'Eliza McDonald, you'll do,' she murmured, and her eyes shut again.

As sleep took her mind away to another place, she fancied she heard the call of a curlew and was content.

Eric came quietly to the door and saw the smile on her face. He blew her a kiss and tiptoed away.

Their dreaming had come full circle.

ACKNOWLEDGEMENTS

Firstly, I wish to thank Greg Barron for having the faith in my ability to write novels worthy of publication in his stable. His advice and assistance with manuscript preparation has been invaluable.

I am also grateful to John Morrison and Janette De Sousa Roque for permission to use John's wonderful painting for the cover of this novel. I have known John for over forty years.

Also, James Barron has demonstrated his design skills in transforming John's painting into an excellent cover for Curlew Dreaming.

John Armstrong's input regarding Top End matters and his knowledge of World War II warbirds was a valuable contribution.

Thanks to my wife and best mate Gillian for her constant support and valuable criticism.